Aberystwyth Mon Amour

Aberystwyth Mon Amour

Malcolm Pryce

BLOOMSBURY

First published in Great Britain 2001
This paperback edition published 2002

Bloomsbury Publishing Plc, 36 Soho Square, London W1D 3QY

A CIP catalogue record is available from the British Library

ISBN 0 7475 5786 1
ISBN-13 9780747557869

12

All papers used by Bloomsbury Publishing are natural, recyclable products made from wood grown in well-managed forests. The manufacturing processes conform to the environmental regulations of the country of origin.

Typeset by Palimpsest Book Production Limited,
Polmont, Stirlingshire
Printed in Great Britain by Clays Limited, St Ives plc

www.bloomsbury.com/malcolmpryce

For Mum and Dad, Andy and Pepys

LET'S BE CLEAR about it then: Aberystwyth in the Eighties was no Babylon. Even when the flood came there was nothing Biblical about the matter, despite what some fools are saying now. I spent the years before the deluge operating out of an office on Canticle Street, above the Orthopaedic Boot shop. And you know what that means: take two lefts outside the door and you were on the Old Prom. That was where it all happened: the bars, the dives, the gambling dens, the 24-hour Whelk Stall, and Sospan's ice-cream kiosk. That's where the tea-cosy shops were, the ones that never sold tea cosies; and the toffee-apple dens, the ones that never sold toffee. And that was where those latter day Canutes, the ladies from the Sweet Jesus League, had their stall. I saw a lot of things along that part of the Prom, but I don't remember seeing any hanging gardens. Just those round concrete tubs of hydrangeas the Council put out so the drunks would have something to throw up in. I also spent a lot of my time at the Druid-run Moulin Club in Patriarch Street and I'm well aware of what the girls got up to there. Sure, you can call it harlotry if it makes you feel better, but I was there the night Bianca died and I'm just as happy with the word prostitution. And as for idolatry, well, if you ask me, the only thing men worshipped on a regular basis in the days before the flood was money. That, and the singer down at the Moulin, Myfanwy Montez. And I know that for certain, because although I never had any money in my office in those days, I did once have Myfanwy Montez . . .

Chapter 1

I can't afford friends in this town, I lose too many working days attending the funerals

Sospan, the ice-cream seller

THE THING I remember most about it was walking the entire length of the Prom that morning and not seeing a Druid. Normally when I made my stroll shortly before 9am I would see a few hanging around at Sospan's ice-cream stall, preening themselves in their sharp Swansea suits and teardrop aviator shades. Or they would be standing outside Dai the Custard Pie's joke shop, waiting for him to open so they could buy some more of that soap that makes a person's face go black. But on that day in June there wasn't a bard in sight. It was as if nature had forgotten one of the ingredients of the day and was carrying on in the hope that no one would notice. Looking back, it's hard for people who weren't there to appreciate how strange it felt. In those days, everything in town was controlled by the Druids. Sure, the Bronzinis controlled the ice cream, the tailoring and the haircuts; and the Llewellyns controlled the crazy golf, the toffee apples and the bingo. But we all know who controlled the Bronzinis and the Llewellyns. And, of course, the police got to push a few poets around now and again; but that was just for show. Like those little fish that are allowed to swim around inside the shark's jaw to clean his teeth.

When I arrived at Canticle Street Mrs Llantrisant was already there swabbing the step. She did this every morning as well as tidying up in my office and doing a number of other things, all of which I had forbidden her to do. But she took no notice. Her mother had swabbed this step and so had her mother and her mother before that. There had probably been a Mrs Llantrisant covered in woad soaping the menhirs in the iron-age hill fort south of the town. You just had to accept the fact that she came with the premises like the electricity supply.

'*Bore da*, Mr Knight!'

'*Bore da*, Mrs Llantrisant! Lovely day?'

'Oh isn't it just!'

At this point the usual formula was for us to spend a few minutes pinning down exactly how lovely a day it was. We did this by cross-referencing it with its counterparts in previous years, the records of which Mrs Llantrisant kept in her head like those people who know all the FA Cup goal-scorers since 1909. But on this occasion she was distracted by an impatient excitement which made her bob up and down on the spot like a toddler aching to divulge a secret. She placed a white bony finger on my forearm.

'You'll never guess what!' she said excitedly.

'What?' I said.

'You've got a customer!'

Though rare, this wasn't quite the novelty that her excitement suggested.

'You'll never guess in a million years who it is!'

'Well, I'd better go and see then, hadn't I?'

I stepped over the gleaming slate doorstep, but Mrs Llantrisant held on to my arm, her finger digging in like a talon. She glanced furtively up and down the street and then lowered her voice, as if there was a danger someone would steal the client if word got out.

'It's Myfanwy Montez,' she hissed. 'The famous singer!'

Bonfires of excitement burned in her eyes; you'd never guess that Mrs Llantrisant spent three nights a week outside the night club where Myfanwy Montez worked, handing out pamphlets and calling the singer a strumpet.

My office was divided into an outer waiting area and the inner office. But Mrs Llantrisant usually let clients straight into the main room even though I had told her not to. Miss Montez was already sitting in the client's chair with her back to the door; she jumped when I entered then half stood up and half turned round.

'I hope you don't mind, the cleaning lady told me to come in.'

'I know, she does that.'

She looked across to the coat stand in the corner of the room; there was a wide-brimmed straw hat hanging from it.

'I used your hat stand.'

'Did you take a ticket?'

'No.'

'Always insist on a ticket, Miss Montez – it could get confusing if another client turns up.'

She peered at me for a second puzzled, and then giggled.

'Mrs Llantrisant said you would tease me!'

I sat down in the chair opposite her. 'What else did she say when she should have been swabbing my step?'

'Are you angry with her?'

'Who?'

'Mrs Llantrisant.'

I shook my head. 'No point. It doesn't work.'

'How did you know my name?'

'You know as well as I do it's fly-posted on every spare wall between here and the station.'

She smiled at the compliment, if indeed it was one, and leaned forward with her hands placed palms down underneath her thighs. Her luxuriant hair cascaded forward and had the colour and sheen of conkers fresh out of the shell. Yes, I would have recognised her anywhere. Her features were a lot softer than the harsh black and white advertising images that were pasted around town, but there was one thing which marked her out instantly as Aberystwyth's celebrated night-club singer: the mole which sat at the exact point where her lip ended and the cheek began. She was facing the window and squinting so I walked over and closed the blinds. The view looked out across the slate roofs of downtown Aberystwyth towards the iron-age hill fort on Pen Dinas; and beyond that to the four chimneys of the rock factory, now belching out pink smoke.

It didn't usually take long for a client to lay the goods on the table, but Myfanwy seemed in no hurry. She sat in the seat like a child and looked wonderingly around the room. There was not much to look at: a battered chesterfield sofa, a mono record player, and a nineteenth-century sea chest. The connecting door to the outer office had a top half of frosted glass upon which were stencilled the words 'Knight Errant Investigations' and the name 'Louie Knight' in smaller letters. When I set up the practice a few years ago the name had struck me as a clever conceit, but now it made me wince every time I saw it. On the desk there was a pre-war fan with Bakelite knobs; a desk lamp from the Fifties; a modern phone and an answering machine . . . people thought the styling was deliberate and ironic but actually the whole office had been rented from the library and the furniture came as part of the deal; along with Mrs Llantrisant. The bathroom door still had the lock on the outside from the days when the room had been used to house sensitive items like the anatomy books and the *Colour Atlas of Eye Surgery*. There were two photos on the desk, in cheap stand-up frames. A black and white snap of my mother and father on a windswept promenade in 1950s Llandudno. My father, fresh-faced and Brylcreemed, leaning into the wind and shielding his new wife; and my mother the eternal bride with a smile that held no inkling that she'd be dead in a year. The other picture was a blurred Kodakolor image of Marty, my school friend who was sent on a cross-country run in a blizzard and never came back. The only other photo in the room hung next to the door: great-great-uncle Noel Bartholomew – the Victorian eccentric and romantic whose rogue gene for undertaking daft crusades had been passed on to me. On the walls either side of the door, facing each other and flanking uncle Noel, were two maps: one of Aberystwyth and environs; one of Borneo.

'I've never been in a private detective's office before.'

'Don't expect too much.'

'What's in the trunk?'

'Some charts of the South China Sea, a Burmese tribal headdress and a shrunken head.'

She gasped. 'Really?'

'Really.'

'Is that Caldy Island?' she asked pointing at the map of Borneo.

'No, it's Borneo.'

She paused, bit her lip and said, 'I expect you're wondering why I'm here.'

'It had crossed my mind.'

'They say you're the best private detective in town.'

'Did they tell you about the others?'

'What about them?'

'There aren't any.'

She smiled. 'That must make you the best then. Anyway, I want to hire you.'

'Have you got any job in mind, or do you just want to take me for a walk?'

'I want you to find a missing person.'

I nodded thoughtfully. 'Anyone I know?'

'Evans the Boot.'

I didn't say anything, just raised my eyebrows. Very high. I could have whistled as well, but I decided to stick with the eyebrows.

'Evans the Boot?'

Myfanwy looked at me and fidgeted awkwardly.

'Is he a friend of yours?'

'He's my cousin.'

'And he's gone missing?'

'About a week now.'

'Are you sure you want to find him?'

She sighed. 'Yes, I know he's a bad lad, but his mother doesn't see it that way.'

'That's the great thing about mothers.' I leaned back and folded my arms behind my head. 'Have you been to the police?'

'Yes.'

'What did they say?'

'They said it was the best news they'd had all week.'

I laughed but stopped myself as soon as I noticed her glaring at me.

'It's not funny!'

'No, sorry. I suppose not.'

'Will you help me?'

What was I supposed to say? That she was better off going to the police, who would have the resources and the connections? That with missing persons you need a lot of patience because quite often they don't want to be found? That Evans the Boot was almost certainly dead? Instead I said, 'I don't like Evans the Boot.'

'I'm not asking you to like him, just find him.'

'And I don't like the sort of people he goes round with. If I go poking my nose into their affairs I could go missing too.'

'I see, so you're scared.'

'No, I'm not scared!'

'Sounds like it to me.'

'Well I'm not.'

She shrugged. We glared at each other for a while.

'I'll admit that looking for Evans the Boot is not a healthy way to earn a living,' I said, looking away, unable to hold her stare.

'Fair enough.' Her tone suggested I was a failure.

'I mean, I'm sorry and all that.'

'Don't bother, I know what the real reason is.' She stood up and walked over to the door.

'What is that supposed to mean?'

She picked up her hat. 'You just don't want a girl like me as a client.'

I opened my mouth to speak but she carried on.

'It's OK, you don't need to explain,' she said breezily. 'I'm used to it.'

I scooted across the room to the door. 'What are you talking about?'

She flashed a look of scorn. 'Moulin girls!'

'Moulin girls?'

'That's it, isn't it? You despise us.'

'No I don't!'

'You wouldn't want to be seen with me when you're playing golf with the Grand Wizard.'

'Hey hold on!' I cried. 'You think I play golf with the Druids?'

She stopped at the map of Borneo on her way out and said, as if her previous remarks had been about the weather, 'What do the little red dots mean?'

'Sorry?' I said, still reeling.

'These little red dots on the map?'

'It's the route taken by my great-great-uncle Noel on his expedition.'

'What was he doing?'

'He was looking for an Englishwoman rumoured to be lost in the jungle.'

'Did he fancy her?'

'No, he'd never met her; he'd just read about the case and it fascinated him.'

She traced her finger along the route – up the Rajang river and across the Bungan rapids, covering in two seconds what took Noel six months.

'Where is this place?' she said to the map.

'It's near Australia.'

'He went all the way to Australia to help a woman?'

'Yes. I suppose you could say that.'

She looked up at me and said slyly, 'Are you sure he was your uncle?'

Before I could answer she had skipped through the doorway and was off down the stairs. I ran out and leaned over the balcony to toss a comment down, but I couldn't think of anything to say. The front door slammed.

I walked back, put my feet up on the desk and contemplated the morning. As usual clients were thin on the ground and I had just turned down one whose cheques would probably be honoured by the bank. The framed sepia image of Noel Bartholomew stared down and chided me with an expression that many have described as enigmatic but which has always struck me as supercilious. Starched tropical whites, pith helmet, a dead tiger at his feet and jungle behind him. Even in 1870 the camera was busy lying: the tiger was stuffed, the jungle ferns picked in Danycoed wood and the whole scene composed in a studio before he left Town. I gave a wan smile and thought about Evans the Boot. I knew him of course. An opportunistic thief with an eye for a climbable drainpipe or an easily opened back door. Still in school but broad-shouldered and bearded. Capable of seducing the wives of his school masters and then boasting to them of it afterwards. A violent thug who invoked a tingling, visceral fear. That same fear you feel when in a strange town you enter an underpass and hear from up ahead the primaeval, ritual chanting of football hooligans. Yes, I knew him, we were both creatures of the same nocturnal landscape. But our paths seldom crossed. His evenings would be mapped out by the various intricate routes from pub to pub that characterised the night out in town. While I would be sitting in cold cars, clammy with breath and condensation, watching bedroom curtains. A professional snoop in a world where most people did it as a hobby. I looked again at Noel. It was obvious now what I should have shouted down the stairs to Myfanwy: uncle Noel never came back alive. That's where misplaced chivalry gets you. But the thought didn't comfort me; the morning's peace had been disturbed, and there was only one place to re-establish it.

*

Et in Arcadia ego. The fibreglass ice-cream cone was five feet high and the Latin motto curved around the base in copperplate neon. Sitting on top of Sospan's stall, and visible to the sun-parched fisherman from ten miles out to sea, it was as much an Aberystwyth icon as the Cliff Railway or Myfanwy's mole. I too was in Arcady. I knew what it meant because I had once looked it up at the library; but if you asked Sospan he would shrug and say he found it in a book and thought it had something to do with the amusement arcade. That was his story and he stuck to it. But he knew better than anyone what strange demons brought the troubled souls to his counter.

'Morning, Mr Knight! Usual is it?'

'Make it a double with extra ripple.'

He tut-tutted. 'And not even ten o'clock! Heavy night was it?'

'No, just something on my mind.'

'Well you've come to the right place.'

His hands fluttered like seagull wings at the dispenser while he stared back over his shoulder at me, inscrutable behind that rictus of smarm the ice man calls a smile. A lot of people claimed to find in his face a resemblance to the notorious Nazi Angel of Death, Josef Mengele, but I struggled to see it myself. Although there was about him an air of moral neutrality that could on occasion be quite unnerving. He placed the ice cream down on the counter in front of me and stared edgily at the troubled expression on my face. For some reason the interview in my office had upset me.

'You get that inside you, it'll make you feel a lot better.'

'What's it all about, then, Sospan?' I asked as I picked up the cone.

'Search me.'

'Don't you ever think about things?'

'What sort of things would that be then?' he asked guardedly.

'Oh I don't know. What it all means. This town. The things that go on . . .'

He sucked in his breath, starting to get alarmed at the way the conversation was heading. I struggled to find the right words.

'Moral things, Sospan, you know! Good and bad and the rôle you play in it. The sense that by doing nothing, or not enough, you might be a . . . a . . . I don't know . . . an accomplice or something . . .'

'I don't have a lot of time for thinking about things,' he said with a defensive edge creeping into his tone. 'I just scatter my hundreds and thousands before the public. Philosophy I leave to the drunks.'

I could see that I had lost him. Or I had led the conversation in a direction which threatened the protocol. People came here to escape their cares, not to relive them. They came to buy his vanilla-soaked tickets back to a world where pain was just a grazed knee and a mother's caring hand was never far away.

* * *

I took a slurp and then turned, leaning my back against the counter and staring out to sea. The surface of the water glittered like the shards of a shattered mirror. It was going to be a scorcher.

'Seen much of Evans the Boot lately?' I asked casually.

'No. And I don't want to.'

'I heard he'd done a bunk.'

'Has he? I don't expect many people will be sorry to hear that.'

'You hear anything about it?'

He scratched his chin in a pantomime of a man struggling to remember.

'Can't say that I have.'

I put a 50p piece on the counter and the smiling ice man removed it with a nonchalance that took years of polishing.

'I didn't hear anything myself, but they do say that the kid at the bingo parlour knows about these things.'

I nodded and walked off, flicking the remainder of the half-finished cone into the bin.

The mangled ironwork of Aberystwyth Pier points out across the waters of Cardigan Bay like a skeletal finger. In happier times it had been a brightly painted boulevard of kiosks and sideshows where the ladies and gentlemen of the day came to enjoy the restorative properties of the seaside air. Parasols were twirled, moustaches waxed and ships bound for Shanghai, Honolulu, Papeete and 'Frisco' could be embarked from the end of the jetty. But the intervening years had seen a sad, slow fall from grace. The ships had all been turned into garden sheds and the Pier now lay stunted and truncated like a bridge to the Promised Land that had run out of funds.

I walked under an arch of flashing, coloured lights past a cobweb-covered RSPCA dog who stood sentinel. He regarded me with a glazed look and a shocked expression on his fibreglass face and I patted him before entering. Inside it was bedlam: a flashing labyrinth of fruit machines at which boys, who should have been in school, stood chewing like cows in the late-afternoon sun and examining the reels with the concentration of chess players. Sullen girls slouched next to them with heavy kohl-rimmed eyes like handmaidens from Egyptian tombs. I walked quickly past to the back and through the fluttering door of plastic strips into Bingoland. Here the same girls, fifty years down the line, could be found wearing dishwater-coloured coats and peering intently at the electro-illuminated screens. Each searching in the depths of the TV tube for the string of numbers that would unlock the doors of the glass-fronted cabinet of prizes. Goblin Teasmades, picnic hampers, sets of wine glasses or, for those granite-hearted ones with the resolve to save up the vouchers, the Colt 45 and Roy Rogers hat. Any line from top to bottom, side to side or from corner to corner.

At the far end of the room, next to a window looking out on to a forlorn ocean, there was a player who differed from the rest. Dressed in school uniform, she looked about fifteen or sixteen years old, and had a turned-up nose, a mass of freckles, spiky blonde hair and a chocolate-rimmed mouth. Although she was sliding the plastic shutters across on her console, she hadn't put any money in. Without the background illumination you couldn't see the numbers, but she didn't look like she needed to. I walked over to her. She gave me a brief glance and then returned her attention to the game.

'Wouldn't it be better if you put some money in?'

She answered mechanically without removing her gaze from the screen. 'No point. This machine isn't going to come up for another fifty games. Lady over there in the blue scarf is going to win this one.'

I looked across to the lady in question. She didn't seem the lucky type.

'She'd probably pay a lot of money for a piece of information like that.'

'She already did. Why do you think she's sitting there?'

'How do you work it out?'

'I got a system.'

'Oh.'

'Wanna buy into it?'

'No thanks. I don't believe in systems.'

She shrugged. 'Suit yourself.'

'How old are you?'

'Old enough.'

The lady in the blue scarf shouted, 'House!'

Twenty jaws dropped and the crack of Mintos hitting lower dental plates was like a Mexican firing squad taking aim. The compère walked over and started checking off the numbers as the rest of the room held its breath and watched through rheum-filled eyes of hate. Everyone prayed that there had been a mistake: a wrong number or maybe the lady would turn out to be one of those sickos who drifted in off the street to make hoax calls. The caller gave the 'OK' and the bubble burst. The lady in the blue scarf squealed with glee and twenty handbags snapped open in unison as everyone delved for more coins.

I looked at the kid with renewed respect.

'Pretty good! What's your name?'

'Calamity Jane, what's yours?'

'Louie Knight.'

'What can I do for you, Louie?'

'Evans the Boot.'

The kid pursed her lips and shook her head.

'Sorry, never heard of him.'

I took a 50p piece and laid it on top of the bingo console.

She reconsidered. 'I've got a friend who might.'

I nodded.

Kelly's eye, number one. They were off again.

'I'd like to meet him.'

Calamity Jane tut-tutted at the enormity of the task.

'That might not be easy, boss.'

'Of course.'

'Tough assignment.'

Two fat ladies, eighty-eight.

'You look like a tough kid.'

She considered again.

'Maybe I can arrange something. I'll need some help to cover my bus fare.'

I put a 20p piece down on top of the 50p piece.

'I live in Machynlleth.'

I put another 20p down.

'And sundry expenses.'

'Well, let's just begin with the bus fare.'

Calamity Jane looked at the coins disdainfully.

'Generally, my friend doesn't get out of bed for less than two pound.'

'Must be a big bed.'

'Fills the whole room.'

I put another 50p piece down.

'Always glad to help a man get out of bed.'

'Looks to me like you want him to stay there the whole day.'

I sighed and took out my card. 'I tell you what, why don't you pin this to his teddy bear. If he's got any information about Evans the Boot, we can discuss terms then.'

She picked up the card and examined it.

'You're a gumshoe!' she said, her face lighting up. 'That's what I'm going to be when I grow up.'

'Good for you!'

She slid the card into her breast pocket and slipped off the stool.

'I'll be in touch.'

Two things struck me when I got back to the office in Canticle Street: the light was flashing on the answerphone; and the office had been ransacked.

Chapter 2

THERE WAS NO sign to indicate the presence of Wales's most notorious night club. Just a plain black door, standing quietly amid the Dickensian bow windows of Patriarch Street. On the one side were the shops selling Welsh fudge, slate barometers and paperweights made out of polished fossils from the beach. And on the other, the Salvation Army second-hand clothing store, 'Army Surplice'. The door to the club itself was featureless except for a Judas window and the number six in scarlet and only if you looked closely at the doorbell on the right would you see the simple words: Moulin Goch, Boîte de Nuit. When I arrived shortly after 10pm Mrs Llantrisant and Mrs Abergynolwen from the Sweet Jesus League against Turpitude had just started setting up their stall.

'Evening, Mr Knight!'

'Evening, Mrs Llantrisant! You're looking very glamorous tonight, new hair-do is it?'

'Guess again, Mr Knight, new something else.' She lifted her left heel and did a pirouette to show off her wares. I studied her keenly; what was new?

'Go on! Can't you tell? Honestly, you men!'

'It's those orthopaedic boots, isn't it?'

She beamed and bent forward to look at them. 'Got them this morning; imported from Milan they are: calfskin with sheepskin lining – hypo-allergenic, as well, so's the cat doesn't get a cough.'

Mrs Abergynolwen came over. 'Going into the Club, is it?'

'I thought I might.'

'Like a nice little sedative to put in your drink, Mr Knight? You'll need it.'

'Not with my luck, ladies.'

'Just in case now. Keep the lid on those raging hormones. Better safe than sorry.'

'Honestly, it would be like locking the stable door when you haven't got a horse!'

The Club was a dimly lit basement made up of adjoining cellars knocked into one. The theme was nautical: fishing nets hung from the ceiling and other maritime bric-à-brac littered the room. To one side there was a small dais that acted as the stage. It was edged with sequins that glittered in the spotlights, and an unattended microphone stood in the middle. Nearer to the stage there were closely packed wooden tables, each with an oil lamp on top, while further back there was more elaborate seating made up of coracles and rowing boats sawn in half and padded to form intimate sofas. In the far corner there was an entire fishing boat washed up behind a crimson rope, accessible only to Druids and high-ranking party functionaries. Between the tables a sea of dry ice billowed, dyed blue and turquoise by the luminous plastic fish entangled in the ceiling nets. The effect was wonderful and outshone only by the club's most famous assets of all: the Entertainment Officers, or, as we all affectionately knew them, the Moulin girls. Their job was to keep everybody happy; their uniform, anything to do with the sea that they could dig up from Dai the Custard Pie's fancy dress basement. There were cabin boys and pirates; captains, smugglers and mermaids. And also, inexplicably, a girl in Welsh national dress and two Marie Antoinettes.

I was shown to a table near the front by a door officer in a dinner jacket. Myfanwy was advertised as coming on at 8pm, but never appeared before 11pm, so I ordered a rum and pondered the significance of my ransacked office. The man from the Orthopaedic Boot shop said he'd seen a group of men leaving the premises hurriedly and driving off in a mauve Montego with blacked-out windows. Only one group of people drove cars like that – the Druids. I thought of how completely the tentacles of their organisation now encircled our town; how they reached into every nook and crevice, and controlled all aspects of life – the public affairs and those goings-on that dare not show their face to the sun. How they organised the crime and also those people put in office to stop it; and how they took a cut from both. It was so familiar now it was easy to forget that it hadn't always been like this. There was a time when they just organised the Eisteddfod, licensed the application of spells and judged the poetry. When I was in school we would eagerly push ourselves forward outside assembly to have our hair tousled by the Grand Wizard when he came from the temple to deliver an address. When did it change? When did mothers start pulling their kids into shop doorways as the men of the shroud passed? When did they become gangsters in mistletoe? Was it the time they started wearing the specially tailored surplices? That day when the usual sheets, pillow cases and Wellington boots painted white with emulsion no longer sufficed? Or was it when Lovespoon the messianic Welsh teacher became Grand Wizard? And the high-ranking officers started staining their cloaks red and black to distinguish the hierarchy like the Daleks on TV? Now, of course, they eschewed sheets altogether in favour of sharp Swansea suits and silk handkerchiefs.

I ordered another drink and pondered the damage to my office. What had they been searching for? Did it have something to do with Myfanwy's visit? Nothing had been stolen. Admittedly there wasn't much to steal, but there were a few things in the attic that I didn't want disturbed. The attic still connected to the main building of the public library and I had secreted a store of cash and a disguise up there as an emergency escape route.

* * *

And then there was the message on the answerphone. Short and to the point: a boy with an Italian accent claimed to have information to sell about Evans the Boot and told me to go to the 24-hour Whelk Stall tonight at 1am.

The girl in the Welsh national dress appeared in front of me, blocking off the light.

'Hi, handsome!'

I looked up warily. 'Hi.' At close quarters I could see her outfit was only a faint echo of Welsh national dress: a basque, fishnet tights, a shawl and a stovepipe hat sitting at a jaunty angle on a mass of black curls.

She held out her hand. 'I'm Bianca.'

It would have been ungracious not to shake her hand, but I knew that once shook, that arm would act like a drawbridge enabling her to gallop across and sack the citadel of my wallet whenever she pleased. I hesitated which made her wiggle her hand impatiently in front of my face, grinning. Reluctantly I took her hand and shook. There was no resisting these girls, and if you wanted to – went the unvoiced accusation in their mocking smiles – why bother coming in the first place? She grinned and spun round excitedly before seating herself on the empty chair opposite me.

'Myfanwy told me to look after you.'

My heart fluttered unaccountably. 'She did?'

'Mmmm,' she giggled. 'She'll be along later, so she made me her deputy; only she didn't give me a star – boo hoo!'

'Are you sure she meant me?'

'Of course. You're Louie aren't you?'

I opened my mouth to speak but only managed a croak. She reached across and tousled my hair. As she did so, her basque slipped forward and I stared into the shadowy abyss of her cleavage. I groaned unintentionally before finally dragging my eyes back up to the safety zone of her face. But the damage was done: the cheeky expression poised halfway between a grin and a smirk made it clear she had registered the kill.

'Naughty boy!' she said and flicked my nose.

She moved her stool closer so we were sitting side by side, arms touching and her hair spilling out on to my shoulder, tickling my face. Her skin was hot next to mine and the moist animal scent of hair filled my nostrils like incense.

'Mmmm, I can see why she likes you!'

'But how did she know I was coming?' I said weakly.

'I don't know, I suppose you told her.'

'No I didn't.'

A waiter appeared.

'Did you tell her you weren't coming?'

'No.'

'Well, same thing then.' And then looking up at the waiter, 'Brandy-coke and another of whatever he's having.' The waiter nodded and moved off.

In a panic I shouted after him, 'Hey wait a minute!' He stopped and turned, but only slightly.

'What's wrong?' asked Bianca, her brow clouding.

I wanted to ask how much a brandy-coke cost, but thought better of it. Bianca waved the waiter away.

'Don't you want to have a nice time?' she cooed.

'Yes of course, but . . .' The words were lost as I considered the implications of what Bianca had just said. Myfanwy knew I would come. I hadn't said I was going to, and she hadn't invited me or anything; we hadn't even discussed it. In fact, I didn't even know myself until this afternoon. But she had known. Not just assumed it, which was bad enough, but had been so confident of it she had even appointed a friend to look after me. And damn it, here I was.

As the minutes ticked away after 11.15 the Club filled up quickly. Just before Myfanwy came on, one of the Druids from the roped off section got up and made for the gents and I followed him. I stood next to him in the stall and looked at him, but made no attempt to piss. After a few seconds he looked over. I smiled.

'That your Montego outside?'

'What the fuck's it to you?'

'Some people driving a car that like smashed up my place this afternoon. Wondered if you knew anything about it?'

He shrugged. 'Nothing to do with me.'

'It looked like they were searching for something.'

'You don't say.'

'Well tell your friends if they want anything from me, they should come and ask. It's more polite.'

'Dunno what you're talking about.' He shook his dick and walked out. I went back to my table.

By the time I returned to my seat, a change had come over the room. As if reacting to an unseen signal, the private conversations started to fizzle out, one by one, until in just a few seconds there were only three or four people talking. Then two, then none. We all looked to the stage like children who have scented that Father Christmas is in the building. A wave of restlessness then swept through the gathering like a breeze through a field of corn. A man appeared on the stage, clutching a microphone and holding out a supplicatory arm, admonishing the restless crowd into silence.

'All right, settle down, settle down!'

There was an outbreak of chair-squeaking as people turned their seats to face the stage.

'Settle down. We've got a long show ahead of us tonight, we can't start until you let us.'

The compère paused, as if to leave a respectable gap between his persona and the new one he was about to adopt. He adjusted his bow tie and then spoke in a voice borrowed from the days of Old Time Music Hall.

'My Lords, ladies, gentlemen!' he began to a huge roar of delight. 'Bards and High Priests, it's time once again to welcome our sweet little songstress from St Asaph . . .'

The audience went 'Ooooh!'

'The little lamb chop from Lampeter . . . the farmer's favourite and Druid's delight . . .'

The audience went 'Aaah!'

'The babe that makes the bards bubble at the brim with the basest beastliness . . .'

The room thundered a delighted 'Whooah!'

'Ladies and gentlemen I give you the cute, the candy-coated, the coracle-sized crackerjack from Cwmtydu! The legendary, leek-scented lovespoon from Llanfihangel-y-Creuddyn, the one and only legendary Welsh chanteuse – Myfanwy M-o-n-t-e-z!'

It took a full three minutes for the applause to die down. During that time, the already dim lights were dimmed further, until nothing could be made out in the room except the cigarette ends in the faces of the audience and shadowy movements on the stage. Then, all of a sudden, dawn broke in the form of a single spotlight trained on Myfanwy, shimmering in an evening gown of pale blue silk.

She sang all the old favourites: 'David of White Rock'; the ancient Welsh hymn 'Calon Lan'; 'Una Paloma Blanca'; and, of course, 'Myfanwy'. Everyone had heard it a thousand times before, and no one cared. It was a class act and lasted for well over an hour. Towards the end she came down from the stage and wandered like a minstrel among the tables, teasing the men who made good-natured grabs for her. I tried not to catch her eye, but it was impossible. For the final chorus of 'Myfanwy' she came and stood at my table. I looked slowly up from my glass, our gazes locked, and to the everlasting grief of the yearning audience, she delicately plucked the rosebud from her hair and threw it into my lap. Then the lights went out.

Outside, much later, the night had turned cold and the air was full of that moisture that hangs halfway between drizzle and rain. It was about five or so minutes to one and the streets were deserted except for the occasional lone figure lurching drunkenly home. I pulled up my collar and walked along the Prom past the old university building and towards Constitution Hill. Above my head, illuminated cartoon figures shone with electric smiles in the night, and on the other side of the road, high up on the wall of the old college, Father Time sat preserved in a mosaic. His long white beard and hour glass warning everyone who looked up – and in a language they could all understand – that, for every man alive, the hours left before closing time were short.

By the time I reached the Whelk Stall the drizzle had finally made up its mind and turned into rain, driving full and hard off the sea and into my face. The booth was quiet: no one there except the kid in charge – a pimply adolescent in a grubby white coat and a silly cardboard hat. I ordered the special and waited, as the youth kept a wary eye on me; trouble was never far away at this time of night. Some instinct had long ago told me that the kid on the answerphone was not going to turn up, but I had to stay just in case. So I waited, grimly crunching the gritty pickled delicacies. After half an hour, and soaked to the skin, I gave up and left.

When I got home there was someone in the office, standing at the window with his back to me. It was Detective Inspector Llunos. Short and portly with a permanent look of weary sadness.

'You keep late hours,' he said without turning.

'Is that a police matter?'

'Depends what you get up to during them.'

I went into the kitchenette, picked up two glasses from the draining board and poured us both a rum. By the time I returned he was sitting in the client's chair, just like Myfanwy had done earlier in the day. It seemed like last year.

'What did you get up to?'

I waited a few seconds and let the fire of the rum chase out the late-night damp.

'I was at the Moulin.'

'I know. What did you do after that?'

'Went for a walk.'

'A walk?' He pretended to consider my answer. 'That's nice. Anywhere in particular?'

'No, just around.'

I wondered what he was getting at; he wasn't here for a chat.

'With a girl were you?'

I shook my head.

'Or was it little boys?'

I poured another drink and looked at him sleepily.

He sighed. During his years on the Force in Aberystwyth he'd seen everything there was to see and had long ago lost the energy to be offended by it. Just as the man who cleans up after the donkeys on the Prom no longer notices what it is he sweeps up. I'd run into him a number of times before. There was a sort of uneasy truce between us. Like any cop he didn't like having private operatives sniffing around on his turf. I didn't blame him for it; when I was walking the beat in Swansea I didn't like them either. But I had a right to operate, as long as I kept within certain limits; and as long as I did, he tolerated me. The key requirement was that I dealt straight with him; if I did, things ran smoothly enough. But if I played what he called 'silly buggers', he could be very, very hard. Sadly, my instinct was telling me that on this case I was going to be playing silly buggers.

He drank his rum slowly and then started again.

'Did you have an appointment with anyone tonight?'

I shook my head.

'An appointment with Giuseppe Bronzini?'

I paused for a second, and then said, 'Who?'

He laughed. The hesitation had been for the tiniest fraction of a second but the wily cop had seen it. I didn't like where this was heading.

'We spoke to his mother earlier; he told her he was going to meet you this evening. Know anything about that?'

'Llunos, what the fuck do you want?'

He reached into his pocket and pulled out the business card I had given Calamity Jane in the afternoon.

'Recognise this?'

'It looks like one of my cards.'

Llunos examined it as if he'd only just noticed it. 'Yes it does, doesn't it?' He flicked the card with his thumb. 'We found it on Bronzini earlier this evening. I don't suppose you can explain that?'

'Bronzini?'

'Yes. He was dead, by the way.'

I stared at him across the desk, fear starting to flutter in my stomach. He raised one eyebrow, prompting me to explain.

'I went to the Moulin, I left and went for a walk. I had some whelks and came home. I had no meeting arranged. And I've never met this kid.' It was silly buggers time.

'Any idea how he came to have your card?'

'I don't know. Maybe he picked it up off the floor.'

The tired detective stared at the ceiling and considered my reply with an air of sarcastic thoughtfulness.

'I see,' he continued. 'So you've never seen the dead boy. You didn't have any arrangement to see him this evening, you were just out walking. Hmmm.' He examined my story like someone trying on a hat they know doesn't fit, just to be fair to the hat. 'And you say he probably picked your card up off the floor. Hmmm. Any idea why he stuck it up his arse?'

Chapter 3

THE CELL DOOR clanged open and banged shut throughout the night as rhythmically as a pile-driver. I sat in the corner and gazed through red throbbing eyes at the lurid pageant: drunks and punks and pimps and ponces; young farmers and old farmers; pool-hall hustlers and pick pockets; Vimto louts, card sharps and shove ha'penny sharps; sailors and lobster fisherman and hookers from the putting green; the one-armed man from the all-night sweet shop, dandies and dish-washers and drunken school teachers; fire-walkers and whelk-eaters, high priests and low priests; footpads and cut-throats; waifs, strays, vanilla thieves and peat stealers; the clerk from the library, the engineer from the Great Little Train of Wales . . . it rolled on without end. At about 2am they brought in the caretaker from the school, Mr Giles, wearing the same tree-coloured tweeds he wore when I had been in school two decades ago. He slumped on to one of the benches lining the wall and held his head in his hands. Everyone was in a bad way here, but he looked more unhappy than most. I went over to him.

'Mr Giles?' I said placing a gentle hand on his broad back. I could feel silent sobs quivering through his large frame.

'Mr Giles?'

He looked up. He was a friend of my father and knew me well.

'Louie!'

'You OK?'

'Oh no, no, no, no I'm not.'

'Did they beat you?'

He shook his head.

'What did they get you for?'

'They haven't told me.'

I nodded. It was the usual way. You wouldn't find the procedure outlined in any of the pamphlets issued by Her Majesty's Stationery Office, but Llunos had his own methods. Most people were picked up, thrown in and thrown out again the following morning without being charged or any sort of paperwork involved. It helped keep the crime figures down.

'I know what he's up to, though,' Mr Giles said. 'It's about that dog.'

'What dog?'

'At the school. He's going to pin it on me. It just isn't fair.' He buried his face in his hands again. It was unusual to see Mr Giles as upset as this. For a man who spent his life stockaded into a potting shed at the corner of the rugby field at St Luddite's, his hoe swapped for a night-stick, fortitude was a way of life. It was probably the drink making him emotional.

'What's this about a dog?'

He answered into the palms of his hands. 'One of the Bronzini boys killed Mrs Morgan's dog and they're blaming me.'

There was a fresh bout of silent sobbing; I patted him gently and moved off, leaving him to his pain.

Just before breakfast, Llunos released me. I stood blinking in the bright morning sunshine on the steps of the jail.

'You're letting me go?'

He nodded. 'You've got friends in high places.'

'News to me.'

He turned to go back inside. 'Not the sort of friends I'd like to have, though.'

I stepped down on to the pavement.

'One thing, Peeper!' he called after me.

I stopped and looked round.

'This Bronzini kid . . . was murder. Serious stuff. No room here for a private operative, you understand?'

'Sure.'

'If I find you sniffing round it, we might have to arrange for you to fall down the police station steps.'

I said nothing and walked away. An awful lot of people in this town had fallen down those steps.

'Kierkegaard or Heidegger, Mr Knight?'

'Sorry, you've got me there, Sospan.'

'It's Existentialist week; my latest promotion.'

'Give me a mint choc chip with a wafer of the Absurd.'

'Coming up.'

A Sospan Special: the only over-the-counter preparation effective against the sarcasm of an Aberystwyth cop.

Sospan pushed my money back across the counter.

'Already paid for; gentleman over there.' He motioned with the ice-cream scoop towards one of the benches near the railings. A man in a white Crimplene safari suit was seated there, incandescent in the early morning sun. It was Valentine from the boutique, the 'fixer' for the Druids. I walked over.

'Nice suit.'

He looked at the material on his arm as if surprised to see it there.

'Quality stuff thith,' he lisped. 'You should come down the thop, I'll do you a nice price.'

'If I ever go on safari, I will.'

'Thit down.'

'I'm OK standing, thanks. What do you want?' He paused for a moment as if weighing each word carefully.

'You have a . . . a . . . shall we thay an "item" in your possession which is of interest to my organisation.'

I took another lick. 'Is that so?'

'You know what I'm referring to?'

'Maybe.' I had no idea.

'It was given to you by Myfanwy.'

'Oh that!' I still had no idea.

'We'd like to buy it.'

'That's nice.'

'We're nice people, Mr Knight.'

'Is that why you smashed up my office?'

He raised an apologetic hand.

'A mithtake, very regrettable. We'll be more than happy to compenthate you in return, of course, for the item in question.'

I pursed my lips thoughtfully.

'How much?'

Valentine smiled, revealing a gap between the front two teeth.

'We're reasonable men; we wouldn't want to fall out over a few pounds. Thay two grand?'

I considered. 'That won't pay for the broken furniture.'

He laughed and slapped his knees in the action of standing up.

'From what I hear, 50p would be more than enough to pay for the furniture in your office. Two is very generous.'

'Let's say five.'

'I'm afraid not. There are also hidden costs to be taken into account; costs which you would have to bear if we found we could no longer afford to be nice.'

My gaze followed him as he walked briskly up the Prom towards the Bandstand. When I turned round there was a Labrador sitting at my feet, staring up and politely licking his muzzle. I looked at the ice cream.

'You sure? Paid for by the Druids, you know.'

He gave a lick of affirmation and I threw the ice into the air. The dog leaped up and caught it while it was still rising.

* * *

When I got back to the office Calamity Jane was sitting in the client's chair.

'Tough break about the Bronzini kid,' she said nonchalantly.

'So you heard?'

'Was it you?'

'Was it me what?'

'Was it you that killed him? The word is, the police took you in. That makes you a suspect doesn't it?'

I choked for a second. 'Why you little – scallywag!'

'Nothing personal, I just deal in facts.'

'Yeah? Well perhaps you'd like to explain the fact that they found that card I gave you on his body?'

She looked puzzled for a second, then she reached into her pocket and pulled out my card.

'Been with me the whole time; you mention my name to the police?'

'No.'

She gave me a look of deep scrutiny.

'Sure?

'Scout's honour.'

'Hmmm. OK. So who do you reckon did it?'

'I've no idea.'

'It shouldn't take us long to find out.'

'Hang on, kiddo, what's all this "we" business?'

'I thought I'd help you out on this one.'

'Did you now!'

'As a partner.'

'Do I look like I need a partner?'

'From where I'm sitting you do.'

'Oh really!'

'Yep.'

'Shouldn't you be in school?'

She ignored that and slid off the chair; then started pacing around the room.

'I won't ask for much. 50p a day.'

I laughed. 'That's 50p more than I earn most days.'

She walked over to the map of the town.

'We'll need some red pins.'

'What for?'

'To plot all the murders. We'll need bus timetables, witness statements, a computer database and some fresh coffee. Oh yeah,' she said turning from the map, 'if it's OK with you I might need to use your sofa, there's going to be some late nights on this one.'

'What happens if there aren't any more murders?'

She stared at me. 'What are you talking about?'

'Bronzini dead, that's one red pin – I reckon I could find one in the drawer somewhere. No need to waste money on a box. Does it have to be red?'

She took out a pack of cigarettes and said matter-of-factly, 'Boy, you're really good; you've almost got me fooled.'

'Did anyone say you could smoke in here?'

'Don't worry, I'll open a window.'

'I mean you're too young to smoke.'

'How can you be a private dick if you don't smoke?' She rolled her eyes and made a big deal of petulantly putting away the cigarettes. Then she sat down.

For a while neither of us spoke; a mild air of antagonism growing in the silence. We both knew whoever spoke first would lose. She started drumming her fingers on the table-top. I was damned if I was going to speak. I shifted in my seat and rested my elbow on the back of the chair. She copied me, the little minx.

'I mean, come on, kid . . .' I said finally.

She started counting off names on her fingers with exaggerated childishness. 'Bronzini, Brainbocs, Llewellyn and Evans the Boot.'

I stared at her suspiciously. 'What?'

'That's four pins, wouldn't you say?'

'W . . . what's that you're saying?'

'OK I'll admit Evans isn't officially dead. Maybe half a pin, but I'm only saying that to be kind to you. Won't be long before he's a whole pin.'

'Evans the Boot?'

'Probably trying to jemmy open them pearly gates as we speak.'

'Calamity!' I said sharply.

'St Peter better get himself an Alsatian.'

I banged my fist on the table. 'Calamity, stop it! What are you talking about? Who are these other people?'

'I'm sure you must have them on file. The police are keeping a blanket on it, but you being a private dick would have your own sources, wouldn't you?'

She gave me a look of crushing superiority.

Aberystwyth was a great place for a connoisseur of irony. The most underworked man in town was Meirion, the crime reporter on the *Gazette*: he worked fewer hours in a year than Father Christmas. Not because of a lack of material. There was enough going on to keep an entire department on overtime, but the money that owned the newspaper also owned the seafront hotels and the ghost train and the putting green and various other bits of tourist infrastructure. To read the *Gazette* you'd think we were a town full of Tibetan monks. We were sitting now on the terrace of the Seaside Rock Café, overlooking the crazy golf course.

'So far there have been three dead schoolchildren,' he said sucking thoughtfully on a stick of Blackpool humbug. 'All in the same class at school. Bronzini, Llewellyn and Brainbocs; and Evans the Boot is still missing.'

The waitress appeared and I ordered the assiette.

'It's all being kept under wraps of course. And you didn't hear any of this from me.'

'So how did they die?'

He took the rock out of his mouth. 'Brainbocs fell into one of the slurry vats at the cheese yards. Bronzini and Llewellyn were both given "squirty flowers".'

'Cobra venom?'

'Some sort of neurotoxin.'

I whistled. It was an old trick. Send a kid one of those squirt-water-in-your-eye flowers from the joke shop and fill it with cobra venom.

'Any idea who's doing it?'

'Hard to tell. Three of the kids were all of a bunch. Llewellyn, Bronzini, Evans the Boot were all hooligans. And we know there was no love lost between them and some of those South Aberystwyth gangs – posses or whatever it is they call themselves these days. But Brainbocs doesn't fit in. This kid was a child prodigy. The Cambrian Mozart they called him. Brilliant at history and just about everything else he turned his hand to. He spent last summer transcribing Proust's *À la recherche du temps perdu* into runes.'

I gasped. 'Wow! I couldn't even manage the cat sat on the mat!'

'Normally Brainbocs wouldn't go near kids like that, not unless he wanted his head kicked in.'

'So Bronzini and Llewellyn would have had plenty of enemies, and Brainbocs wouldn't say boo to a goose?'

'Just about. Although even Brainbocs had a few enemies.'

'Really?'

'Brainbocs got a Saturday job working at the rock factory – helping out in the R&D unit after hours. He became interested in the great age-old puzzle of rock manufacturing, called De Quincey's Theorem. It's very complicated, but basically it concerns the attempt to change the wording of the letters midway through the rock. You know, so it starts off saying Blackpool and then after a few mouthfuls it says Zanzibar or something. It's one of the last great challenges of the rock-maker's art. And he cracked it. Just like that. Sat down with a pen and paper and a set of log tables and worked it out. So then the management make him head of R&D and within a week – and the kid is still in school, don't forget, hasn't even done his O levels – within a week he'd found a way of computer type-setting the letters. Saved a fortune: twenty old-timers were thrown out of work the same afternoon. Entire factory closes down on strike. The Unions say, "Get rid of the kid, or you'll never make another stick of rock in this town." So they fire the kid. His parting shot was forty cases of rock that said "Aberystwyth" and then after two mouthfuls read: "I've pissed in this rock".'

If you walk south past the Pier and the Bandstand you come to Castle Point where the Promenade turns sharply as if on a hinge. After that the town takes on a different character: an exposed, wind-beaten strip leading down to the harbour with a down-at-heel air where life seems a constant battle with discarded newspapers flying in the wind. The buildings are mostly guesthouses or the sad annexes used by the hotels on the main Prom when they are full. The only people you see are beachcombers and dog-walkers in their flapping macs.

It was down this stretch that I found Mr Giles sitting in the harbour-side pub, the Ship's Biscuit.

'Morning Mr Giles!'

He gave me a sheepish look as if embarrassed about the other night.

'Oh hello. Everything OK?'

'Fine, and yourself?'

'Oh, can't complain,' he said stoically in a tone that stabbed the heart. He was a gentle man who had dedicated his years to the nurturing of tender shoots and seedlings, yet now some cruel trick of fate had led to him spending the autumn of his life as caretaker at St Luddite's. Who in the world had a right to complain if he didn't?

I bought him a pint and asked about the Bronzini incident.

After taking a long drink he spoke quietly to his glass.

'Few weeks ago Mrs Morgan went walking with her dog Lucky across the school grounds. You know we've got a sign up, says "Beware of your Dog", but they never read it, do they? You see a sign like that every day, so you read it but you don't really read it, if you know what I mean. You miss the difference in the wording. So she takes Lucky for a walk, and the dog disappears. Can't find him anywhere. All afternoon she's wandering around, shouting "Lucky, Lucky, Lucky!", but he's gone without a trace. Come nightfall, she has to give up. Never mind, she thinks; he'll turn up. But he doesn't. Next week Mrs Morgan's walking past the school and Bronzini appears at the gate and offers to sell her some fur gloves. Said he'd made them himself. Well, she was only too pleased to encourage a bit of industry and self-reliance among the youth, especially after all those terrible things she's been hearing about the school. So she buys the gloves. Nicely made they were, and there's something about the pattern she likes, something familiar, but she can't quite put her finger on it. They say when she got home she put the gloves on the reading table next to the fireplace and goes to make a cup of tea. When she comes back in she finds Sheba – the dog's mother – standing at the foot of the table staring up at the gloves and making this pitiful whining sound, and pawing at the ground. Terrible thing it was.'

I shook my head, appalled at the crime.

'Of course,' the caretaker added, 'the kids have their own theory about the murders.'

'Yes?'

'They think it's the Welsh teacher.'

Chapter 4

I THINK MY great-great-uncle Noel must have been in love with the woman in the jungle, Hermione Wilberforce, even though he had never met her – or at least, if he did, he only met her years after he fell in love with her. Is such a thing possible? I leaned back in the chair and listened as the scratchy strains of *Myfanwy Live at the Moulin* filled the room. Mrs Llantrisant had brought the LP round that morning. She said she'd found it in her garage but the cover didn't look like it had been gathering dust anywhere. So typical of Mrs Llantrisant to fib like that. After spending months at her stall every night calling the celebrated night-club singer a flibbertigibbet, she couldn't bring herself to admit that she liked her music as much as anyone else. I looked up at the portrait of great-great-uncle Noel, now sadly defaced by a hairline crack in the picture glass – a legacy of the recent ransacking. Those Druid tough guys would never have manhandled him like that if he'd been alive, that was for sure. He was, by all accounts, a man to be reckoned with. A man who liked nothing better than to enter the ring at county fairs to take on the roving pugilist. When friends and family and several members of the Borneo Society condemned his quest to rescue the white woman lost in the jungle as a romantic fool's errand, it just made him more determined. And so on 14 January 1868 he set off from Aberystwyth for Shrewsbury, en route to Singapore. Five years later the bishop's wife traded two brass kettles for his journal which had been found gathering dust under a chandelier of skulls in the corner of a longhouse.

Further contemplation of his fate was halted by the arrival in the office of a man who looked liked he'd just stepped out of an

Al Capone movie: double-breasted suit in dark blue pinstripe, baggy parallel seamed trousers, silk tie, fedora hat – it was Tutti-frutti, the eldest Bronzini son. Two muscle-bound henchmen followed him in.

'The boss wants to talk to you,' he said simply.

'Would he like to make an appointment?'

The two henchmen walked round the desk, grabbed my arms, and held me pinned against the back of my seat.

'Just sit down and keep your mouth shut.'

Papa Bronzini walked in, leaning heavily on a cane. Tutti-frutti eased the old man's coat off his shoulders and helped him into the client's chair. He took his time making himself comfortable but did not seem bothered by the fact that a roomful of people was waiting for him. It came naturally to him. Once he'd made himself at ease he looked slowly up at me.

'*Buon giorno*.'

'*Bore da*. I'm sorry about your boy.'

He raised a hand as if to indicate my condolences were taken for granted. 'It's been a great shock for the family.'

'I'm sure.'

'Naturally we would like to find out who did this thing.'

'Naturally.'

For a while no one spoke. The Papa seemed to be pondering the right way to broach the subject.

'You will forgive the impertinence, I hear you were a recent guest at the police station?'

'Yes, that's right.'

'May I ask why?'

It was my turn to ponder. What should I tell him? Protecting client confidentiality was a ground rule of the profession. It was true that technically Myfanwy wasn't a client because I wasn't getting paid, but that was only a technicality. Morally I was beholden to protect her interests. I knew, too, that Papa Bronzini was no fool. He had connections; he would already know why Llunos took me in.

'Are you having trouble remembering?' The question was politely put, but the undertone of impatience was clear.

'I can't tell you,' I said.

The thug on my left took out a small rubber cosh and cradled it casually in both hands.

Papa Bronzini looked at me sadly. 'I'm dismayed to hear that.'

'I'm sorry,' I said. 'Especially about your boy; but Llunos wanted to speak to me about a different matter.'

'Is that so?' he asked simply. Again there was silence. This time with an edge of tension. 'You should understand Mr Knight, no one is accusing anyone of anything. It's simply a matter of fact-finding. You're a father yourself, you must understand –'

'No I'm not.'

Papa Bronzini looked confused.

'I'm not a father.'

He picked up the photo of Marty.

'He's not my son. He was a school friend of mine; he died when I was fourteen.'

Bronzini put the photo frame back on the desk with exaggerated respect. 'You must have been very close to him, to keep the picture on your desk all these years.'

'I suppose you could say so. Although it's a bit more complicated than that.' I didn't tell him Marty died for starting a mutiny during a PE lesson.

Bronzini raised a hand. 'Even so, someone with such sensitivity would surely understand my feelings as a father. We're talking simple courtesy and decency here –'

'I do understand, Mr Bronzini, but I can't tell you what Llunos wanted to see me about. It's a matter of honour. As a Sicilian you would surely –'

Papa Bronzini banged the desk with his fist. 'You talk of honour and lie to me in the same breath!'

I wondered how long it would be before they used the cosh. Suddenly I became angry; who were these cheap gangsters to force their way into my office and give me a lecture on manners?

'Look, Mr Bronzini!' I snapped. 'I sympathise about your son, but let's not get carried away; we both know what you and your boys get up to round this town, so don't come here preaching to me about courtesy –'

The cosh landed on the side of my head; sparks shot across my field of vision and the room turned on its side. I lay sideways on the floor for a few seconds before the two thugs dragged me back up and put me in the chair.

Tutti-frutti leaped round the desk and shouted into my face as the two brutes held me back.

'Don't disrespect our son, he was a good boy!'

'Oh yeah!' I shouted, anger blowing away the last remnant of good judgment. 'Try telling that to Mrs Morgan whose gloves bark every time she goes past the butcher's!'

The cosh landed again.

Papa Bronzini sighed and then stood up slowly, signalling with a slight waft of his hand that the interview was over.

'You are a fool, Mr Knight,' he said. 'You will regret your insult to our family.'

After they left, I lay on the floor looking at the room sideways, so angry that I didn't notice for quite some time the large tender bump starting to form on the side of my head. The phone rang and I climbed back on to my chair to answer it.

'Yeah?'

'Hey Peeper!'

'Calamity?'

'I thought I'd check if you've changed your mind yet.'

'About what?'

'The partnership.'

I rested the phone against my cheek and said nothing.

'You still there?'

'Look, Calamity –'

'I know you think I'm just a kid and all that, but I think I know who's behind all this.'

'Look, Calamity –'

'Police are baffled, but –'

'Calamity!' I said sharply. There was a second's silence on the line. 'This isn't a game. If you know anything about this you should go to the authorities.'

She made a derisory farting sound. 'Police! If we left it to them the whole school would be dead.'

'It's not a game, kid.'

'50p a day. That's all.'

I shook my head. 'No dice.'

'I'll be down the Pier if you change your mind.' The line clicked dead.

After sunset the night got hotter rather than cooler until by ten o'clock the people wandering the Prom were sweating more than they had been in the afternoon. As the heat increased, the paving slabs, like flowers opening at dusk, started to release the distinctive perfume of the summer night. It was a mixture that would have kept a wine-taster happy for days unravelling the different notes. Heavier tones of fried onions, spilled beer and the salty tang of sun-dried sea weed; and on top of that coconut oil, sweat, spilled ice cream, cheap aftershave and dog piss. It was a smell that belonged to the overhead lights just as assuredly as the scent of pine belonged to Christmas-tree lights; a smell which would always be linked in the photo album of the soul with three particular sounds: the muted roar of the sea; the electronic chimes of the amusement arcades; and the demented banshee wail of the police sirens.

At the Moulin I was shown to a table only two rows from the front. It meant nothing to me at the time, it was just a table: in the same way that youth means nothing to those who obliviously possess it. I was unaware then of that forlorn army of Myfanwy-worshippers sitting at the back behind the pillars who would have been craning their necks to follow my progress with envy.

Bianca came over with another girl.

'Hi, this is Pandora.'

'Pandy!' the girl announced holding out her hand to shake. She was very small, probably not much over five foot, cute and dressed as a cabin girl. I shook her hand.

'Pleased to meet you.'

Bianca turned to Pandora. 'Perhaps now we can get some peace at last.'

'Not before time,' said Pandora.

'Why, what's wrong?' I asked.

'You of course,' said Pandora. 'Myfanwy won't stop talking about you.'

'Get away!'

'It's been Louie this and Louie that –'

'We're sick of it.'

'Oh you should listen to her!' Pandora rolled her eyes as she forced herself to remember the tedium of hearing my name mentioned every minute of the day.

'We had to tell her to shut up. "Who cares how handsome he is?" we said.'

I laughed off their nonsense. 'You must think I was born yesterday!'

'It's true!' they chimed in chorus.

Myfanwy arrived. 'OK scram, kids, go and find your own man!'

'Pardon us I'm sure!' Pandora and Bianca minced off through the tables, making an exaggerated show of being put out. Myfanwy watched them go.

'That one's Pandy. All the men fancy her. They like her white socks. You wouldn't think she keeps a flick-knife in the right one, would you?'

She kissed me on the cheek, sat down and said, 'I didn't think you'd be back.'

'Why?'

'I don't know, I just didn't. I suppose because I wanted you to come back.'

'You did?'

'Of course! I'm sorry I was rude to you in your office.'

'You weren't, were you?'

'Wasn't I?'

'I don't think so.'

A waiter appeared.

'I'm on stage in a little while, but we'll have a quick drink. Order something.'

'What do you want?'

'Anything, whatever you're having.'

I ordered two straight rums.

'I mean, I understand why you wouldn't want to take the case and that.'

'Have you heard any more about your cousin?'

She shook her head sadly. 'No, his Mam's going out of her mind.'

'I asked around a bit, to see if anyone has heard anything.'

She looked at me wide-eyed. 'You did?'

'Here and there, nothing special.'

'How much do I owe you?'

'Nothing, of course.'

'But I must give you something.' She picked up her handbag and I put a restraining hand on her forearm.

'There's something I need to ask you. That afternoon you came to see me, the Druids broke into my office – they were looking for something. Something important to them, which they seem to think you gave me. You don't know what it is do you?'

She looked puzzled. 'No, I've no idea.' She tried to open her bag. 'I must give you something.'

'No,' I said again.

A frown furrowed her brow and then she brightened. 'I know, I'll tell them not to charge you for the time.'

Now I looked puzzled. 'What time?'

'For me sitting here.'

My eyes widened. 'You mean you're going to charge me?'

'But of course! I have to!'

'But I thought . . . I thought . . .' The words trailed off. What did I think? 'Damn it, Myfanwy, I thought you were sitting here because you wanted to!'

'But I do!'

'And you're going to charge me?'

'Of course . . . Oh Louie . . .' She wrapped her arms around mine and pulled herself close to me. 'Don't be like that. It's my job, don't you see?'

'But –'

'It doesn't mean I don't want to sit here. Look at it this way: imagine I was serving behind a bar. When you turn up I'm really pleased because you're my favourite customer. But I still have to charge you for the drink, don't I?'

'That's completely different.'

'Why?'

'I don't know, it just is. It's not the same.'

'Oh Louie!'

'I can't believe this. I thought . . .'

'What?'

I struggled for the words. What was I supposed to say? I who had only known her a few days thought for some unknown reason that she might actually like me? Because I couldn't find the right words, I said the wrong ones.

'So basically you're just renting yourself out to me, are you? I'm no better than all those other sad losers who come here.'

'Hmmm!' she snorted.

I sighed and stared at the table. 'If that's the case, then I don't want you sitting here.'

'Louie!'

'Go away.'

'Louie! Oooh you!' she stood up and stormed away.

When the two rums came I drank them both down in one and ordered two more. After that I had four more. And then another two. It probably explained what happened later. I was wandering back from the toilet sometime towards the end of the evening, past the roped-off section, as Bianca got into a fight with Pickel, the dwarf. Something was said and she slipped angrily off his knee and sat on the knee of one of the other Druids. More words were exchanged and the dwarf flung a hand out to cuff her. Pickel, who wound the town hall clock, always had large bunches of keys hanging from his belt like a cartoon gaoler and his movement unleashed an eerie jingling sound. Bianca dodged the blow and he took aim to do it again. I stepped over the rope and caught his hand.

'Didn't anyone ever tell you not to hit a lady?'

Hate filled his eyes and his orchestra of keys became silent for once, as the passion immobilised him. Even here, in the thick nicotine-heavy fug of the basement bar, I could detect the faint whiff of gin. It was an odour that had oozed out of Pickel all his life, since the days of a childhood spent clinging to his gin-soaked Mam.

'I would tell you to pick on someone your own size,' I quipped, 'but they might not be easy to find.' It was a cheap remark, and showed how drunk I was.

Pickel jumped up but allowed himself to be easily stopped by Valentine's ivory-handled cane which was now resting against his chest.

'Pickel!' snapped Valentine.

Furious, Pickel looked at Valentine, then me, then back to Valentine. 'Who's he think he is, talking to me like that?'

Valentine responded in a cold, businesslike tone. 'The gentleman is right, Pickel. You muthn't mithtreat the ladies.'

Pickel was boiling, but some instinct stopped him from pushing it too far. 'What ladies? They're all slags!'

'Pah!' Bianca stood up and pranced haughtily through the crowd over to the other girls. At that point the manager appeared and interposed himself between me and the argument.

'Sorry sir,' he said politely, 'only Druids allowed in this section.'

It was a watershed. A single wrong syllable here and I would never be allowed back in the Moulin again. Whether or not I paid a visit to the Accident and Emergency department on the way home would depend on the syllable.

'That's OK,' I smiled cheerfully, 'my mistake. Wouldn't want to be mistaken for a Druid.'

I decided to leave. As I retrieved my coat the manager reappeared carrying a silver tray which he proffered to me.

'For you sir.'

There was a mobile phone on it. I picked it up.

'Yes?'

'Now that you have established your credentials ath a gentleman, maybe you will be tho good as to honour our little agreement.' It was Valentine.

'I'm still considering.'

'No, you don't have that luxury. My organisation is getting rather impatient. We've been very fair with you, but time is in very limited thupply in thith matter.'

'Who do you represent?'

'That doesn't concern you.'

'Tell Lovespoon that I'll only deal with him directly.'

'Please, Mithter Knight, you really aren't in a position to make conditions.'

'No meeting with Lovespoon, no deal.'

He sighed. 'You're one man. You know the power of our organisation. Why be tho foolhardy?'

'It's the way I was brought up.'

'You've got until thunthet tomorrow. After that we can forget about being "gentlemanly".'

He hung up.

The next day was Sunday, and as usual I went to meet my father for a pint down at the Ship's Biscuit. I arrived shortly after eleven and Eeyore was already there sitting outside at one of the tables. He was wearing his trademark raincoat and cap despite the warm weather and there was straw on his coat from the donkeys. Another trademark. We looked at each other and nodded; no other greeting was necessary. I went in to fetch two pints and then joined my father in the sun.

'You just missed Mr Giles.'

'I saw him the other day. He wasn't doing too well.'

Eeyore made a sympathetic grimace into his pint glass. 'It's this thing about the dog.'

'I know, but why's he so upset about it? He's seen plenty of worse things up at that school.'

I looked across the harbour and over the rooftops. Aberystwyth was overshadowed by two hills: Pen Dinas with its iron-age hill fort; and Pen-y-Graig with its iron-age school.

Eeyore sighed. 'It's just one thing after another for him, though, isn't it? What do they need a gardener up there for anyway? There's no garden.'

'You seem thirsty today.'

He shrugged.

'Something on your mind?'

'Not really, apart from where the next bale of hay is coming from.'

It was the best time of day to enjoy a drink. The doors were wedged open to allow the fumes of the previous night to escape and in their place was the sharp, reassuring tang of disinfectant. The juke box and fruit machines were silent. The only sounds were the silvery tinkle of someone across the street practising scales on a piano; and the occasional cry of a gull.

Eeyore took a gulp from his pint and then spoke.

'How about you? Got any work?'

I thought about the answer. 'Someone came round on Friday with a case. Missing person. Evans the Boot.'

Eeyore made the sort of hissing sound you make when you burn your finger. 'Did you take it?'

'I'm not sure. I think I turned it down.'

He nodded. 'Probably wisest move.'

I shook my head. 'I don't know. I told the client "no", but I seem to be mixed up in it all the same. I'm not getting paid for it, though; so I don't call that very wise.'

'That's good.'

I looked at him. He was still staring ahead, but talking to me. Which bit did he mean was good?

'What is?'

'If you're helping someone and it's not for money, stands to reason it must be for a reason that's a lot better than money. When I was on the Force we did things because they were right, not because of the money. We'd have been stupid if we'd exposed ourselves to all that danger for money, because they didn't give us any. Not much anyway.'

I took a deep drink. The beer was good.

'The trouble is, I'm not sure if I'm doing it for good motives or just pigheadedness.

'Often there's no difference,' said Eeyore.

On my way back I cut across past the town hall and heard from up ahead the jingling of Pickel and his keys, although it was too far for the smell of gin. He was scurrying with that strange bobbing, bent-over gait reminiscent of the gorillas in the *Planet of the Apes* movies. Some instinct made me stop halfway across the square and hide behind the slate plinth of Lovespoon's equestrian statue. I waited as Pickel entered the side door to the clock tower. It was a strange life he lived up there in the belfry: washing in an old tin tub that collected rainwater and cooking in a cauldron donated by the Shawl & Sorcery Society. Pickel was in school at the same time as me, but we seldom saw him there. Mostly, he would be playing truant and loafing around the Square, looking up at the clock with a curious love; an emotion that was hard to explain except in the terms of the saloon bar psychologist who saw it as the surrogate for a mother's love. The real commodity had been sold long ago to the sailors down at the harbour. Pickel got the job as clock-keeper when the previous incumbent, Mr Dombey, died after falling into the workings. It was the Aberystywth version of the Kennedy assassination, and since it took a week to clean all his flesh off the teeth of the clockwork, time really did stand still for a while. There were many in town for whom the prospect of Mr Dombey dying that way seemed as unlikely as a fireman being run over by his own fire engine. But the police were satisfied that there were no suspicious circumstances surrounding the accident. Yet even they could not deny that there was a strange whiff of gin in the clock tower that day, and Dombey never drank. Still, someone had to wind that clock.

A voice interrupted my chain of thought.

'Hi!' It was Calamity.

'Hi!'

'Where have you been?'

'The pub.'

'You drunk?'

I laughed. 'No!'

She stood beside me twisting her body round to look at my face.

'Have you changed your mind yet?'

'Nope.'

'Aren't you even curious to know who it is?'

'Who what is?'

'The murderer?'

'All right. Who is it?'

By way of answer she looked up, craning her neck and squinting into the bright blue sky.

'Him.'

I followed her gaze up at the leaf-green bronze statue of Lovespoon astride his sturdy cob. Around the hoofs at the base there was a Latin inscription recording the well-known story of how as an infant he refused his mother's teat during Lent.

'The Welsh teacher?'

'Yep.'

'He's murdering his own pupils?'

'You knew him didn't you?'

'Yes,' I sighed, as my thoughts drifted back through the fog of years. 'Yes, he taught me Welsh many years ago.'

'You know what he's like then.'

'I remember he used to hit a lot of people. I don't recall him ever murdering anyone. I could have been away that day, though.'

I could sense the frustration gradually squelching her high spirits.

'Why won't you take me seriously?

But before I could say anything, she started walking away, across the road.

I leaned against the plinth, overcome by an unaccountable weariness. How could I take such a story seriously? It was just a piece of playground nonsense, the sort kids made up all the time. In school we had all been terrified of him, of course. When he appeared in the corridor we used to hurl ourselves aside like Chinese peasants caught by the sudden arrival of the Emperor. Pressed tightly against the wall, we would wait with averted gaze until he swept past, his white hair billowing like the sails of a clipper ship. But apart from dispensing thick ears he never did anything to justify such fear. Now he was Grand Wizard and ran the town from behind a veneer of solid civic respectability. But we all knew how thin the veneer was. Ask the men who mix the concrete in this town – those gaunt-eyed, haunted men who dare not speak of the things secretly added to their concrete during the night. Ask them about the bodies in the foundations. What was it Sospan said? The town is built on honest men. Or ask why Meirion the crime correspondent also covers the fishing industry. Why he reports so assiduously on the foreign objects that frequently snag the nets. Or ask the fishmonger about the human teeth found in the bellies of the fish. Or ask Lovespoon's cousin about his second-hand clothing store 'Dead Men's Shoes'. Ask him where he gets his stock from. Yes, Lovespoon was not a man to be meddled with. And the only reason I or Llunos had not also ended up in a lobster pot was because it suited his purpose to allow us to operate. Like Stalinist show-trials it added a gloss of legitimacy to his regime. All the same. Would he turn on his own pupils? Wouldn't they be sacrosanct? I pressed my cheek against the warm slate of the plinth. Who could say? How do you judge a man, anyway, who commissions an equestrian statue of himself after a pony trekking trip to Tregaron?

Calamity shouted from across the road. 'Would you like to know who the next victim is going to be?'

She grinned and skipped down the street, adding just before she got out of earshot: 'The fireman's son!'

Chapter 5

When I returned from my early-morning stroll the following day, Myfanwy was in the office sitting on a wicker picnic hamper. It squeaked loudly as she stood up.

'Hi! The door was open so –'

I waved away her explanations. We both looked at the hamper.

'It was such a lovely day I thought we could go to Ynyslas; I hope it's OK. Besides, I wanted to apologise.'

'What for?'

She pulled the band from her hair and shook it loose. 'Last night – our little misunderstanding. I didn't want you to think I was after your money.'

'Don't worry about it. I was drunk.'

She lifted the lid to the hamper. 'So I thought I'd treat you.'

My face lit up. 'Wow! Champagne, strawberries, chicken . . . you shouldn't waste your money on me.'

'Oh that's OK, it didn't cost much.'

'Of course it didn't, champagne's really cheap in this town.'

'No, really, it was nothing.'

I looked at her with a stern, schoolmasterly expression. 'Now don't you tell tales like that.'

Myfanwy looked at me awkwardly. 'Honestly, it cost nothing.'

It took a second or two before I understood what she was saying.

'You didn't steal it?'

'No, of course not! I put it on . . . on . . . a slate.'

'A slate?'

She twisted her hands.

'A slate?' I repeated.

'Yes . . . yours actually,' she said brightly.

'Where?'

'At the Deli.'

'I haven't got one.'

She joined her hands together in front of her, stretched the arms and smiled sheepishly.

'Well, I suppose you have now.'

We wedged the hamper into the back seat of my Wolsely Hornet and drove through town and up Penglais Hill. I suppose I should have been annoyed but really I felt like a kid on a school trip. I didn't need to ask how she managed to get the man at the Deli to put thirty pounds' worth of food on to the slate of someone who never visited his shop. I could picture the scene only too clearly: Mr Griffiths standing there looking awe-struck and imbecilic as if an angel had appeared in front of the counter; his thick-rimmed spectacles misting up and his pink sausagey face, edged on either side by two broom-heads of wiry black hair, turning crimson. I could see him shooing away the assistant and adjusting his tie as he assumed command of the situation. He probably didn't dare look at her, in case he mistakenly looked at the wrong place. She probably told him he was handsome and he probably lost control of his bladder for a second. I could see the shaking of his hands as he put the produce into the hamper, and then the slight pause when she asks for the champagne, and then the shakes getting worse. He was lucky she didn't ask for the deeds to the shop.

At the top of Penglais Hill we turned left and took the old route to Borth. The sun was hot, the windows were open and Myfanwy sang as we drove. It was like sailing a ship over an ocean of grass as the road went up and down over the hills and dales. Every hillside was chequer-boarded with cows. The constant rising and falling of the landscape had a hypnotic regularity and you thought it would never end. But then the car mounted the final hill with that suddenness that never fails to surprise and we were on the roof of the world, staring at nothing but blue: the washed-out blue of the hot sky, and the darker indigo of the cold sea rolling in from the Bay. We pulled into a driveway in front of a five-bar gate and got out. The hillside curved steeply away down to Borth and the wind was fierce, buffeting the car and making the loose cloth of my shirt flap with a sharp sound. Down below us, extending for almost ten miles, was the huge flat expanse of the Dovey estuary and stretched across it in a thin straight line was a straggle of houses. This was the town of Borth: tinselled up with inflatable swimming hoops, buckets and spades in summer; and in winter nothing but dust and creaking shutters. At the far northern extreme, lost in the haze and a desert of sand dunes was Ynyslas, goal of our picnic; and beyond that, on the other side of the estuary, were the dot-sized houses of Aberdovey. From here they looked achingly close, but so formidable a barrier were the estuarial tides, that Aberdovey often seemed like another country.

Myfanwy inserted herself between my arm and my body, to shelter from the wind, and pointed out toward the dunes of Ynyslas.

'That's where Evans the Boot's Mam lives. I thought we could drop in and say hello.'

I looked at her with a mild sensation of having been subtly manipulated.

'That's if you don't mind.'

We parked midway along the main street and climbed on to the high concrete sea wall, which neatly divided town and beach and blocked any prospect of a sea view from the guest houses on the road. On the beach holidaymakers from the Midlands were encamped in three-sided tents made of deck-chair material, but so wide and long were the golden sands, the illusion of being alone was not hard to enjoy. It was a beach created for buckets and spades and sons burying dads.

The land between Borth and Ynyslas is taken up by a golf course and we strolled gently between the rough of the links and the smooth of the ocean. Fifty yards ahead of us a lone figure could be seen tramping through the knee-high grass. His tattered army greatcoat and forlorn demeanour marked him out as one of the veterans from the war in Patagonia in 1961. We stopped walking and watched his slow, dreamy progress. Patagonia: the Welsh Vietnam. Even after a quarter of a century the scars on the collective heart had still not fully healed. Patagonia, a harsh tract of land on the tip of South America, a world of searing beauty and withering cold; difficult to find on an atlas and known only because Welsh settlers went out there in the nineteenth century. A story that began in adversity and ended in tragedy seventy years later when the Indians turned against them. It was a war of independence that soured a generation and left behind the legacy of the Vets: soldiers in a ghost army that haunted the lanes of West Wales. Each carrying in his heart the story of a military adventure that no one wanted to hear.

He was looking for lost golf balls which he could sell for his evening's meal. There was a sudden shout, a sharp crack, and the old soldier spun to the ground; felled by a golf ball. We ran towards him and from the fairway the party responsible for his misfortune came over at a more leisurely pace.

He was sitting up rubbing his head when we arrived.

'Are you OK?' said Myfanwy putting her hand on his shoulder.

'Sure, sure,' the soldier said distantly. 'Not the first time I've been hit by a golf ball.'

As he spoke we looked up to watch the arrival of the golfers. There were five of them, although we could only see four because the fifth was inside a sedan chair. The Druidic crest at the front told us it belonged to Lovespoon. The first of the party to arrive was Pickel who cartwheeled towards us like a circus tumbler. Behind him came Valentine in tartan slacks, three-tone golfing brogues and a sleeveless diamond motif sweater over a floral pattern shirt. He was pulling a squeaking trolley. At the back of the group, standing by the sedan chair, was the school games teacher, Herod Jenkins.

'I think he may be concussed,' I said looking up.

'Bloody idiot!' Valentine spluttered. 'I'll give him thomething to be concuthed about. Tell him to move his arse tho we can get on with the game.'

'He needs to rest a while.'

'Not here he doesn't.'

Myfanwy spoke: 'You should say sorry to him, you could have killed him.'

'You can shut your mouth you little tart!' said Pickel.

'Why don't you try and make me you smelly little piss-pot!'

'OK, OK,' I cried trying to wrest control of the situation. 'This man is injured –'

'Well he shouldn't go jumping in front of golf balls, then, should he?'

'Oh he jumped did he?'

'Of course he did, didn't you thee? He dived, tho he could make an inthurance claim or something.'

'Does he look like the sort of guy who has insurance?'

'Don't you be fooled by him, I know his sort –'

There was a sharp clicking sound and we all looked round to the sedan chair. A hand protruded through the curtains, like that of a Bourbon monarch. The hand waved impatiently and Valentine hurried over and poked his head inside. An uneasy silence ensued, broken occasionally by the sound of Herod Jenkins cracking his knuckles. I found myself unable to resist staring at him. Even after twenty years the sight of the man who sent Marty to his death on that cross-country run sent tremors of fear through my soul.

Valentine returned and spoke to me. 'Mr Lovethpoon extends his compliments and has asked me to remind you of the deadline we agreed for thunthet this evening. He says the thun thets at 21.17.' Then, turning to the rest of the party, 'OK, we'll drop a thtroke and move on.' They sauntered off.

'Ooh they give me the creeps!' shivered Myfanwy.

The soldier sat up and crossed his arms over his knees. His coat was torn and stained and his hair long and matted, splaying out from beneath the famous green beret.

'Thanks for your help. My name's Cadwaladr.'

'Louie and Myfanwy.'

He nodded. 'I know, the singer. I've seen the posters.'

Myfanwy smiled. 'Are you feeling all right now?'

'Oh sure. It was only a little knock.'

'It sounded pretty loud to me,' I laughed.

'No, no. It was nothing. It was the hunger that did it, y'see. I fell over from weakness, not because of the golf ball.'

There was a moment of puzzlement until we realised that the old soldier was staring longingly at the hamper.

'Of course!' I reached inside and broke off a chicken leg and handed it to him.

'No no!' he protested. 'I didn't mean that. I wouldn't dream of taking your picnic.'

'It's all right,' said Myfanwy, 'honestly it is!'

'Yes, please be our guest.'

'Absolutely not,' he insisted, 'I won't hear of it; although if it's all the same to you I wouldn't mind just trying the chicken to remind myself what they taste like. It's been so long you see.'

Myfanwy and I exchanged glances.

'Well, I suppose here is as good a place as anywhere.' We dragged the hamper off the fairway and up to the top of one of the dunes. Then we found a sandy spot with a commanding view of the ocean and began our picnic. Cadwaladr ate with the hunger of one who no longer has to worry about keeping the wolf from his door, because the beast has grown so thin you can fend him off with a stick. Chicken and bread, champagne, strawberries, ice cream and gateaux, it all disappeared.

'That Welsh teacher,' said Myfanwy after she finished eating, 'he really thinks he's something.'

I laughed. 'That's because he *is* something. Grand Wizard on the Druid council, head-teacher, prize-winning poet, scholar . . . war hero as well, so I hear.'

Cadwaladr spat out a piece of chicken gristle. 'War hero my foot!'

We both looked at him.

'I fought alongside him in '61. I don't remember him being carried around in a sedan chair then. He was just like the rest of us, a scared, skinny kid who just wanted to go home to his Mam.'

'It must have been terrible,' said Myfanwy.

The old soldier nodded. 'I was seventeen at the time, never been further than Swansea before, and then only to see Father Christmas. The thing I remember most is the cold. And the food – all that school potato.' He laughed bitterly. 'As a gesture of solidarity the school kids at home were going without their dinners so they could send them to us. Until we wrote asking them to stop.'

He chuckled and took out a scrap of newspaper and some tobacco and proceeded to roll a cigarette.

'Lovespoon won the Cross of Asaph, didn't he?' said Myfanwy brightly.

The soldier nodded. 'For sitting on his backside the whole war in a plane.'

'He won it for the raid over Rio Caeriog.' A shadow of pain passed across the soldier's face on hearing Myfanwy's words and she added quickly, 'We . . . we . . . we did it in school.'

Cadwaladr laughed bitterly. 'I bet they didn't teach you my version of it.' He paused, as if about to recall the bitter events of those far-off times, and then thought better of it. He shook his head and said in a tone of remote sadness, 'No, I bet they didn't tell you that one.'

He didn't say any more and concentrated his attention on the cigarette. The rolling paper added a faint rustling to the sighing of the wind in the marram grass. We stared at the old soldier and Myfanwy gave me a helpless look, angry with herself for having mentioned the one battle that no one wanted to talk about. Rio Caeriog, a slowly meandering river in the foothills of the Sierra Machynlleth mountains. The most famous or infamous battle of the conflict. They said it was a great victory and handed out medals like sweets. But no one who came back ever wanted to talk about it.

I started to pack away the remains of the picnic and Cadwaladr stood up.

'Thanks for the meal, it was lovely.'

'Where you going?' I asked. 'Maybe we could give you a lift.'

'Don't see how. Not unless you're going nowhere.'

'Just tell us where you're going, we can drop you off.'

'No, really, I'm going nowhere. As long as I don't reach there too soon, I'll be fine.'

Myfanwy looked at me and I shrugged. 'We'll see you around anyway.'

He nodded and then trudged off. We watched as he walked down the wall of stones to the sand and on to the water's edge.

Then he turned in the direction of Borth and followed the line of the sea; he didn't look back.

Half an hour later we were sitting on the veranda of Evans the Boot's dilapidated wooden bungalow, drinking tea. The garden looked out on to the estuary and was filled with bric-à-brac: a rusting child's swing; an upturned boat with rotten planks; a swampy pond with an old pram in it; and a number of car tyres strewn around the spiky grass. A channel filled with slate-coloured water and a simple piece of wire strung between two concrete posts served as a fence. In the distance across the constantly sliding estuarial waters, was Aberdovey, that Shangri-la of restless Aberystwyth misfits.

Surprisingly, given the temperament of the son she had borne, Ma Evans was a gentle and thoughtful lady: two soft grey eyes, a bun of fine white hair and a face worn with the myriad cares that came from bringing a rebel into the world alone. She shook her head sadly.

'Nope. This time it's different. He's gone before, but this time it's different, I can feel it.'

'You mustn't give up hope, dear,' said Myfanwy.

'You can't fool me. A mother knows. I knew it as soon as the police came round. You know why? They were polite. First time in fifty years they've been polite to me. Called me "Madam". I knew then something bad had happened to the boy.'

Myfanwy picked up the tea pot and refreshed the cups. 'That still doesn't prove anything.'

'They had a special dog with them. Wanted to put it in his bedroom. "What for?" I said, "you'll frighten the cat." They said it was a whiffer dog or something. Had a very delicate sense of smell. "Well, you don't want to be sending him into my boy's room then," I said, "the pong in there!" Well, of course they wouldn't listen to me. I wouldn't let them but they had a warrant, so what could I do? That was a novelty as well, going to the trouble of getting some paperwork. So they send the dog in and he's sick. Wouldn't go back neither, just sat in the garden howling. So then they went themselves. Should have seen them when they came out. Green as Martians, they were.'

She enjoyed a mild snicker and sipped her tea. Then she opened her handbag with a snap and pulled out a scrap of purple cloth.

'They found this under the bed. They put it in a plastic bag and gave me a receipt for it. "Suspected tea cosy", it said. "He's never been involved in anything like that," I said. "That's for the judge to decide," they said. Then they went.'

I took the cloth and looked at it.

It was just a scrap of wool, about the size of a postage stamp.

'I suppose you know your son had a few enemies?'

She snorted. 'Bloomin' millions. If it wasn't for Myfanwy coming round here once in a while, I don't think we'd ever see another human face. We're not a very popular family –'

'Now don't go saying that,' interjected Myfanwy.

'Ha! you don't have to waste any time trying to fool me. I know the things they say.'

'What do they say?' I asked.

'You know very well. Don't you go teasing me. They say I'm a witch.'

Myfanwy gasped and put her hand to her mouth. It fooled no one. Everyone knew Evans the Boot's Mam was a witch.

'Are they right?' I joked.

She pulled a face as if trying to dismiss any significance that might attach to her words. 'Well, as you know, if a young girl's in trouble and she doesn't want her parents to learn of it, she can always come here for some advice, and maybe a few herbs if you know what I mean. But that hardly makes you a witch now does it?'

Myfanwy sympathised. 'Of course not.'

'It's not like I use a knitting needle. Just a few boiled leaves, no harm in that.'

'No different from aromatherapy,' said Myfanwy.

'And then there's the runes. I do a bit of translating, now and again, you know. Nothing fancy of course.'

Myfanwy turned to me. 'Mrs Evans is the best rune-translater for miles around.'

She nodded to the chimney breast where a piece of framed runic script hung decoratively over the mantelpiece. It made my mind wander back to those desolate Friday afternoons in the third year when the double-period of rune composition made the time until 4 o'clock seem like a life sentence.

'She used to translate for the County,' Myfanwy added.

I smiled at Mrs Evans but she waved the compliment aside.

'Or if someone can't sleep,' she continued, taking care not to overlook any piece of evidence against her, 'well I know a few herbs which can be useful there, too, don't I?'

'And they call you a witch just for that!' scoffed Myfanwy.

'And there's the love potions, of course, and the Saturday mornings at the Witches' Co-op. But only on the till.'

Myfanwy scoffed again. 'No different from working in the sweet shop. Mrs Abergynolwen works on the till on Wednesdays, too.'

Ma Evans spat in contempt. 'Mrs Abergynolwen! She doesn't know her mandragora from her henbane!'

'Anyway,' said Myfanwy soothingly, 'you shouldn't let them call you a witch. I'd put a spell on them if I were you.'

'Oh I do! You should see the rash I give 'em! All over – like spotted dick. All I need is a bit of their clothing, or something they've touched. Menstrual fluid and nail clippings work best; or sometimes Julian brings me a vole and I can –'

The cat jumped up from within the house on to the window frame and mewed.

'No not you, I was just talking to Myfanwy.'

Julian mewed again.

'I didn't! I just mentioned your name! I was telling her about the voles.'

The cat made a short exasperated mew and leaped back into the house.

As we walked back along the dunes, the sky in the west became molten and the far-off windows of Borth burned with golden fire. The heat of the day had slipped away, and the rising breeze had a sudden chill edge to it which brought goosebumps to Myfanwy's back. We quickened our step and I reflected on the extra significance that today's sunset had acquired. Why hadn't I just told them I didn't know what they were looking for? I began to regret having been so cocky with them.

'Let's go for a drink,' said Myfanwy.

'Don't you have to work tonight?'

'I phoned in sick this morning.'

'You shouldn't do that.'

'Oh don't be such a misery. Aren't you having fun?'

'Of course I am.'

I led the way across the road to the Schooner Inn. We sat on a sofa in the lounge and drank beer as the setting sun turned the windows to stained glass.

'I've had a really, really, really lovely day,' said Myfanwy simply.

I nodded.

'Later we can have fish and chips.'

I said nothing and Myfanwy put her hand on my arm.

'What's wrong? You've gone all quiet.'

I sighed and took a drink. 'Do you know what has happened to Evans the Boot?'

She shook her head. 'No, of course not.'

'Haven't you any idea at all?'

'Don't you believe me?'

'After you left my office, some Druids came and ransacked it. I don't know what they were looking for but they told me I had until sunset this evening to give it to them.'

'What will they do to you?'

I shrugged. 'You know their methods.'

She twisted a beer mat between her fingers. 'And I've got you into this. I'm such a cow, I should never have involved you.'

'What could they be after?'

'Louie, I really don't know what it could be.'

A glittering drop of rain spattered against the window.

It must have been just after midnight; the rain was sluicing down from the sky in torrents and we took cover beneath a coat from the back of the car and ran across the street to my office. Once inside I went into the kitchen to fetch the bottle of rum and two glasses. When I returned to the office Myfanwy was standing in the doorway to the bedroom.

'Mmmm . . . how many poor girls have you undone in this room?'

'Not many.'

'Don't lie to me you wicked man.'

'No honest.'

'You're a private detective, you must get women throwing themselves at you all the time.'

I laughed. 'In Aberystwyth?'

'You surely don't expect me to believe you?'

'It's up to you.'

She disappeared into the bedroom and I followed her in. She sat down on the bed and ran her hand across the covers, and then stopped with a puzzled look on her face. We both looked across to her hand, which was resting on an odd-looking mound in the duvet. Gingerly she pulled back the covers, her expression deepening from one of puzzlement to fear and then, as she let out a long, shrill, ear-piercing scream, to one of horror. Lying on the pillow, in a dark sticky pool, was the head of a donkey.

Chapter 6

'HERE YOU ARE, Mr Knight, my multi-vitamin special to pick you up.'

I took the ice cream and wandered disconsolately along the Prom in the direction of Eeyore's stable, the donkey's head in a cardboard box under my arm. Sospan had said I looked tired and it was hardly surprising really. Friday night had been spent in the police cell. And last night, after I had calmed Myfanwy down and driven her home, my attempts at catching a few hours' sleep met with little success. And when I did finally manage to fall asleep shortly before dawn, I had slipped into the nightmare which has visited me, on and off, for the past twenty years. A cold, rainswept late Friday afternoon in January, the light fading so fast behind the lowering cloud that it is almost dusk, and there's still half an hour to go before the last school bell. The world is a symphony of greys: slate sky, grass the colour of the sea in winter, the mobile classrooms and metalwork blocks discernible only as black shapes containing yellow postage stamps of warm, yellow light – the light from which we are exiled. Reaching into the sky the white totemic masts of the rugby posts. And walking towards me through a herd of muddy boys in rugby jerseys is Herod Jenkins. I don't know why, among all the many episodes of misery, it is always this one that haunts me. Why, for example, it is not the terrible day when Marty went off on that cross-country run and didn't return. Or why it isn't that time in the summer downpour when Herod ordered the other boys to bowl cricket balls at me and to aim for my nose. But it is always this particular scene: that cold, rainy January afternoon when he walked towards me through the jeering boys and said, 'Come on then, son, do you want some?' And I was faced with the

Hobson's choice of trying to take the ball off him and suffering the battering which that would entail, or of disobeying him, which was even worse. 'Come on then, son, do you want some?' As the kids jeered and Herod's face widened with that horizontal crease he called a smile.

*

Eeyore sat on a bale of hay, his head resting in his hands, and stared gloomily at the decapitated head.

'In your bed?'

I nodded.

The early-morning sun made the dust in the stable dance and sparkle.

He shook his head sadly. 'It's Esmeralda.'

'Yes, I know. I recognised the white ear. I'm sorry.'

He made a dismissive expression. 'I thought at first it was one of those gangs, you know, the ones that smuggle them into Holland for those movies they do.'

I picked up a sack and laid it over the donkey's head, silencing the withering gleam of accusation in her eye.

'I don't think she suffered much,' I offered uselessly.

'No, it's us who remain who are fated to suffer.'

'Dad! Don't be like that.'

He rose to his feet with the desperate weariness of the prize fighter who would really prefer to stay down on the canvas.

'Come, I want to give you something.'

He led me through the stable, past the quietly shuffling donkeys and into an outhouse where he removed a brick from the wall and reached inside. He pulled out a key.

'There's not much I can do for you. Too old for that now. But I can give you this.'

He placed the key in my hand.

'It's to a caravan in Ynyslas. A ghost van, built from two sections of crash write-offs welded together. No records exist for it anywhere. Not the police, not the Council, not the Chirpy Caravaners of Britain Association. It's ice-cold. You can't see it from the road, it's hidden behind the Borth Lagoons Holiday Camp sign. Even the caretaker doesn't know about it. If things get too hot for you, you could hang out there for a while. No one would find you.'

I closed my hand around the key.

'There's food and water and a brand new ludo set. It's not much but it might help.'

'Thanks.'

He waved my gratitude impatiently away. 'Now you get out of here and find those guys. I've got a donkey to bury.'

From the harbour I walked up through the Castle to the top of town and turned right just before the market to KnitWits the wool shop. The bell tinkled and I walked through the aisle of displays stacked to the ceiling with wool in every shade and grade that the shepherd could offer. I put the scrap of wool from Evans the Boot's Mam on the counter and waited as Mildred Crickhowell examined it with a jeweller's loupe. It made her look like a Cyclops: one watery jellyfish-sized eye criss-crossed with spidery red veins.

'It's tea cosy all right,' she laughed. 'Funny, you don't look the type!'

'It's . . . it's not mine,' I said lamely.

She laughed again. 'No, it never is! Don't tell me, it belongs to a friend!'

I squirmed. Visitors to the town were often surprised by the amount of shops selling tea cosies, especially as most of them were concentrated down by the harbour. Just when this harmless piece of tea-pot furniture became a front for another form of spout-warming activity was a mystery lost in history.

I picked up the scrap of wool. 'Can you be sure it's cosy? I mean it's just a piece of wool, it could be from a cardigan or something.'

The woman leaned her shoulders back and tilted her head in the sort of look which said: 'What do you mean sure?! This is KnitWits you've come to, you know?'

She handed me the eyepiece. 'See for yourself.'

As I held the cloth up to the light and examined the weave, she explained to me the various features.

'See the fine dust particles in the yarn? That's tea dust. Now look at the way the threads are woven together. See? Like figure-of-eights intertwined with zigzags? That's pretty fancy crocheting. You don't see that sort of thing very often. That's what's known as the Hildegaard Purl after the Hildegaardian Order of the Sisters of Deiniol. They invented it. Now that tells us something very interesting.'

There was a pause as I struggled to see the things she was talking about.

'Very interesting,' she repeated.

'Yeah, why?'

'Dates it, doesn't it. Surer than carbon dating, that is. It's from 1958.'

'How can you tell?'

'Hildegaard Purl was invented that year, and then not long after the sisters abjured the vice of amusement and stopped the knitting. No one else can do it like they could. And there's more. Look at the curved edge with the elaborate stitching. See it?'

'Yes!' I said, amazed at how much the woman had seen through her magnifying glass.

'See how the fibres are shrivelled and discoloured?'

'Yes.'

'That's classic scorching. That's where the spout would have gone. Now see around that rim those funny symbols?'

'Yes! Like hieroglyphics.'

'Ha!' She laughed and smacked me on the back with a force you wouldn't have expected from a lady of her age. 'Not bad for someone who claims not to know anything about tea cosies. They're not hieroglyphics, but you're not far wrong. Early Mayan alphabet. Which means what you've got here is the *Mhexuataacahuatcxl*. It's from a limited edition set of cosies knitted by the Sisters of Deiniol for Ma Prytherch's Tea Cosy Emporium in 1958. Creation Legends of the World series. This is *Mhexuataacahuatcxl*, the Mayan fertility god.'

I put the eyepiece down and stared at her in wonder.

She was grinning with delight; it wasn't often she got a chance to show off like this.

She picked up the eyepiece and had another look herself.

'And, if I'm not mistaken, this little crescent shape at the edge is all that remains of his loin cloth. The design is chiefly based on source material uncovered by the 1935 Oxford University Expedition to the Cordillera Oriental. *Mhexuataacahuatcxl* was the deity responsible for the renewal of vegetation and patron god of the corporation of goldsmiths. Human victims were killed and flayed to honour him twice a year. The loin cloth is a bit of licence. He could assume the form of man or woman, you see. Obviously that was a bit racy for those sisters so they left the precise details to our imaginations.'

She put down the loupe and beamed at me. 'Remarkable people: very accomplished mathematicians, invented the concept of the zero, yet curiously they never discovered the wheel.'

'That is absolutely amazing,' I said.

'Pah!' She waved a contemptuously dismissive hand in front of her face. 'Child's play. If they'd hurry up and send me that replacement part for my scanning electron microscope I'd really be able to tell you something.'

She started tapping the counter top.

'Of course, if it really is *Mhexuataacahuatcxl*, I ought, by rights, to report you to the police.'

There was a pause. I could tell the woman was observing me keenly, while pretending not to.

'The police?'

'There were only four *Mhexuataacahuatcxls*.'

'Go on.'

Three of those four are in private collections, and the fourth until fairly recently was in the Museum.'

'And it's not any more?'

'It was stolen a few weeks ago.'

It rained for the rest of the week, and I sat in my office with my feet on the desk and stared up at the picture of Noel Bartholomew. I wondered how the gene for risking one's life on stupid causes could survive in the gene pool. Here I was on the trail of a missing boy and running headlong into a confrontation with the Druids. Evans the Boot wasn't even worth saving. His Mam might think he was, but no one else in town did. I wondered why he stole the tea cosy from the Museum. I couldn't begin to imagine but I knew it wasn't because he liked tea. I was also haunted by Calamity's parting words about the fireman's son. It was stupid, I knew that, but I couldn't get the image of the lady in the bingo hall out of my head, the lady in the blue scarf. That was a pretty damned accurate prediction. What if Calamity really did know who was going to be next? I reached for an umbrella.

Terrace Road was glossy with rain and the pavements thick with holidaymakers forced from their caravans in search of stimulus. In their clear plastic macs they jostled each other and stared with disconsolate, rain-washed faces into shop windows. I shook my head sadly. What sort of life must they have come from, I wondered, if this represented a holiday? On Penglais Hill the cars queued to get into town. Later in the afternoon they would be heading back the other way, to camping-gas meals and long nights of ludo.

At the school I pulled into the lay-by behind the rugby field. Far off in the gloom, on the other side of the pitch, I could see the squat, Neanderthal figure of Herod Jenkins leading a file of small rugby-kitted boys through sheets of rain. The man who sent Marty on the run from which he never returned. The scene had hardly changed at all in twenty years except for a new wooden building that had recently appeared in the south-western corner. I looked at it, a strange skeleton of wood shaped vaguely like an upturned beetle. Seeing Herod again had robbed me of all desire to enter the school grounds. And it occurred to me that if I wanted to see the school secretary I would probably bump into Lovespoon as well. I sat for a while listening to the drumbeat of the rain on the car's roof. Then I drove home and rang the school secretary.

'Fireman's son?' said a puzzled voice on the other end of the line.

'Yes, it's for a jamboree in Oslo. He'd be an honoured guest of Crown Prince Gustav.'

'We've got one in the first year.'

'No, too young. Must be about fifteen or sixteen.'

'What about an ambulance driver's son?'

I hung up. The next day the *Cambrian Gazette* landed on my doorstep with the front-page news that the Ghost Train would be cancelled for a week. The fireman who shovelled the coal into the boiler had been given compassionate leave: his son had died the previous night in a hit-and-run accident.

*

'"Should I, after tea and cake and ices, have the strength to force the moment to its crisis?" That's T.S. Eliot, that is, Mr Knight,' said Sospan smiling as he put the two ninety-nines down on the stand. 'From Prufrock!'

Calamity and I picked up the ices and walked over to the railings. She was now my assistant with on-target earnings of 50p a day and an ice-cream allowance.

'OK,' I said after we had shaken on the deal, 'what's the story?'

She looked at me with an insufferably smug grin and said, 'Cartographer's folly.'

'Cartographer's what?'

'Folly.'

I licked the vanilla slowly.

'You see,' continued Calamity, 'everyone knew there had to be a link to all these murders, but no one could see what it was. The kids were chalk and cheese: Evans and Bronzini and Llewellyn on one hand, Brainbocs on the other.'

'Right. So what was the link?'

She paused for effect and took a long slow deliberate slurp. 'The police couldn't see it at all.'

'I know; and you could. Now what is it?'

'Boy, they were all over the place. Not a clue.'

'Are you going to tell me or not?'

She stopped slurping and turned to look at me. 'The school bus.'

'The school bus?'

'It really fooled me for a while. You see, the police were talking a load of nonsense about them all living in the same area. But you only had to look at a map to see that wasn't true. I know, because I did look at a map. In fact, I spent hours looking at one. And the funny thing was, although it was plain the police were barking up the wrong tree, I kept getting this feeling that there was something there. And then I saw it, they were all on the same bus route. Maybe, I thought, the school bus was the link. But then, if it was as simple as that, why not arrange for the bus to crash? That way you get everybody in one hit. Then it struck me.'

I finished my ice and threw the empty cone into the bin. 'Are you going to get to the point before sunset?'

'You have to follow the reasoning behind what I'm telling you. Do you think I'm going through all this for fun?'

'Yes, I do. But go on in your own time.'

'I have to tell you, I was foxed.'

I threw my head back and groaned.

'So I went back to the map a second time, and stared, and stared and stared. And then I had it. "Eureka!" I shouted.'

She looked at me with a mixture of triumph and the impudent knowledge that I still had no idea what she was talking about.

'You're fired.'

'Aw! Don't be a misery!'

'You've got one minute.'

She tutted and rolled her eyes. 'Do you know how map makers protect their work against illegal copying?'

'No.'

'You've got to understand with a map it's very difficult to prove copyright infringement. If someone wants to publish a map but is too lazy to put on their wellies and go out with a measuring stick, they can just buy someone else's map and copy it. Save themselves a lot of walking around in the mud. After all, the landscape is already there and you're just recording it. So everyone's map should be the same anyway, shouldn't it?'

I nodded, with a puzzled look slowly creeping across my brow.

'So if you are an honest map maker, how do you protect yourself?'

'I give in.'

'I'll tell you. You put things in which don't exist. For example, you make up a hill and call it Louie's Knoll. There's no such thing in real life, so if it appears on someone else's map, the implication is, they copied yours.' She looked at me with the fire of discovery in her eyes. 'It's called a cartographer's folly.'

'I'm still lost. Was Brainbocs a map maker?'

Calamity put a conspiratorial hand on my arm, looked round and then continued in a lowered voice, 'Brainbocs was smarter than Einstein. Normally, he would get 100 per cent for every piece of homework he did. Trouble was, although he had the brains of Einstein, he had the fighting ability of a squirrel. Just about anyone could copy his homework and there was nothing he could do about it. So he would deliberately put in weird errors. The sort which no one who had actually done the homework could possibly make. Then when the same mistakes cropped up in other people's work, the teacher would guess what was going on. It was like his personal watermark.'

'And Evans, Llewellyn and Bronzini copied his homework on the bus to school each morning?'

'That's right. Everyone knows Lovespoon warned Brainbocs to steer clear of whatever it was he was writing about. But Brainbocs wouldn't listen. He must have stumbled on something; something so awful that the Welsh teacher had to kill him. But when he gets three more pieces of homework with Brainbocs's watermark he has to kill the other three as well.'

'And what was it Brainbocs writing about?'

Calamity leaned closer and said in her best cloak-and-daggery voice: 'No idea.'

Chapter 7

NO ONE KNEW what Dai Brainbocs wrote in that essay. Or, at least, if they did they weren't telling. Could a fifth-form kid write something so bad his teacher was obliged to kill him? I didn't know but I didn't have any other angle to work on and I spent the following week asking around. So did Calamity. Meirion sent me some cuttings from the *Gazette* and I pored over them. Brainbocs had been the first victim; the story went that he handed the essay in just before the 9am bell and disappeared sometime during lunch time. Two weeks later they found his calliper and some of his teeth at the bottom of one of the vats of Cardiganshire Green at the cheese yards. Everything else had been eaten away by the lactic acid. It was a well-known way of disposing of a body. There were two articles on Brainbocs: a factual piece about the discovery of the body and a rather florid essay discussing the remarkable short career of the schoolboy genius. It was signed off by Iolo Davies, the Museum curator, but was almost certainly ghost-written by Meirion. 'With hair the colour of museum dust and one leg that wouldn't bend at the knee, he'd spent so much of his life in the twilight of Aberystwyth public library he'd become translucent, like those grotesque deep sea creatures you see in *National Geographic* . . .' It was difficult to imagine Iolo Davies writing like that. There were also a few words from his teacher, Lovespoon, who described him as the finest scholar the school had ever produced; a remark that made it sound as if he were part of a proud tradition, rather than a freak that had somehow slipped through the net. Lovespoon had been so upset by the incident that he needed a week's leave and had lost the essay.

*   *   *

The week after Brainbocs's corpse was found in the cheese, Evans the Boot disappeared from the scene. The date was hard to pinpoint because he was such an elusive character, it took a while before anyone realised he had gone. And even then it was some time before people dared believe it. Not long after that a member of his gang, Llewellyn Morgan, received the 'squirt water in your eye' flower anonymously through the post. He tested it out on the balcony of his council estate flat and was so maddened by the cobra venom that he fell over the edge, digging at his eyes with his fingers in such a frenzy that they later found eyeball jelly under the nails. He fell nineteen floors but according to the pathologist would have been dead by the time he passed the eighth or ninth. Bronzini and the fireman's son – both members of the same gang – were the most recent victims. Whoever killed Bronzini must presumably also have been the one who stuck my business card up his backside, which suggested they already knew I was investigating the case, even before I did. None of the articles mentioned the stolen tea cosy.

I put the newspaper articles down flat on the window ledge of the Tropicana Milk Bar and took a drink from my strawberry milk shake. It was nearing the end and the straw made that loud plug-hole sound, which filled the whole restaurant with a grotesque burbling. Perhaps if Brainbocs had still been alive he could have turned the attention of his genius to solving that one.

The Tropicana was a great place to sit and watch the world go by. Like a lot of cafes round town it hadn't succeeded in making the leap into the last quarter of the twentieth century by acknowledging the existence of cappuccinos and espressos, but the shakes in lurid, primary colours were good and you could also get burgers and hot dogs and the juke box wasn't too loud. There was a set of Formica tables in the centre, with seats screwed to the floor, and along the window where I was sitting there was a shelf at chest height with stools covered in red vinyl. Pandora and Bianca walked past the window and waved when they saw me but they didn't stop. I watched them mincing down the Prom, Bianca with such an exaggeratedly impudent gait it was if she had springs inside her legs. And Pandy the cabin girl with the knife in her sock.

As I watched their two behinds wiggling up the street a hand passed in front of my gaze and waved about as if checking whether I was blind or not.

'Sorry,' said Calamity, 'I thought you'd turned to stone.'

'I was thinking.'

'And I know what about as well.'

She climbed on to a stool and I offered her a shake.

'No thanks, I can't stay, I've got double maths after morning break.'

'You're actually going for once?'

'This one, no choice. He checks.'

'So what have you got for me?'

'Actually, I will have that shake. Strawberry.'

I groaned, but went and fetched it all the same. Calamity unloaded the fruits of her research between sips.

'It's pretty clear the other kids were all done in because they copied Brainbocs's homework,' she began, reminding me of what I already knew.

'I know that.'

'I know you know, I'm just being thorough. Point is,' she continued, 'what was he writing about? The word on the playground is, there's a copy floating around.'

'Copy of what?'

'The essay. It's probably what the Druids were looking for when they turned your place over.'

'He made a copy of it?'

'He always did. It was his *modus operandi*.'

I looked at her askance and she gave her nose the sort of tilt that suggested she used the expression every day.

'OK, he made a copy. Now what was the essay about?'

Calamity took a long, tension-inducing slurp and then said casually, 'Cantref-y-Gwaelod.'

I said nothing.

'Cantref-y-Gwaelod,' she repeated.

'Cantref-y-Gwaelod?'

'The fabled dark-age kingdom. They say Lovespoon warned him off, told him to write about something else. But Brainbocs wouldn't listen.'

I was so surprised I said nothing for a while. Calamity stared nonchalantly out of the window as if the revelation that the Welsh teacher had killed a pupil for writing about a mythical kingdom was nothing more than you'd expect.

'This is the legendary kingdom that lay between here and Ireland? The one that sank beneath the waves ten thousand years ago?'

'Yes. They say on moonlit nights you can hear ghostly bells ringing across the sea.'

'I know.'

Do you believe that?'

'No.'

'Neither do I.'

'It's just a folk tale.'

'I'm just telling you what I hear.'

'But I can't see what's so bad about it.'

'Me neither. I once painted a picture of Cantref-y-Gwaelod in art. Scary.'

She slipped off the stool as if to leave and put a scrap of paper down on the counter.

'I got this, too. It's the address of Dai Brainbocs's Mam.'

*   *   *

I put the paper in my pocket and walked down Terrace Road towards the station. Like most kids who went to school in Aberystwyth I was familiar with the Cantref-y-Gwaelod myth. The folk tale version told how the kingdom lying in the lowland to the west had been protected from the sea by dykes and during a feast one night someone had left the sluice gates open. Similar stories were found all round the coast of Britain and seemed to be a folk memory of the land that was lost with the rising seas following the last ice age. A process that would have taken thousands of years, but which was telescoped into an overnight party in the popular version. Ghostly bells pealing across the waters on moonlit nights were also an integral part of the stories. The stories had some basis in fact – at low tide you could see the remains of an ancient forest on Borth Beach. And Mrs Pugh from Ynyslas had once famously won a rent rebate because of the bells keeping her awake at night. But there had never been any suggestion before that writing about it was bad for your health. Out of curiosity I walked through town to the Dragon's Lair on Station Square. A bell tinkled as I entered; it was one of those shops where you had to stoop to look around because there was so much stock, half of it hanging from the ceiling: a mixture of carved slate barometers, fudge and tea towels with recipes and, towards the back, a more serious selection of books. I headed for the tea towel section where I knew I could find a potted history of the kingdom which wouldn't make too many demands on my attention span. Geraint, the owner, came out from the back to greet me and we exchanged *bore da*s.

'Haven't seen you here for a while, Louie! Are you looking for anything in particular?'

I picked up a tea towel depicting a history of the lost kingdom of Cantref-y-Gwaelod.

'Well, now,' said Geraint, 'you DO surprise me!'

'Really?'

'You're the last person I would expect to be asking about that.

How many shall I put you down for? Two, three? Or is it just for yourself?'

'Sorry?'

'Tickets?'

'What are you talking about?'

'Tickets for Cantref-y-Gwaelod – that's what you meant isn't it?'

'You're selling tickets?'

'I can't promise anything, I can just put you on the list like everyone else.'

'I thought the place sank ten thousand years ago?'

'Oh yes.'

'Day out on a submarine, is it?'

'Not quite. Exodus.'

'Exodus?'

'Lovespoon is taking his people back.'

'Back where?'

'Back to Cantref-y-Gwaelod of course. Look, if you're not interested, that's fine. I've got plenty who are.'

'But how can he take people back. They don't come from there.'

'They did originally. Everyone did. Don't you know the story? When the place was flooded everyone who escaped went east. We're all descended from them. Even you.'

Geraint was grinning from ear to ear, but he usually did that anyway.

'So Lovespoon is masterminding an Exodus?'

'Take the folks out of servitude, like. Let my people go!'

'Who's in servitude round here?'

'You don't need chains to be in servitude, Louie. You should know that.'

'I suppose not. Won't it be a bit wet?'

'They're going to reclaim the land. Don't worry, it's all worked out. They're going to rebuild the sea defences and drain the land like in Holland.'

'How are they going to get there?'

'Ark.' Geraint crossed his arms with an air of smug satisfaction. 'It's not finished yet of course, but she'll be a real beauty when she is – four stabilisers, two hundred cabins with en suite, global positioning system and four cappuccino machines.'

'And all made out of gopher wood, I suppose.'

'Gopher wood and South American hardwoods from sustainable plantations. And modern high-performance plastics for below the water line.'

'Where's the ship?'

'Up at the school; special woodwork project.'

'And you're selling tickets for it.'

'Me and the other travel agents.'

'Are you going?'

Geraint faltered. 'Er . . . not immediately! Someone has to mind the shop.' He burst out laughing. 'Hey don't be going on at me! I get ten per cent on each ticket, so where's the harm? At worst they'll have a nice day out on Lovespoon's new boat. Come on. I've just put the kettle on.'

Outside the shop I took out the slip of paper Calamity had given me and looked at the address. Clarach. Four miles out of town and I could make a detour past the school on the way. It was lunch break when I arrived but though the playgrounds were full of children the games field was deserted. It was one of those numerous paradoxes that govern school life. Vast stretches of green fields which the municipality had set aside for play were out of bounds during playtime. Armed with the knowledge from Geraint I could see now that the new building, which I had initially thought resembled an upturned beetle, did indeed look like the beginnings of a ship. An Ark. Brainbocs, the finest schoolboy scholar of the century, had written an essay about the lost kingdom of Cantref-y-Gwaelod. Now his teacher Lovespoon was masterminding a scheme to reclaim the land and sail there in an Ark. What did it all mean? And, more to the point, how on earth were they going to get the boat to the sea? It was five miles away.

*

I found Dai Brainbocs's Mam in her cottage overlooking Clarach. It was the side which faced north and, permanently shielded from the sun, lived in sodden perma-gloom like the homeland of the Snow Queen. I parked my Wolsely Hornet in a lay-by set aside for undiscriminating picnickers and walked along the path cut into the side of the hill. The leaves underfoot squelched and the air had the cloying dampness of a tropical rainforest. The stones of the mouldering cottage had a cheesy consistency and water dripped from the eaves; where the drops fell there were malevolent looking white flowers that probably didn't grow anywhere else in Britain outside Kew Botanical Gardens. I knocked and called out, but getting no answer I pushed the door and went in.

Ma Brainbocs sat moving rhythmically back and forth on a rocking chair in the kitchen. She didn't see me, her head had fallen forward on to her chest and as she rocked she intoned the words 'all gone, all gone' softly to herself. I stood in the kitchen doorway and watched, aware as I did of a dark rheumatic chill seeping insistently up my legs from the floor.

'All gone,' she moaned, 'all gone, my lovely boy.'

'Mrs Brainbocs?'

'All gone, all gone.'

I placed a hand gently on her shoulder and she looked up with unfocused eyes.

'All gone, my boy, all gone.'

'Yes,' I said. 'He's gone. I've come to talk to you about him, about David.'

A gleam of comprehension appeared in the waters of her eyes and the mauve iris of her mouth slowly opened like a sea anemone's vagina.

'Dai?'

I nodded.

'He's gone.'

'Yes.'

'They took him.'

I knelt down and looked into her eyes.

'Who took him, Mrs Brainbocs?'

'That teacher.'

'Lovespoon?'

'Yes!'

'Do you know why?'

She looked at me now, her eyes slightly narrowing and whispered, 'Because of what he wrote.'

'About Cantref-y-Gwaelod?'

There was no answer and for a while there was silence in the room except for the sound of her hoarse rasping breath. I looked around. There was not much: a spinning wheel; a festering mattress in the corner; empty sherry bottles. I walked over to the stove to make her a cup of tea. There was no food in the house; instead I picked up a baked beans tin from the floor and washed it out under the tap, then I filled it with rum from my hip flask.

'This will do you good,' I said, holding it under her nose.

Two cold trembling hands gripped mine and drew the tin upwards. As the fiery spirit flowed inside her, she began to speak again with renewed strength.

'It was the Druids.'

'They took your boy?'

'Killed him.'

'Are you sure?'

She nodded and looked up at me, with a new determination.

'Of course I'm sure.'

'What was the essay about, Mrs Brainbocs? Can you remember?'

Her eyes dropped and focused on the hip flask in my coat pocket. I refilled the tin and handed it to her. She snatched at it and drank too greedily. A cough erupted from her throat and the pale warm liquor mixed with her saliva and dribbled down her bearded chin. I patted her on the back as if she were a baby.

'Please try and remember!'

'I don't know,' she said when the coughing subsided, 'I told the police everything I know.'

'Did he make a copy of it?'

This time she looked directly me with the fire of certainty burning in her eyes. 'Of course he did. Boy always did that. Always made a copy. 'Case anything happened.'

'Do you know where he put the copy?'

'Yes.'

My heart leaped. 'Yes!? Where?'

She grabbed my forearm and pressed weakly as if confiding her last secret. 'He hid it in a well-known beauty spot.'

'Well-known beauty spot?'

'Yes.'

'Which one?'

She shook her head. 'I don't know. He didn't say.' She reached out again for the baked beans tin. I refilled it but this time held it out of her reach.

'Which one?'

She shook her head back and forth like a frisky horse.

'I don't know. I don't know . . . !'

I poured some of the rum on to the floor and she gasped in horror.

'No . . . no . . . please don't!'

'Which beauty spot, Mrs Brainbocs?'

Fear crept into her eyes. 'Please give me a drink. Please!'

I turned the rum flask upside down. The liquid started to gush out. She jerked herself forward and the words tumbled out as she said anything that might stop me wasting the precious rum.

'I don't know. He wouldn't tell me. He couldn't. Boy was so excited he could hardly talk. Wouldn't hardly eat. Then he went away for a whole week. That's when he met her, y'see. That's how he knew for sure. Wouldn't eat at all when he got back.'

'Knew what?'

'Everything. Knew it all then, after he saw her. Knew the lot. She told him, y'see. Told him everything. Why shouldn't she? She didn't care. Bitch. When he got back he was pale as a ghost. Wouldn't sleep or eat or anything. Just walked up and down all night. I told him he'd wear out the hinge on his calliper, but the boy wouldn't listen. Said: Ma if something happens to me in school tomorrow, remember: I want to be buried next to Dad.'

I let her grab the rum and watched in pity as she sucked it down making a noise like water emptying from a bath. She paused for a second.

'Who was this person he met?'

'Gwenno.'

'Gwenno who?'

'Just Gwenno.'

There was another pause; Ma Brainbocs was panting like an athlete now.

I patted her gently on the shoulder. 'Mrs Brainbocs, are you saying this Gwenno told him something? Something Lovespoon didn't like?'

She looked at me, the fire in her eyes declining like an oil lamp being turned down for the night. 'Yes.' For a moment, her forlorn gaze held mine and then her head slumped forward on to her chest.

The faint light of understanding had gone out. 'All gone,' she intoned monotonously once more, 'all gone.'

As I started to leave, the rocking began again, rhythmically in accompaniment to the forlorn mantra of a mother's woe: 'All gone, my boy, all gone.'

Chapter 8

DID NOEL FIND her? After the typhoon the family of Hermione Wilberforce was dragged dead from the sea by local fishermen but Hermione was not among them. A search was conducted and nothing was found. And that should have been the end of the matter. If she wasn't dead the pirates infesting the coast off Borneo would soon make her wish she was. But then the strange stories started filtering out of the jungle. Absurd, impossible tales of a white woman seen residing there. No one who knew anything about these things believed them. Not the authorities in Singapore; nor the Rajah in Sarawak. But Bartholomew did – that daft Sir Galahad who soldiered on against all advice, even after all his guides and bearers abandoned him. The journal for which the bishop's wife traded the brass kettles peters out, after six weeks alone, in a fevered, malarial scrawl. 'I have seen her' he wrote in the final week, riddled with sickness and unable to move. I have seen her, and after that the last words, 'faith is to believe what you do not yet see'. Was it just a hallucination brought on by the madness of fever? Of course. There can be no other explanation. The chances that the woman was even there in the jungle in the first place were incalculably small. The possibility that he managed to locate her was zero. There was no real surprise about his fate, no mystery at all. Except for one thing: he took a camera with him.

*

I drove slowly round the large expanse of lawn that fronted the Museum and blinked as the sun flashed off the plexiglass nose of the Lancaster. Acquired in 1961 from the famous 617 'Dambusters' squadron, it had stood on Victory Square since the end of hostilities, its majesty never dimming despite the passage of time. Somewhere beneath the waters of the Rio Caeriog lay her sister plane. I pulled over and switched off the engine and watched a party of school children pair off and climb up the ladder, through the entrance under the dorsal turret and into the fuselage. All through school they told us how the people left Wales in the nineteenth century to settle in Patagonia, but no one ever told us why. A shilling from the end of the Pier to start a new life in a land of milk and honey. What they found wasn't even a land of bread and jam, but a barren, desolate, ice-covered wilderness. I was too young to remember the war of independence, but like everybody else I was familiar with the Pathé news footage of the queues snaking down the street outside the recruitment offices. The initial euphoria. And then the disillusionment. The body bags and policy U-turns; the sobering discovery that the boys weren't the men in white hats as everybody had supposed. Weren't liberators at all. Opinion at home turned against the ill-advised military adventure, people changed their minds. But the troops – entrenched in a war from which it was now impossible to extricate them – were not allowed such a luxury. And then came the famous Rio Caeriog campaign; a turning point and famous victory, in the same way that Dunkirk was a victory.

I found the Museum curator, Rhiannon Jones, in the Combinations and Corsetry section which ran the length of the top floor of a building that was more interesting than the exhibits it housed. The Devil's Bridge Tin & Lead Steam Railway Co. had built it during the middle of the last century, a magnificent neo-Gothic pile filled with cherubs and gargoyles, turrets, archways and crenellations. The lingerie that now shimmered in the prismatic light from the stained glass windows was said to be the largest collection of its kind in Europe and when I was young they employed a man specially to chase away the schoolboys who tried to sneak in. A job that had now gone the same way as workhouses and beadles. Although deserted, it was a pleasant enough place to take a stroll on a summer's day. I wandered through the shafts of late-afternoon sun that streamed in tenderly caressing the exhibits and making the dust dance. The tea-cosy section was at the far end under the Great South Window overlooking the Square. It was not a famous collection – a few shabby pieces in ancient cases that gave not the slightest hint at the infamous goings on of the harbour-side tea-cosy shops. It was easy to see where the Mayan piece had been stolen from. A newly replaced pane of glass and a tea cosy-shaped discolouration on the background paper in the display cabinet. A new card lay next to it bearing the fib: 'On temporary loan to the Leipziger Staatsgalerie.'

Rhiannon Jones walked over and stood next to me, admiring the cosies.

'*Prynhawn da*, Mr Knight!'

I turned and smiled. '*Prynhawn da*, Mrs Jones, lovely day!'

She put on an epiphanic expression. 'Oh isn't it!'

I needed to pump her for information but first I had to negotiate my way graciously through the introductory pleasantries. Too much haste here and she might stonewall me later.

'Oh yes, turned out beautiful, it has,' I said. 'Let's hope it stays like this for July.'

The sun slid behind a cloud on Mrs Jones's brow as some long-forgotten trauma from her childhood rose to the surface. 'Ooh you wouldn't say that if you'd seen it in '32! Lovely June that was, then first day of July it rained and didn't stop until August Bank Holiday.' She shuddered. 'I still haven't got over it!'

'Still,' I said consolingly, 'we can't complain about today.'

'Oh no,' she smiled, 'it's turned out nice all right. But then . . .'

She paused and slowly lifted her index finger to the bridge of her nose in a gesture that the women of Aberystwyth absorb at their grandmother's knee. It was a gesture designed to add a courtroom emphasis to a certain caveat that was coming. Coming unavoidably, and with the predestined certainty of a piano falling on to the head of a cartoon cat. I watched mesmerised. Oh yes, it was indeed a lovely day, she conceded, her rib cage filling up with air. 'But!' She wagged her finger in front of my face. 'But . . . but then it was nice yesterday, too, *chwarae teg*!'

Her eyes sparkled with the fire of victory. It was nice yesterday too. Of course it was. Or was it? To be honest I couldn't remember, but it didn't really matter. We were dealing here with that linguistic get-out-of-jail-free card '*chwarae teg*'. It translated as 'fair-play' and if you put one in your sentence there was nothing, no solecism, platitude or canyon-bridging leap of logic you couldn't get away with.

Having verbally checkmated me, Mrs Jones returned her attention to the tea cosies, becoming a model of magnanimity towards her vanquished foe.

'Oh yes, beauties these are,' she said. 'This set was knitted by the Sisters of Deiniol at the Hospice in '61. It was part of the war effort to buy the Lancaster.' She gave a slight nod towards the window that looked out on to Victory Square.

'It was because we didn't have any air cover, you see.'

'Must have taken a lot of knitting to buy a bomber.'

'Oh yes, but those Sisters of Deiniol are nothing if not disciplined. Ever so strict they are. You know Mrs Beynon from the lighthouse? They wouldn't let her work in the gift shop when her monthly courses were on her!'

*

The cream in the cakes was mashed up from margarine and sugar. The tables and chairs came from a school assembly hall. And the high, church-like ceiling was filled with an echoey din, softened by the fug of steam and accumulated minto-flavoured breath that resides in places like this even in the depths of summer. It was the Museum café. Red plastic tomato-shaped ketchup dispenser on the table. Polished tea urn on the counter along from the display where canoe-shaped doughnuts bore scars of fake jam. In the corner there was a one-armed bandit for which you had to change money into old pennies at the till.

Mrs Jones wiped her little finger along the rim of her prune-like mouth. Traces of cream still clung stubbornly to the grey moss-like growth on her upper lip.

'You know,' I said, 'I used to come here a lot as a kid.'

'Oh yes, we used to be very popular with the schools.'

'My favourite part', I added with exaggerated casualness, 'was the Cantref-y-Gwaelod section.'

Mrs Jones stopped chewing her doughnut and put it down on the plate. Her hand shook. 'I'm afraid', she said softly, 'that's not one of my specialities.'

'Still over by the section on two-headed calves is it?'

The trembling got worse. 'Y . . . Yes, I 'spect it is.'

'Perhaps we can walk over there, later.'

'I . . . I . . . I think it's closed'

'Oh what a pity, I've been thinking of doing some research; a sort of twentieth-century reassessment –'

Mrs Jones cut me off sharply. 'I'm sorry, I can't help you.'

'It wouldn't be any bother. Mostly theory. I'd be approaching the subject from a modern oceanographical perspective. I'd need the tide tables for the Dark Ages, of course –'

She put her hands to her ears and whined like a child.

'No, no, please stop, I don't know anything about Cantref-y-Gwaelod, really I don't.'

'What are you scared of?'

'Nothing, nothing . . . I . . . please, I have to get back.'

She stood up suddenly, the squeal of her stool making the whole room stop talking and look round. Then, lowering her voice to a harsh whisper, she hissed: 'Just fuck off, right?'

I grabbed her arm before she could escape, the dirty white wool coarse under my hand. 'Not until you tell me what you're hiding.' I tightened my grip on her bony arm and she winced in pain. Everyone in the room was watching in astonishment.

'Nothing!' she hissed. 'I'm not hiding anything. I know nothing about Cantref-y-Gwaelod.' Again she tried to struggle free, but I held on grimly.

'Who killed Brainbocs?' It was wild card thrown in to see if it had any effect on her. It did.

She gasped and cast an involuntary glance over to the fireplace by the door. I followed her gaze. There was a rectangle of bright paper above the mantelpiece where a picture which had been hanging a long time had recently been removed.

'You want me to end up like him? Like Mr Davies? Is that it? Is that what you want?'

'The old curator?'

'Yes!'

'Did he help Brainbocs with his essay?'

She whined and struggled like a cat caught in a trap.

'Where is he now? Mr Davies?'

'Just fuck off!'

My grip broke and Mrs Jones rushed through the tables, knocking drinks over as she went. Oblivious to the stares, I sat looking at the fireplace and the spot where Mr Davies's portrait used to hang.

* * *

The next day they re-opened the Ghost Train and Myfanwy rang to tell me she had two tickets. I met her outside the railway station, next to the sign saying 'What is the purpose of your journey to England?' There was something I wanted to ask her, but it was such a stupid question, I kept avoiding it. 'After Myfanwy's next scream,' I told myself. And then when she screamed, I put it off until the next. There was no shortage of screams; this was the only ghost train in the world with real ghosts. Before privatisation it had been the only ghost train operated by British Rail. It started life as an educational project by the Cardiganshire Heritage Foundation. A disused lead working had been turned into a theme ride depicting the history of lead mining in Cardiganshire. Narrow-gauge steam trains hauled holiday-makers and school-trippers up to the mine and then were exchanged for pit ponies which pulled the wagons through the galleries. It even won an award from UNESCO for responsible tourism, but then came the terrible accident. A wheel spun off and hit a pit prop bringing the roof down and killing a party of day-trippers from the Midlands. When the place re-opened two months later funny things started happening. The ponies whinnied eerily from their stables every night and in the morning they shied and refused to enter the mine. Strange sounds were heard and disembodied lights were seen floating inside the tunnels. Soon passenger numbers dwindled and it looked like the train had reached the end of the line. But then word began to spread and a new breed of passenger arrived: not people with an interest in industrial archaeology, but UFO-hunters, megalith lovers, spontaneous human combustion ghouls and lads on stag nights. And so was born the world's only genuine ghost train. In addition to the curtains of fluorescent sea weed, and plastic skeletons through which the electrically driven wagons now trundled, thrill-seekers could also look out for a woman carrying a head under her arm with peroxide blonde hair. Or a man asleep on a bench with a copy of the *Daily Mirror* over his face. And, in the cafeteria, an ectoplasmic woman breast-feeding her baby.

Myfanwy screamed and buried her head on my chest as we swept round a corner and through a curtain of fluorescent sea weed. I wanted to see if she knew any reason why her cousin Evans should have a piece of tea cosy with a Mayan pattern on it. The train crashed out through the final gate and into the warm sunshine.

'Myfawny?'

'Mmmm?'

'I know this sounds silly, but did your cousin Evans have any interest in the Incas?'

'The who?'

'Or the Aztecs; or anything like that?'

She leaned her head against my chest and looked up, smiling. 'I'm so disappointed, we never saw the woman breast-feeding.'

'You screamed enough, anyway.'

'I know but that was at the fake ghosts.'

'If they were fake, why did you scream?'

The train ground slowly to a halt and the rest of the passengers started taking off the hard hats.

'They were fake screams.' She sat up and started unbuckling the safety belt. 'Next time you can take Pandy.'

I sighed. 'Look, will you stop trying to pair me up with your friends!'

'I'm not, but she wants to go, and she's too frightened as well.'

'What about the knife in her sock?'

She put her arm round my neck and pulled herself on to me. Hair pressed warmly against my face cutting off all the light and filling me with an overwhelming urge to sleep; I pushed her gently back and asked her again.

'Was he into the Aztecs?'

She pursed her lips in a pretence of thinking and then said: 'To tell the truth I don't think he listened to groups much.'

I dropped Myfanwy off at her flat overlooking Tan-y-Bwlch and drove uphill to Southgate and then turned left into the mountainous hinterland beyond. The sun was shining in Aberystwyth but as I climbed it clouded over until soon I was driving through a chilly fog, in a world of drystone walls and cattle grids. Frightened sheep clung to the banks on either side of the road, wondering desperately how they were going to get back into the fields from which they had somehow escaped. As the mist thickened, I drove through sad unenchanted forests of conifers planted in uniform rows by the Forestry Commission, occasionally passing sticks set in the fence, with rubber shovels to beat out fires. From time to time glimpses of Nant-y-moch reservoir glinted in staccato bursts through the trees. And then the trees stopped and I found myself at a crumbling, weed-filled church yard on the slopes overlooking the reservoir. The church where Marty lies buried. I parked and made my way through the crooked slate teeth of the graves.

It was never officially established that he had been consumptive. And so many well-meaning friends have since tried to assure me that he wasn't. But how would they know? Were they there that day in primary school when we had our BCG jabs? When Marty was so terrified of the needle that I took his place in return for a month's supply of Mars bars? Perhaps if he had lived in town things might have been different. But he lived here on this sunless northern hillside overlooking the reservoir. I looked down at the simple headstone and then let my eyes wander across to the placid gunmetal waters pent up behind Nant-y-moch dam. Marty once told me that there was a village lying at the bottom of the lake; he said that it had been flooded when they built the dam and the man who printed the leaflets telling the people to quit their homes had got the dates mixed up and they all drowned. Marty said he never got any wedding invitations to do after that. It still makes me laugh.

The blizzard that took Marty had held Aberystwyth in its grip for three days and for once we had made the tragic mistake of allowing the candle of hope to flicker in our hearts. Experience had taught us, years before we were to go out into the real world to find the lesson confirmed, that the best policy is always to expect the worst. But this time as we watched the TV footage of helicopters air-lifting bales of hay to stranded livestock we thought that this Friday, at least, games would be called off. But Herod Jenkins was not one to be so easily cheated of his sport. In his book the only meteorological conditions severe enough to cancel games were to be found on Saturn. Marty hated rugby. For him it was a pagan game, a modern embodiment of the ritual rape-fest of the Beltane feasts. The goal posts represented the vulva of the fertility goddess Wicca and the ball was a symbolic sperm. It was a compelling thesis but didn't save him from being sacrificed on the altar of Herod's madness.

Nothing could ever have prepared us for the shock of that day. We were used to the fact that the normal laws of the land didn't operate on the games field, but this time the physical laws seemed suspended as well. It was as if we woke up in the morning on the ceiling to find that gravity had been reversed overnight. Marty stood there holding the one talisman known to grant immunity from persecution – the note from your Ma – and Herod rejected it. A bit of running around would be good for a cold he said in words which have gone down in medical history. And so saying he went inside to don his arctic parka. Marty stood there whiter than a ghost and shaking. The inquiry would later find that the note had been forged which meant that Herod was morally absolved. But

Marty wasn't fit, even if the note was false. He looked at me, his one friend, for help and I said, 'Marty, we won't go.' Four words that would shape my thoughts and deeds for the rest of my life. 'Marty, we won't go.' What could be simpler? It was plainly madness to go out on the field that day and if we all refused, what could he do? If we all stuck together our will could prevail. We would simply refuse to move. Marty embraced the plan with enthusiasm and managed to unite the whole class behind his mutiny. Herod came back outside with his whistle and Marty stepped forward and said, 'Sir, we're not going.' Herod blinked in astonishment and turned his full attention on the boy: fragile and shivering, awkward and scholastic – all crimes in a games teacher's eyes – and then he smiled and turned to the rest of us. 'Oh really?' he said. 'And who else is too cold to go for a little run?' There followed a split-second's silence and then everyone jeered; it was plain that Marty had been tricked and no one else had had the slightest intention of refusing to play. Not one of them stepped forward. Finally, drunk on the glee of victory, Herod turned his gaze to me, whom he knew to be Marty's confederate, and said, 'Well darling?' And I cringed like a beaten dog and said nothing. We all played rugby that day and Marty was sent on a cross-country run, alone. He looked at me just before he left and in his eye was that unforgettable heart-breaking look. Not of reproach, which would be so much more easy to live with, but of understanding. And also something else: that searing farewell of the prisoner as they apply the blindfold, and his eyes take their last drink of this beautiful world.

Chapter 9

DORIS PUGH SAT in her official tourist information blazer and spat the word across the desk like a cherry stone: 'Semen!'

I gasped.

'On an apricot satin camisole.'

'Old?'

'Flapper years. Of course he said it wasn't his, but then they all say that don't they? Thirty years he'd been there. Two more years and he would have retired on full pension with a gold clock.'

The job of a private detective in Aberystwyth was full of ironies. If you asked people politely for information they would normally clam up and begrudge you even the time of day. But if you stood on the other side of a garden hedge to them you couldn't shut them up. And sometimes the simplest way to find out what you wanted was to ask the lady at the tourist information kiosk.

'Well you can't be too careful,' she continued, 'can you? What with all these overseas students we get now? I mean, look at those girls we get from Brunei, wearing those things over the face that's like looking through a letterbox. Imagine it!'

I thanked her and wandered off down the Prom shaking my head sadly at the cruelty of Lovespoon. All his life Iolo Davies had served at that Museum, with never a blemish on his record. But he helped Brainbocs with his school essay and so he had to be punished. The method chosen was breathtakingly effective: a rogue semen stain found on one of the exhibits in the Combinations and Corsetry section. I didn't need to know the exact details to know how it was done. All very hush-hush, but not quite. Nothing crudely dramatic. Just a minor detail that would do far more damage than any gross slander. Plant the seed – ha! the cruelty of the phrase – and allow the gentle winds of scandal to blow. Everything would follow with a bleak inevitability: allegations of impropriety, rumours of extra-curricular loans of the exhibits . . . and in no time they would be removing the portrait that had hung in the Museum café for a generation. And what struck me with the most force was this: the sheer artistry of Lovespoon's evil. Because the truth was, Iolo probably had been involved in something pornographic with the combinations. Such things were commonplace. A select group of trusted high-ranking townsfolk. Envelopes of money passed discreetly under restaurant tables. He'd probably been doing it for years and they probably knew all about it and let him do it. But when they moved against him the allegations would have been impossible to refute.

Where was he now? There was one man in Aberystwyth who would know: Archie Smalls. But of course he wouldn't tell me. Not unless he was forced to. I sighed. To make him squeal I would need to find someone else; someone most people went out of their way to avoid. Her name was Siani-y-Blojob, probably the most unpleasant girl in the whole of Wales. But first I would need to get drunk.

*

It was one of those occasions which strike you as a mistake the moment you walk in. You just don't have the strength to listen to the voice in your heart and turn round and walk away. But I needed to talk to Siani and to do that I needed to go to the Indian, and to do either of those two things I needed to get drunk. So I went to the Moulin.

* * *

Myfanwy was sitting and laughing with the Druids and looked up when I entered and quickly looked away. I was shown to a table further back than previously, squashed up against a pillar with a bad view. I ordered a drink and told the waiter to tell Myfanwy I was here. He gave me a look of scarcely concealed derision. Bianca came and joined me instead.

'Hi, handsome.'

I nodded.

'Don't I even get a little smile?'

I turned to her and smiled weakly.

'Can I have a drink?'

I shrugged.

She stopped a waiter and ordered a drink.

'I bet I know why you're sad. It's Myfanwy. You're angry because she's talking to the Druids.'

'No I'm not.'

'You have to understand, Louie, she really likes you but this is a job.'

'I do understand.'

'I know how you feel. Believe me she'd much rather be here with you.'

'You couldn't even imagine how I feel.'

Bianca shrugged and we both sat in silence for a while. Then she stood up without a word and left. As soon as she went I started to wish she hadn't. I picked up her glass and sniffed it. Genuine rum – no coloured water. In the Moulin that passed as a real compliment.

I ordered more drinks and thought unhappily about Siani-y-Blojob. Every town has its hard cases just as every town has its whore and its bore. They come and go like the bluebells. And if, as some people suggest, there are good and bad years, like wines, then Siani represented one of the finest vintages in the history of the châteaux.

A girl about whom people would tell fireside tales to their children in years to come, vainly trying to convey the essence in the same way some fathers try to give their children an appreciation of the glories of Tom Finney and Stanley Matthews.

After a while, Myfanwy came over. I'd been watching her out of the corner of my eye the whole time.

'Hi, Louie!'

'Hi.'

'Sorry, I'm busy with clients.'

I took a drink.

'You don't mind do you?'

'No.'

She looked uncertainly and then offered brightly: 'I tell you what, why don't you take Bianca home with you tonight?'

It was as if she were suggesting I stop off for a takeaway.

'It's on the house.'

I looked up into her face. She was smiling happily.

'How can you say that?'

Her jaw dropped and the happy grin seeped away. 'I mean, I thought . . .' She sat down and interlinked her arm with mine. 'Oh Louie, don't get like all the others.'

'All what others?'

'You'll be calling me a tart next.'

The word hit like a meat hook.

'How can you accuse me of that and in the same breath tell me to go home with Bianca?'

A look of exasperation crossed her face.

'No one's forcing you.'

I've thought about that night many times in the years since. Wondering whether, had I altered certain details of it, certain phrases or order of words, or even if I'd been in a better mood, it might have changed the course of subsequent events. It's an easy trap to fall into – the habit of parcelling up the past into a series of neat turning points; to load incidents with a power to alter the course of events which they never possessed. Not seeing that a moment which appears pivotal in the context of an evening is really only reflecting a process which has been unfolding unseen for many months. Like a heart seizure is just the sudden outward manifestation of a lifestyle. Sometimes I ask myself if I really believe that and I realise I have no choice. The alternative scenario: that my actions that night might have made a difference, is too painful to examine in view of how that evening ended. I took Bianca home.

Maybe it was simply the power of the phrase 'on the house' that did it. Words that initially filled me with contempt, but which became less offensive and more attractive with every drink. Or maybe it was just the drink. My original plan of going on to the Indian to find Siani had lost all appeal. And it didn't have any to start with. What for anyway? I already knew where Evans was: at the bottom of the harbour or somewhere similar. There could be no other explanation. It was just a matter of time before he floated to the surface. I didn't care anyway. Or maybe it was something to do with Bianca. She was a sweet girl. Not just pretty. But something else, which I only really came to understand long after she died. She was more honest than Myfanwy. She wasn't very smart, and that was probably why. But she was a lot nicer for it.

For a long time we sat in my car, parked on the Prom just across from the mosaic of Father Time. The windows were wound down and out in the blackness we could hear the ocean throbbing; roaring and shuddering and gnawing at the boulders of the sea wall. I asked her why she hung around with Pickel and she shrugged.

'It's not like you think.'

'But he's horrible, isn't he?'

'He repairs the clocks for the pensioners for nothing. You wouldn't believe how shy he is about it; they have to leave them on the back step and in the morning they're fixed – like the tooth fairy.'

She shifted in the seat, the shiny black plastic coat crackling as she moved. 'And if they get locked out, he opens their door for them. He can open any lock . . . besides, you don't know what it's like for him.'

'Do you?'

'He spent his childhood waiting for his mum to come home from the pub. I know what that's like.'

In the darkness the glare from the streetlights glistened on the pillar-box red of her lips and the whites of her eyes.

'You make things so difficult.'

'What things?'

'You know I like you?'

'No.'

'Well, I do.'

'Thanks.'

'I didn't mean it like that.'

'Nor did I.'

She looked across at me and smiled weakly. 'I know you're a nice guy.'

'Don't get carried away, I'm not that nice.'

She squeezed my hand in the darkness.

I asked, 'Why did Myfanwy tell you to come home with me?'

'She didn't. I wanted to.'

'I just don't get it.'

'Does everything always have to be something you can get?

I pondered that one for a while. Then she put her hand on my shoulder and said, 'Can we talk about something else?'

But we didn't talk; instead we drove round the block to Canticle

Street and climbed the bare wooden stairs to the scrap of destiny which seemed so like a turning point but was probably nothing of the sort.

The following night I stayed home and drank half a bottle of rum and booked a table at the Indian restaurant.

'Do you have a reservation?' Two dark eyes studied me through the Judas hole in the door.

'Yes, Kreuzenfeld.'

The waiter nodded and pulled back the bolts.

'We've been expecting you.'

The door opened and I was shown past a sign saying 'Please guard your artificial limb against theft' and into a lounge packed with tables. The air was foggy with sweat, body odour, beery breath, hot curry spices, vomit and disinfectant. Most of the tables were full; a mixture of locals and nervous tourists. I sat down and the waiter held out a menu, regarding me with a mixture of anxiety and interest. I smiled at him. 'What's good tonight, then?'

He stared at me. 'Good?' he said in a flat Midlands accent.

'Yes, what does the chef recommend?'

'Are you trying to be funny?'

'No. I mean what should I have? What's good?'

It was plainly a request he'd never had to deal with before. He narrowed his eyes and looked at me, suspicion and confusion swimming in his eyes.

'You mean on the menu, like?'

'Yes.'

He laughed.

'Nothing of course, it's all shit.' And then, perhaps feeling a trace of guilt inspired by my guileless expression, he added:

'I mean look at this lot, what's the point?'

I looked round at the screaming hordes and nodded in sympathy.

'No point at all. You might as well open up a few tins of dog food and stir in some curry powder.'

'We do!'

I looked at him startled, and he burst out laughing. 'Just kidding, mate, but it's not a bad idea. They wouldn't know.'

I put the menu down on the table.

'Look, I'll tell you what I can do, mate, I'll ask the chef to do you some egg on toast or something?'

Before I could answer, a fight broke out in the corner of the room and the waiter strode off wearily and without any sense of urgency to attend to the situation. I looked around. On the table next to me a man lay face down in his curry. And over in the bay window, among a group of bikers, sat the girl I was looking for. Siani-y-Blojob: dirty and frayed sleeveless denim vest over the standard-issue leather jacket; hair like wet straw and a pudgy pasty face.

The fight had developed from shouts and abuse to flailing fists as the two protagonists fell heavily on to a neighbouring table, occupied by a group of lads. Paradoxically, it was one of the few things you could do to someone in this restaurant that wouldn't cause offence. Brush their sleeve, look at their girlfriend, or just stare in the wrong direction for a second and you would be issued with a challenge. But throw a body on to a stranger's food and it was OK, the sort of forgivable mistake that could happen to anyone. The only danger was if you spilled their pint of lager and there was no danger of that because it would have been whipped out of harm's way the moment the fight broke out. It was a spectacle of synchronisation and choreography that put the wonders of the natural world to shame. A shout, a scream, the splintering of glass – and suddenly, to the accompanying shouts of 'incoming!' – thirty right arms shot forward like the tentacles of a sea anemone to remove the pints. What made it even more amazing was this: they all knew the difference, like veterans from the trenches in the First World War, between the real and the false alarms. Only the tourists embarrassed themselves by reaching for their pints at the wrong moment.

The fight rolled off the table and on to the floor and the waiters moved in to disengage the flailing limbs. Another late night in Aberystwyth. Over by the window Siani-y-Blojob, like a human oil rig, lit one of her farts with a plume of flame. As she did so a waiter brought three curries on a tray and scraped them all on to one plate for her. Reckoning that this gave me at least an hour's grace, I stood up and left.

I drove fast through the empty streets, along the one-way system which took me past the station, along to the harbour and over Trefechan Bridge out towards the council estate. Calamity had written down the address for me and I found it easily enough: a semi-detached house in a nondescript row with those metal gates and railings which council houses seem always to have painted either blue, red or yellow. There was a small patch of garden to the side and the underwear hung from one of those merry-go-round washing line contraptions. I put on a gardening glove.

*

I knew I would find Archie Smalls at the all-night diner on Llanbadarn Road. It was situated on a patch of waste ground set away from the road with room for the long-distance lorry drivers to pull up for bacon sandwiches and mugs of tea. The other customers – and there were never many at any one time – were the usual misfits you find in the early hours: burglars and drunks sobering up; night-shift workers going home and early-shift workers on their way. And people like Archie who like to start late in the night, long after the rest of the town has fallen into a drunken sleep. There was one waitress on duty in a stained pink tunic and a cook playing cards at the back. The night was hot and all the windows were open, but there was hardly any movement of air to take the edge off the heat from the kitchen. Archie was sitting morosely, staring into a cold mug of tea at a table just inside the doorway. I sat down opposite him. I could see he didn't want company.

'Morning!'

He looked up sourly, but said nothing.

'Fancy a chat?'

'No.'

'Don't worry, you will.'

He looked up again and stared at me.

'I hear you've been spending a lot of time in this neighbourhood.'

'If I have, it's my business, isn't it?'

'Not now I've made it mine.'

He put a grubby index finger in his mouth and gnawed at it and spoke without taking it out. 'What do you want?'

'I was just wondering what Siani-y-Blojob would say if she caught you stealing her knickers.'

He became convulsed with contempt. 'You think I'm stupid?'

He stood up to leave but stopped halfway when I put the panties down on the table-top.

'They're from her garden.'

'Fuck off!'

'I was there about half an hour ago.'

'She'll tear your bollocks off.'

'Why would she suspect me?'

He sat down, slowly, as if there was an egg on the seat beneath him.

I started speaking to no one in particular. 'About an hour ago she was in the curry house; she had three curries. I reckon she'd be on the third by now. Maybe after that she'll go for a few more pints. Maybe she won't, maybe even she has early nights now and again. You've probably got about an hour to put her knickers back. Otherwise, you might as well start packing your suitcase.'

For a while he sat and looked at me without saying anything. I could see he was working it out. I could be lying, but why would I bother? If I wasn't lying, he was in trouble. I hated doing it to him.

'What do you want?' he said finally.

'Iolo Davies, from the Museum.'

He shot up and started to leave again but I grabbed the sleeve of his coat. The waitress looked over and then quickly away again.

'What happened to him?'

'What do you mean?'

'I hear he left the Museum.'

'So?'

'Bit sudden wasn't it?'

He shrugged. 'Maybe he wanted a change of career.'

'Did you do any business with him?'

'Yeah. Some.'

'What happened?'

Archie looked sadly at the panties, thought for a while, and then said, 'That thing with the semen stain was bollocks. He'd never get caught like that. He was a pro; we all were.'

I nodded.

'We had a well-run group – you know, respectable people, vicars and school teachers and the like, none of your riff-raff. Everyone was clean. No stains, no mess. Everyone used protection. It was understood. If anyone got caught we'd all go down. The authorities had known about it for years; they didn't care as long as they all received their fat envelopes of cash at the beginning of every month. Then one day they went for Iolo.'

'What about the rest of the ring?'

'That was the funny part. It was just him. Whatever it was he'd done, it wasn't the underwear.'

'What happened to him?'

'I heard he managed to get out of town; or maybe they let him, I don't know.'

'Do you know where he went?'

He shrugged.

I placed a hand on the panties. 'Don't force me to do this, Archie.'

He shook his head. 'I really don't know where he went, but it's not hard to guess . . . I mean the man's got to make a living hasn't he?'

'So?'

'So years ago, long before he became Mr Big Bollocks, he had a different trade. The sort they don't paint your picture in oils for and hang up in the Rotary Club.'

'What was it?'

Archie looked into my eyes and stared long and hard. He knew he was going to tell me, but he still didn't like it. Eventually he said the three words:

'Punch and Judy.'

Chapter 10

'IF THE PIRATES caught you,' I explained, 'they chained you to an oar and rubbed chillis in your eyes to keep you awake. Unless you were a woman in which case they sold you into slavery.'

Calamity stood in front of the map of Borneo and studied the route of my great-great-uncle.

'What makes you so sure she didn't drown?'

'She probably did.'

Calamity unwrapped a sugar lolly. 'So you just sit here staring at your uncle?'

'It's the second rule of being a private eye.'

She looked at me with interest. 'How does it go?'

'Look after your shoes.'

She frowned.

'It means don't waste shoe leather walking around all over the place when a lot of things can be worked out with your head.'

'What's the first rule of being a private eye?'

'Don't be one.'

She frowned again. 'And the third?'

'I'll tell you later.'

'You mean you haven't thought of it yet.'

I laughed. 'Come on, get your coat, it's time to violate the second rule.'

In Venice a nobleman would arrive at the Duke's palace in furs and silks and half an hour later would exit the back way over the Bridge of Sighs to prison. With Iolo Davies the way led over Trefechan Bridge but the symbolism was the same. For years he had basked in the warm glow of Aberystwyth respectability. Not a duke or a lord, perhaps, but a man occupying an eminent position, enjoying the esteem of the movers and shakers of his little world. Invited every year to the Golf Club Summer Ball and the Rotary Club Christmas Party; holder of a seat on the St Luddite's School board of governors; advisor to the examining boards; publisher of several pieces of research into the lost art of whalebone corsetry. A proud man who had his suits tailored in Swansea, and bespoke aftershave mixed to a personal recipe by the perfumers of Gwent. A man of culture now forced to scratch a living putting on marionette performances in the back rooms of pubs.

Aberaeron was the centre of the Punch and Judy circuit and as we drove south along the coast road, we talked more about Hermione Wilberforce. I explained how years later Bartholomew's journal was found in the jungle. It recorded how his guides and bearers abandoned him one by one, until finally he ploughed on alone; how his last weeks were spent racked by fever and madness. And how in the final delirium before he died he described the day when, alone in the jungle and too ill to move, he was visited by Hermione.

'The thing is,' said Calamity, the lolly still in her mouth, 'that doesn't prove anything, does it?'

'Nope.'

'It could just have been a hallucination.'

'Of course.'

'Or an orang-utan. Or he could have just made it up.'

'Except for one thing.'

There was a slight pause. Calamity looked at me sensing the mild air of melodrama in my voice.

'What?'

'He took a camera with him.'

I could sense her interest quicken.

'It was one of the very first ones – the size of a step-ladder and he lugged it all the way to Borneo and then upriver. He was the first person ever to record images of the headhunting tribes. He once described how he arranged a photo session and had to wait an hour for the women of the tribe to get ready. He said women were the same all over the world.'

Calamity snorted.

'Most of the film was eaten by insects but a few plates survived.'

'Where are they?'

'Sydney University.'

'You're not going to tell me he took a picture of Hermione?'

'I don't know. That's the fascinating thing: the camera was never found – they found his journal and other effects but not the camera. Then fifteen years later it turned up, or so the story goes, in a junk shop in Hong Kong. An American merchant bought it and there was a plate still inside. They say he had it developed and although partially ruined you could still make out the ghostly image of a European woman in the midst of the rainforest.'

'What happened to the picture?'

'He lost it.'

It was late afternoon when we drove into the fishing village of Aberaeron. I pulled up and parked outside the butcher's shop on the main street. A fawn Allegro pulled in and parked about thirty yards behind me. It had been following us most of the way from Aberystwyth.

'How many pubs are there in this town?' Calamity asked.

'Loads.'

'How are we gong to find the right one?'

'Third rule of being a private eye. When confronted with a mystery, don't ask what's the answer, ask what's the question.'

Calamity considered that one for a second. 'That's a good one; better than the first two.'

'Can you see the fawn Allegro behind us?'

'It's been following us since Southgate.'

I squinted at the driver in the rear-view mirror. Trench coat and trilby, beard, dark glasses, newspaper balanced on the steering wheel, it didn't prove anything, but when did an innocent person ever dress like that?

'So what's the question?'

'The question is: not which pub will he be in tonight, but which of these two butchers' shops will he be getting his sausages from.'

Calamity considered this new approach to detective work.

I took out the pamphlet on the history of the Museum that I had picked up from the library. 'Whatever else I know or don't know, I know you can't do Punch and Judy without sausages. There's always a bit where the Chinaman falls into the sausage machine and comes out as a yellow sausage with a pigtail.'

In the list of contributors at the back of the booklet there was a picture of Iolo Davies. They may have removed his portrait from the Museum café but they had done nothing more painstaking than that. Chubby red cheeks, a toothbrush moustache which he may have shaved off and bushy eyebrows which he probably hadn't.

He turned up shortly before closing time at about 5.20pm, sauntering down the sunlit street with the air of someone who has just woken up. The once-sharply tailored suit was now dirty and torn. Both knees were patched with the sort of big ugly stitching you normally only saw on clown's trousers; the handmade shoes were scuffed and open to reveal his toes. He walked into the shop and came out a few minutes later with a bag of sausages under his arm. As he walked off down the street, I eased the car out into the traffic and followed. He walked down the High Street, across the pelican crossing and into a pub overlooking the harbour called the Jolly Roger. I drove a couple of blocks and let Calamity out at the lights. The plan was for her to double back and keep an eye on the pub; I would carry on and try to lose the tail. We agreed to rendezvous at 7.30pm. I drove on and parked on an embankment overlooking the harbour; there was time to kill and the way to do it was wind down the window, let the muggy late-afternoon air in, and snooze to the muted cries of the gulls. The Allegro overtook and turned into a side street.

I awoke at the time when the town was poised between the edge of day and the beginning of night. The shopkeepers and office workers had all walked the few minutes it took them to get home and it would be a while before anyone set out for an early-evening pint. The sky in the west was mauve and one or two street lights were beginning to flicker orange and pink. The scent of fried onions drifted through the car window.

It was a five-minute walk down the main road to the pub, but I took a longer route on foot through the harbour. By early evening it was a deserted stretch of nets, lobster pots and boats hoisted out of the water. The air was sharp and stank of dried fish. Midway along the route, I turned a corner and then stepped into a doorway and waited. A figure in a trench coat and trilby appeared walking quietly and furtively. I stepped out and stood in his path without saying anything.

He froze, and then turned to run just as I lunged forwards and grabbed the front of his coat. We struggled and fell against a pile of fish-smelling cages. In the tussle the man's beard came off. It was a cheap joke-shop one held on with plastic spectacle frames which hooked over the ears. I looked into his face in astonishment. It was a woman. The surprise was enough to give her the split-second she needed. Out of a pocket came a can which she sprayed into my face. Pepper spray. My spine arched backwards with a vicious kick as I struggled to escape the stinging needles of the gas. At the same time, the woman struggled free and ran off, leaving me holding a false beard and the button off the front of her coat.

I couldn't take Calamity into the pub so I gave her some money for fish and chips and told her to make herself scarce. Then I entered the front bar. It had a pleasant careworn air about it, the round wooden tables were ingrained with years of spilled beer and cigarette stains and the plain wooden chairs were worn smooth. It was tricked out with sailors' hats and maritime odds and ends and behind the bar there was a ship's wheel that looked like it had come off a real ship. It was a plain old-fashioned boozer populated by plain old-fashioned people.

I asked the landlord about the Punch and Judy show and he interrupted his polishing of a gleaming pint glass to gesture at a set of double doors leading on to a yard at the back. If it had been slightly less scruffy you could have got away with calling it a terrace. Rows of chairs had already been set and gulls hopped among the seats.

'Should be quite a show,' the landlord said, observing my interest.

I nodded.

'Oh yes, if you like that sort of thing, you should find it most edifying. Very interesting slant it is.'

I raised my eyebrows.

'Oh no, don't get me wrong, sir. It's very traditional. All the old favourites. Nothing too avant-garde. Regulars wouldn't stand for those – what do they call them? – "contemporary interpretations" like you get in Swansea.'

I grimaced politely. 'You can't beat the old way of doing things.'

‘I see you’re a man after my own heart, sir.’

‘When they throw the baby out of the window I expect a visit from the policeman, not the social services.’

‘And that’s exactly what you’ll get here. Although,’ he added, ‘Mr Davies is no dinosaur either. He does make one or two interpretations of his own, but not in such a way as to ram it down your throat, if you’ll pardon the expression.’

I picked up my pint. ‘I think I’ll go and make sure of a good seat.’

‘Very wise. It’ll be standing room only in another quarter of an hour.’

As I started to walk away he called me back and leaned conspiratorially across the counter and took hold of my lapel. ‘Seeing as you’re a bit of sportsman, sir, you might like to know . . .’ He pulled my ear closer to his mouth and whispered, ‘We’ve got a bit of a game going on upstairs afterwards. “Mr Chunky”.’

‘Mr what?’

‘Chunky. Mr Chunky says Parsnip – the drinking game.’

I nodded. ‘Ah!’

He looked cautiously from side to side and added, ‘Llanfihangel-y-Creuddyn rules: vomit once to join the table and twice to leave.’

By 8.15 there were three people in the audience including me. The other two were an old couple, silver-haired and wrinkled and shaking like jelly. The bar man had been lying, of course, but I had known that all along. It was obvious from the state of Davies’s clothes that he wasn’t packing them in every night. Even in Swansea no one ever got rich on the Punch and Judy circuit. The dream of seeing your name in big red type on the wall of the bandstand was just that – a dream from the same tattered rag-bag of empty hopes that had been filling the second-class railway compartments to Shrewsbury for more than a hundred years.

* * *

Davies came on just after 8.30. He made a quick glance at the empty seats, put on a defiant look and went behind the stripey canvas booth. Seconds later the squeaky voices started. I wondered about his life. I wasn't familiar with 'Mr Chunky says Parsnip', but I knew plenty of games like it, and I knew what they did to people. After about ten minutes of the performance the old couple left. Iolo carried on gamely for another fifteen minutes before winding up. It was a very ordinary performance but not as hopeless as it could have been; he had some skill at least. Towards the end he had even indulged in some experimental interpretation with a scene I hadn't seen before where the policeman plants a piece of trumped-up evidence on Mr Punch. The echoes of Iolo's own fate were clear if pathetically pointless.

When the show ended I clapped slowly and deliberately. It took Iolo Davies five minutes to gather his things together, put away the puppets, and emerge from behind the booth. I carried on clapping and he looked over at me.

'You taking the piss?'

'My name's Louie.'

'Did I ask?'

'I thought you might like to know.'

'What do you want?'

'Information about Dai Brainbocs.'

He stopped and looked round. 'Just leave me alone.'

'It won't take long.'

'What do you want to ask about him for? He's dead isn't he?'

'I want to know why.'

He looked at me through narrowed eyes.

'Who are you?'

'I'm a relative of Brainbocs.'

'No you're not.'

'I'm a private detective investigating his death.'

He turned to leave again.

'Look!' I said hurriedly. 'It would only take a few minutes, and I might be able to help you.'

He snorted. 'You're out of your depth.'

I tried a final gambit. 'You think it was right what happened to you?'

He laughed bitterly. 'Does it matter?'

'All I want is a few minutes.'

Iolo Davies put the last chip in his mouth, scrunched the wrapping paper up and threw it out of the car window. Then he turned to me, the light from the street lamp silvering the edge of his face.

'How much do you know?'

'I know Brainbocs was working on Cantref-y-Gwaelod; I know he disappeared shortly after handing his essay in; I know the kids say he stumbled on to something big, something the Welsh teacher didn't like. I know Lovespoon is planning to reclaim the land of Cantref-y-Gwaelod and take a group of pilgrims there in an Ark. I know three other kids working on the same essay are dead and one is missing. I presume they were killed because they copied Brainbocs's homework and found out whatever it was he found out. I know you lost your job about the same time as well. And it's my guess you were punished for helping Brainbocs.'

The old Museum curator wiped his greasy fingers down the thighs of his trousers and shook his head gently in admiration as he recalled Brainbocs's scholarship. His voice took on a sad and distant quality.

'The Cantref-y-Gwaelod stuff was genius. No other word for it. He did it all, you know. This whole Exodus project to build the Ark and settle the land – it was all Brainbocs's idea. He was down the Museum a lot, usually in the archives. He wanted to do things with the school essay that people didn't even dream could be done. He had this idea that you could somehow shake the world with one. I mean, partly it was some sort of compensation for the bad leg. But still, it was more than that. He once said he could wrestle with destiny and force her to her knees.' He laughed without mirth. 'I know, it sounds a load of crap when I say it, but when you listened to him . . . you just . . . well it's funny but it didn't seem so strange.'

'But surely he couldn't really locate this lost iron-age kingdom?'

'This boy could do anything. You know how he pinpointed where it was? Triangulation. He set up recording devices at points along the coast where people claimed they could hear the ghostly bells; then he analysed the Doppler shift in the frequencies and then did a load of sums I wouldn't have a clue about and triangulated the source of the bells. Unbelievable. And that was just the start. Then he took echo soundings to map the terrain and draw up the drainage scheme. And to cap it all he designed the Ark.'

'I don't get it, what did he do wrong? I thought Lovespoon loved the idea. Was he trying to steal the boy's glory?'

Iolo shook his head and took a breath. 'It wasn't anything to do with Cantref-y-Gwaelod. Of course Lovespoon loved the project; he told me to give Brainbocs all the assistance he needed. Not that he needed any. But then one day the kid changed tack. Just like that. Came in with a gleam in his eye that was even crazier than the usual one. He started working in a different section of the Museum. He said he'd had this new idea and that it was going to be his *pièce de résistance*.'

'And the Welsh teacher didn't approve?'

'The kid told me not to tell Lovespoon – it was meant to be a surprise. But the teacher found out anyway.'

'And that's when they put the stain on the camisole?'

'It wasn't a camisole, it was a rare corso-pantaloon in tea rose crêpe de chine.'

'So what was the new area of research? What did he switch to?'

The chair made a low farting sound as Iolo turned to face me. The light glistening on the two sad puddles of his eyes. 'I'll tell you. Only don't ask me to explain it, because even now –'

He paused.

'Yes?'

'Even now I have no idea what was so bad about the new –'

There was a sound from outside the car. The museum curator froze, his jaw agape. I threw my hand across, to grab his arm. To reassure him. But it was too late. He was staring with a wild, transfixed look past the side of my head. I spun round and saw out there in the featureless night, hovering on the threshold of discernibility, dark figures. Like crows or, more accurately, like the woman in the trench coat I had fought with earlier in the day.

'You bastard!' cried Iolo as he tore free of my hand. 'You dirty, double-crossing bastard!' He threw the car door open, and ran out into the night. By the time I too had got out of the car both he and the mysterious figures were gone.

*

It was well after eleven when I picked up Calamity and drove back to Aberystwyth. Just outside Llanrhystyd an ambulance streaked past at full pelt in the opposite direction. With the roads so empty it shot through the darkened countryside like a blue flashing arrow. As things turned out, the high speed was in vain. By that time Iolo Davies was already dead.

Chapter 11

EEYORE PEERED AT the button through the magnifying glass he used for the 'spot the ball' competitions.

'Yep,' he said. 'It's them all right.'

'Sweet Jesus League?'

He nodded.

At first glance it looked like any other black plastic button, the sort all old ladies had on their overcoats, but if you looked closely at the holes for the thread you could see they were arranged differently. There were two large round ones, and underneath that a single triangular one, and then beneath that a rectangular one. The shape of the button wasn't perfectly round, either, but had indentations on either side that made it look vaguely potato-like. Sewn on to a coat these things would be difficult to spot. But hold the button up to the daylight and you saw it straight away: it was a skull. Eeyore handed the button back to me, over the gleaming back of Henrietta. I leaned my arms on her saddle as she stood looking patiently over the railings and out to sea.

According to the newspaper Iolo Davis had been found at the foot of the cliff. Broken turf high up on the cliff's edge had indicated where he lost his footing in a tragic accident. His injuries were entirely consistent with a fall and foul play was not suspected. That was the official version anyway.

'Not the old bags who sell pamphlets outside the Moulin,' Eeyore continued. 'This belongs to the big girls: the ESSJAT.'

'ESSJAT?'

'It's a sort of secret commando unit; an elite force drawn from the ranks of the foot soldiers. The name comes from the initial letters of Sweet Jesus against Turpitude.'

I whistled.

'Officially, they don't exist.'

'And I led them straight to him.'

He scoffed. 'Don't waste time blaming yourself. They would have got him eventually; they always do.'

'I should have taken more care.'

'No Louie!' he snapped with an uncharacteristic edge in his voice. 'Once he was on their list he was dead. It was only a matter of time. You have to accept that.'

'Where do I find them?'

'You don't. I mean you can't. Or, you shouldn't.'

'You know I've got to.'

'No one knows who they are or where they are. They make the postman wear a blindfold.'

'Come on, Dad . . .'

'What business is it of yours, anyway? You think this Evans the Boot chap deserves it?'

'It's not about him, you know that.'

'What is it about then?'

'Lots of things.'

He paused and stroked Henrietta's mane and then said with an air of resignation, 'Well, I suppose you're going to go ahead and look for them whatever I say. But don't go round thinking you killed Davies. If the ESSJAT were after him, he was a dead man walking. It's that simple.'

*

The avuncular white-bearded man kneels at the shore's edge and stares through narrowed eyes out to sea. Around him children gather. The man speaks.

'That's our land out there, beneath those constantly shifting waters. A good land, a rich land. A land where our people can reap and sow and our children's laughter will fill each silver day –'

Calamity Jane picked up the remote control and turned off the TV. 'What crap!'

'Now, now! There's no need for language like that.'

'Who wants to go to Cantref-y-Gwaelod anyway?'

'Quite a lot of people, it seems.'

'Why do they have to do TV commercials then?' She threw the remote control on to the sofa and started pacing up and down the office, counting off points on her fingers. 'Item one: Brainbocs masterminded the plan to reclaim Cantref-y-Gwaelod. Lovespoon loved that scheme. Item two: then he starts researching something else. Lovespoon hates that and tells the Museum curator not to help him. Then the curator loses his job and then . . .' she paused. 'And then he fell off a cliff.'

We exchange glances like guilty children.

'Item three: Brainbocs hid the essay in a well-known beauty spot and was looking for a woman called Gwenno.'

'Item four,' it was my turn, 'Evans the Boot had a piece of Mayan tea cosy in his possession.'

'Not Mayan – Welsh, it was just a Mayan design . . .'

The words trailed off and she looked over to the door. Myfanwy was standing framed in the doorway and she didn't look pleased.

'Hey, come in!'

'I'll stay here, thank you, I'm not staying.'

'Not even for a cup of tea?'

'I just want to tell you to stop investigating my cousin Evans's disappearance. Send me a bill for what you've done up until now.'

'You don't owe me any money, I turned the case down, remember?'

'Yes, but I talked you into it.'

I turned to Calamity. 'Hey, do you think you could put the kettle on for me?'

'She said she didn't want a cup of tea!'

'Well I do.'

'Right now?'

'Yes, right now!'

She looked over to Myfanwy in search of an ally, but Myfanwy simply said, 'Scram, kid.'

Calamity shuffled across to the kitchen. 'If it's about this investigation, it involves me too.'

I turned to Myfanwy. 'You look like a walking thunderstorm.'

'That's hardly surprising, is it?'

I was puzzled. 'I don't know, isn't it?'

'No, it isn't . . . after . . . after . . .'

'After what?'

'After what you did.'

'What did I do?'

'You mean you have to ask?'

I raised my hand as if to indicate a temporary truce and walked over to the kitchen. I closed the door with an exaggerated action.

'Myfanwy, please tell me, what have I done?'

'You mean you don't know?'

'No!'

'That makes it worse.'

'Oh, for God's sake,' I said walking over to the desk because I couldn't think of anything better to do, 'stop playing games and tell me what I am supposed to have done.'

She paused and looked at me. I looked back and smiled encouragingly.

'You slept with Bianca.'

I gaped at her.

'Don't try and deny it, she told me everything.'

'I'm not trying to deny it, I'm just staggered –'

'You think we don't talk to each other or something?'

'Myfanwy!'

'I mean of all the cheek – you think you can just jump into bed with my best friend and she won't tell me?'

'But Myfanwy!' I howled again.

'My best friend, Louie! My best friend!'

'Funny sort of friend!' I shouted.

'And what's that supposed to mean!?'

'I don't know, fuck it all, Myfanwy, it was you who told me to do it!'

'I –' This time it was her turn to stare open-mouthed.

'At the Club, remember?'

'But I didn't mean it!' she screeched, and then flung her hands in the air in exasperation, before turning in the doorway and stomping down the stairs. Her last words, thrown over her shoulder were: 'How can anyone be so stupid!'

I stood rooted to the spot, staring at the empty doorway. Calamity came back in.

'She needs a slap, boss.'

'Don't you start,' I warned her.

'I'm not starting, I'm just observing. She's walking all over you.'

'Is that any of your concern?'

'Yes it is as a matter of fact.'

'Oh really!'

'Yes. Firstly because you're my friend and I don't like to see you acting the doormat; secondly because things like this can interfere with your professional performance; and thirdly because it affects the bottom line.'

'What are you talking about?'

'Didn't I just hear you say you weren't charging her for any of this?'

'That's none of your business.'

She picked up her school satchel adding nonchalantly, 'Fine, but shoe leather's not free. Second rule of being a private eye.'

As she skipped through the door I picked up the phone and called Meirion. After the usual round of pleasantries I asked if he'd heard anything about Iolo. Of course he had. He'd heard everything, he just couldn't print it.

'Most of the injuries seem to have been sustained during the fall from the cliff,' he said.

'Most of them?'

'Well some of them don't look like the sort of mark you'd get from falling off a cliff.'

'What do they look like?'

'More like the sort of holes a hatpin might make.'

I sighed. 'Anything else?'

'Yes, something very strange. Someone's daubed some graffiti on the pavement outside Aberaeron Co-op . . . in blood.'

'Blood?'

'The victim's blood.'

I screwed up my brow and held my breath. I could tell Meirion had more.

'Now I'm no expert,' he laughed, 'but as far as I can see there are only two ways that could happen.'

'Go on.'

'Either some idiot went to the foot of the cliff and collected Iolo's blood. Or Iolo wrote it himself.'

'How could he, he was dead?'

'Ah!' Meirion laughed. 'Depends when he wrote it, doesn't it?'

'All right, Meirion, I know you've got a theory. What is it?'

'If you asked me I'd say he was murdered outside the Co-op and he wrote the graffiti himself. Dipped his finger in his own blood and daubed it on the floor with his dying strength. Then whoever killed him dragged him to the cliff and threw him off to make it look like an accident. Only because it was so dark no one noticed the blood until next morning.'

I could almost feel him beaming on the other end of the phone. He was obviously right.

'So what does the graffiti say?'

'Two words. "Rio Caeriog".'

*

The following afternoon Calamity and I drove to the Museum as Iolo Davies's last words drifted through my thoughts. Had he written the words for me? He must have done. Rio Caeriog. The famous battle from the war in Patagonia. A name once written on the map with the blood of a generation and now inscribed in the Museum curator's blood on the pavements of Aberaeron. Was that the new essay subject Brainbocs had chosen? The one that got him killed? As I parked in the shadow of the Lancaster bomber I mentally reviewed the story of Rio Caeriog. It was well enough known. For months in 1961 the First Expeditionary Force had been taking unsustainable losses in the foothills of the Sierra Machynlleth. Sniped at by day and taunted and ambushed at night by an enemy they couldn't see. And then came the famous raid. A Rolex watch was rigged up by the boffins of Llanelli with a radio beacon inside. The watch was deliberately lost in a card game to one of the bandits in the back room of a cantina. And when the bandit took it home to his base the Lancaster bomber followed. But why did it interest Brainbocs? What was the connection to Cantref-y-Gwaelod? We got out of the car and walked up the steps into a foyer of gilded cherubs and alabaster columns. The Devil's Bridge Tin & Lead Steam Railway Co. had built with a confidence that had long since disappeared from our own age. The grandeur was now sadly defaced by charmless municipal sign boards: Combinations and Corsetry; Two-headed Calves and other Curios; Coelecanths.

Inside the foyer was another of the success stories of that far-off time. A passport photo booth created by the same boffins of the special operations executive at Llanelli Technical College. It was the world's only micro-dot photo booth and gave you your portrait the size of a currant. To see it, you had to buy a special viewer from the gift shop. Most of the micro-dot camera technology familiar from so many spy movies had been developed during the Patagonian War. An animal clinic had been established in Buenos Aires from which the military intelligence, condensed on to micro-dots, had been smuggled out as eye patches for hamsters with lazy eyes. As kids we had polka-dotted the wall of the art class with our drawings of it. Calamity ran to the photo booth and disappeared inside with a swish of orange curtain. I waited patiently for the flashes wondering idly what obscene gestures she was no doubt making to the camera.

Upstairs, in the main gallery, two super-enlarged black and white photographs filled the whole of one wall with a grainy ghostly sea of grey. One was a picture of the two Lancasters leaving Milford Haven aerodrome to cheering crowds. And the other showed five aviators standing in a relaxed circle outside some forgotten South American cantina, drinking tequila and clowning about. They were young and fresh-faced and laughing into the camera lens with a gaiety that suggested the picture must have been taken right at the start of the conflict. It was the Rio Caeriog bomber crew. Lovespoon, Dai the Custard Pie and, with a much younger horizontal crease in his face, Herod Jenkins the games teacher. A triumvirate of the current movers and shakers of Aberystwyth. Did Brainbocs discover something about them that might have taken the glint off those famous medals? Some awkward tidbit that would have wiped that horizontal crease off Herod's face? The smiles frozen in Ilford black and white gave nothing away.

Calamity walked over with the air of one who has made a discovery. I looked up and smiled and she handed me a sheaf of plastic laminated cards bearing the biographies of the airmen. Lovespoon: war hero, school teacher, prize-winning poet and Grand Wizard on the Druid council. Custard Pie: purveyor of fine soaps that make your face go black, and Red Indian arrows that appear to pierce the neck. Herod Jenkins: school games teacher; capped for Wales in his youth and subsequently, although the card did not record this distinction, famous for sending a consumptive schoolboy to his death during a blizzard. The last was Oswald Frobisher. A nobody. One of the handful of English intellectuals who were so dismayed at missing the Spanish Civil War they had signed up for the Patagonian adventure. The card said merely that he died of his wounds when his Lancaster ditched into the Rio Caeriog. There was no clue as to what the wounds were but any schoolkid could tell you: the bandits cut off his John Thomas and stuffed it in his mouth.

Calamity was still holding one card. I looked at her enquiringly and she passed it across. It contained even fewer details than hapless Frobisher's. None at all in fact, just bare white card, and a name. A name that I had last heard from the lips of Dai Brainbocs's Mam. The name of the woman her son had gone to see in the week before he died. Gwenno Guevara, it said simply, freedom fighter.

Chapter 12

BIANCA GINGERLY PULLED out the shards of broken glass from the picture of Noel Bartholomew and wrapped them up in newspaper.

'If I was lost in the jungle would you come looking for me?'

'No, it's too dangerous.'

'Not even to take my picture, like your great-great-uncle?'

I laughed. 'We don't know for sure that he did.'

She carried the parcel of jagged glass through to the kitchen, shouting over her shoulder as she went: 'Of course he did.'

I looked at the portrait. Did he? Did he really find her? Or was it all a hoax played on a gullible American tourist by a wily Chinese shopkeeper? It was Eeyore who gave me the portrait and the chest full of papers and artefacts, back in the days when I believed in common sense and thought the expedition must have ended in failure. But Eeyore had quietly disagreed with a patient conviction he only rarely displayed. It depended on what you considered failure, he said. And added that one day I would understand. But I never really have, even though I return again and again to that diary. Those cracked and yellow pages in which Noel records in a malarial scrawl, growing ever more indecipherable by the day, how she came to see him in his sickness. A passage which ends with the words taken from St Augustine: 'Faith is to believe what you do not yet see.'

Bianca walked back in to the office.

'I think he took her picture in Heaven.'

'He did what?'

'In Heaven. That's where he took her picture.'

I grinned and, seeing the expression, Bianca became suddenly cross.

'You think you know it all, don't you? I suppose you don't believe in ghosts either?'

'No. Do you?'

'Of course. I'm going to be one.'

On our way out we met Mrs Llantrisant. She looked tired and pale, and swabbed robotically.

'*Prynhawn da*, Mr Knight!'

'*Prynhawn da*, Mrs Llantrisant! You look worn out.'

'I'm feeling my age, Mr Knight, that's what I am.'

'Why not take a few days off and put your feet up?'

'And who would fold the serviettes for the Ark if I did that?'

'Is that what you've been doing?'

She stopped and leaned like a drunkard on her mop. 'I'm glad to be able to play my part.'

'You believe in all this then, do you? This Ark business?'

'What's there not to believe?'

'I mean, you'd like to go, would you?'

She grabbed a loose strand of hair and tucked it up beneath the hem of her headscarf. Her hand was shaking.

'It's the kids I'm doing it for. It's too late for us, but the little ones – they deserve it.'

'With Lovespoon as king?'

'Social gerontocracy, Mr Knight, just like in ancient Greece.'

'What's wrong with Aberystwyth?'

She put the mop in the water.

'I'm surprised to hear you ask that, Mr Knight. What do you like about it all of a sudden?'

'It may have its faults but at least it's not currently under ten thousand feet of water.'

'Not ten thousand, less than twenty fathoms. Scarcely a puddle.'

Suddenly, Mrs Llantrisant lost her balance and fell into me. I grabbed her arm and held her upright.

'I'm all right, really I am,' she moaned. 'Just slipped on the wet step, that's all.'

'You're pushing yourself too hard, you are. We don't want another repeat of Easter do we?'

Bianca and I walked along the Prom, heading for Sospan's.

'Silly old bag.'

'There's no need for that.'

'Did you see the look she gave me?'

'She can't help it. She's old and set in her ways.'

'What happened at Easter?'

I ordered a round of ice creams. 'She had a funny turn. Said it was the apples in her pie but she took so bad she called a priest to administer the last rites. She's been all right since, though.'

Bianca leaned her head on my shoulder and said, 'Why didn't you call me?'

'What about?'

'What about!' she cried.

Of course. The last time we met had been the night I took her home.

'I'm sorry, I –'

'Don't apologise.'

I put my palm against the side of her face and ruffled her hair. Sospan handed us the ice creams with the discretion of a brothel madam. We ate them in silence for a while, and then Bianca spoke to the folds of my shirt.

'I've got something for you. I haven't got it yet, but I can get hold of it. That's if you want.'

'What is it?' I spoke to the top of her head.

'Something very, very special.'

'What?'

'Something you'd give your right arm for.'

'There's nothing I'd give my right arm for.'

'I bet you'd give it to marry Myfanwy.'

'No I wouldn't.'

'It's an essay.'

I breathed in sharply and Bianca giggled.

'Really?' I said cautiously. 'What sort of essay?'

'Ooh, just Dai Brainbocs's last essay.' She giggled again.

I pushed her away and looked into her face. 'What are you talking about?'

'Dai Brainbocs's last essay. You are looking for it, aren't you?'

'What makes you think that?'

'Myfanwy told me.'

I closed my eyes in pain.

'It's all right, I won't tell anyone.'

'She shouldn't have told you.'

'What do you expect, she's a big mouth.'

'There's no need for that.'

'I know you think the sun shines out of her backside, but she's not all sugar and spice you know.'

'I'm sure she's not. No one is.'

'So do you want it?'

I didn't answer for a while, just stared at her. 'Are you being serious? You know where Brainbocs's last essay is?'

She nodded. 'I know where there's a copy of it.'

'Where?'

'Pickel's got one.'

'Pickel?'

She nodded again.

'Lovespoon asked him just after Brainbocs died to design a safety box so good, no one in the world could open it, not even the person who made it. Pickel agreed to do it even though he said there wasn't a lock in the world he couldn't open. He said Lovespoon was a wanker. Lovespoon used the box to keep Brainbocs's original essay in – the one he told the papers he'd lost. Pickel took it out when he wasn't looking and made a copy. His insurance policy he called it.'

'Pickel told you this?'

'Yes.'

'How do you know he's not just making it up?'

'Why should he? Besides, I know where he hides it – in the belfry. I could get it, if you wanted.'

I held her head in my hands and stared into her eyes. 'Don't do anything until I've had a chance to think about it.'

The lightning was already flashing in the sky far out over the western horizon when I left for the Moulin that night. I was too late to get a good table and had to sit right at the back with a very bad view of the stage. The showgirls didn't normally venture so far back and I was served by a plain Jane of a waitress in a simple black skirt and white blouse. I had to share the table with a group of men who looked like they had just been picked up off a desert island by the air-sea rescue helicopter. Their hair was wild and unkempt, their clothes torn and ragged. One of the men offered me his hand to shake and, not wishing to offend, I took it gingerly.

'Welcome, brother,' he croaked in the voice of a mariner who hasn't spoken to another soul for ten years. The rest of the group looked at me intently, their gazes playing over my face like searchlights.

'I'm not your brother.'

The man giggled in a way that made my flesh crawl and turned to his companions. 'He says he's not our brother!'

The rest of the group broke into hoarse, wheezing laughter.

The first man looked at me and said, 'I'm Brother Gilbert. This is Brother Frank, and this is Brother Bill. I'll introduce the rest of us later.'

'Don't bother.'

'Oh it's no bother. It's such a pleasure to have you join us. We have so much to talk about.'

My drink arrived and I drank it down in one and ordered another.

'I used to be a bank manager,' said Brother Gilbert. He grabbed my arm and added with a strange urgency, 'And Brother Bill used to be a Justice of the Peace. What do you think of that?'

'I thought you were all fishermen.'

They turned to each other and laughed again.

'We like that,' said Brother Gilbert. 'Fishermen. That's very funny!'

When the laughter died down Brother Gilbert turned to his brothers and said, 'I suppose in a way we are all hooked!' The laughter erupted once more.

I waited patiently, and then said, 'Do you come here a lot, then?'

'Oh yes, every day. Haven't you seen us?'

'No.'

'That explains it then.'

'Explains what?'

'Why you don't understand.'

They all stared at me with a wild glimmer of madness in their eyes, expectantly gauging the effect of Brother Gilbert's words on me. A showgirl passed through the tables halfway between our position and the front and for a moment I thought it was Myfanwy. I craned my neck for a better look.

'She's not here yet,' said Brother Gilbert knowingly.

'Who isn't?'

There was a split-second pause and then the brotherhood fell about laughing again. This time the laughter swept them away. Tears streamed down their cheeks and thighs were slapped. Whenever the laughter looked like petering out, one of the brotherhood would repeat the word 'who?' and it would start all over again.

'You all seem to have a very similar taste in humour.'

'That's because we're a fraternity.'

'We're five people with one mind,' added Brother Bill.

'Like a colony of ants, in a way,' explained Gilbert. 'We're united in suffering.'

'I'm sorry to hear it.'

'Oh no!' cried Gilbert, 'we don't need your sympathy; you're one of us now!'

That took me aback for a second. Again they stared at me like dogs outside a butcher's window display.

'Me? Why?'

Gilbert leaned closer and, as he did, the rest followed suit. His voice took on a cloying, conspiratorial air. 'You mean you don't know?'

I lowered my voice, 'No, what?'

'We're from Myfanwy Anonymous!'

The eyes of the brothers as they scrutinised my face were as wide as children's on bonfire night.

'We used to sit up the front like you,' said Brother Gilbert.

'But not any more,' added Brother Frank forlornly. 'That was a long time ago. Now it's someone else's turn.'

'Now we just sit here and wait for our turn in the sun again,' said Brother Bill.

'I've never heard of your organisation.'

'Not many people have,' hissed Gilbert excitedly, 'you can join if you like!'

'Why would I want to join a bunch of losers like you?'

The brotherhood looked at me sadly. Not with indignation, but with that infuriating understanding that holy men have for other people's human failings.

'Ah, Brother Louie, you're still in denial.'

'Don't give me your cheap armchair psychology,' I shouted.

'Please don't get annoyed,' said Bill. 'For a long time I was just like you.'

'Look, I'm not like you, OK? I'm a good friend of Myfanwy.' It sounded pathetic.

They exchanged glances with a mute understanding but said nothing.

'And don't look at me like that!' I had started to shout again, and to speak faster as if speed would somehow add the conviction that I now felt irresistibly seeping away. 'I'm not like you. This is all a mistake. I came late so there was no room at the front. That's why I'm sitting here; you watch, when she comes she'll come and talk to me!' I was staring around wildly now, almost challenging anyone in the brotherhood to contradict me. But all I met with was a bottomless well of compassion and understanding.

'It's all right, Louie, we understand.'

'No you don't.'

'Oh yes. It's all a mistake. Don't worry, there's no need to get upset.'

'I'm not upset!' And then aware of the passion in my voice I said again in a controlled tone, 'I'm not upset.'

'Of course. But there is one thing you should know. Myfanwy won't come back here to talk to you, the girls don't come back here.'

This time Brother Bill grabbed my arm with sudden urgency, 'But that doesn't mean you don't have a chance. Everyone has a chance.'

'Oh really!' I sneered. 'Is that what you think? Everyone has a chance, do they? Even old Brother what's-his-face over there drooling into his pint?'

They turned and looked sadly at an old man at the end of the table. He was trying desperately to follow the conversation but it was obvious his hearing wasn't good enough. Instead he sat there trembling and forcing himself to laugh when the others did.

'That's Brother Tobias, and he has as good a chance as anyone.' The warmth had left Brother Gilbert's voice now.

Brother Bill leaned across to me. 'You didn't ought to talk about the brothers like that. You didn't ought to disrespect them.'

'Well wise up and see the truth. Brother Tobias doesn't stand a chance with Myfanwy and neither do any of you.'

Brother Frank punched the table and squealed at my heresy. 'No! No! No! It's not true! Everyone has a chance!'

'Because Myfanwy is so good and pure.'

'Is that what you think, is it?' I sneered.

'I can prove it!'

'Yeah! How?' If only I hadn't asked.

Brother Frank brought his face right up to mine, his eyes moist with anger.

'Because . . . because she even went out with that crippled schoolboy!'

'Could have had any man in Wales, as well,' added Gilbert.

I sat there aware that my stomach had just dropped into my shoes. For seconds I couldn't speak, until finally I managed, 'Wh . . . what did you say?'

'The crippled schoolboy – with the bad leg. The one that died. Lovers they were.'

'You mean Dai Brainbocs?'

'Yes!' Gilbert insisted. 'Him!'

'Good God!' I said finally.

I sat unable to speak or move. Twenty minutes later Bianca walked in and told me Myfanwy was up at the hospital. Evans the Boot was dead.

Chapter 13

IT WAS RAINING heavily outside and the streets, glassy and shiny, were largely deserted as I sped down Great Darkgate Street to the hospital. My heart was racing and my mouth dry with fear; the news that Evans the Boot was dead meant nothing, but the revelation that Myfanwy and Brainbocs had been lovers was a pile-driver to the heart. At the hospital I parked as close as I could get to the main door, stepped out and walked across through the driving rain to the garishly lit entrance. A policeman stepped out of the shadows and blocked my way.

'Where you going?'

'Is there a law against visiting the hospital?'

'It's not visiting hours, come back in the morning.'

Another figure stepped out of the shadows. It was Llunos. As usual he didn't look pleased to see me.

'Your mum shag a vulture, or what?'

'What's that mean?'

'Every time I find a corpse, you turn up.'

'I could say the same for you.'

'You could but you'd need to visit the dentist after. What do you want?'

I realised there was no way Llunos was going to let me in, so I decided on a long shot – the truth. 'I need to see Myfanwy.'

I could see he was unused to dealing with it.

'What makes you think she's here?'

'Someone told me they found Evans and she's down at the morgue. I don't need to go in, my business is with her, not Evans the Boot. If you could get a message to her, to tell her I was here, I could wait over there in my car.'

The uniformed policeman started to laugh, 'Oh isn't that sweet! If we could just get a message –'

Llunos shut him up by waving an impatient hand at him. Then he looked at me, 'In your car?'

I nodded.

'OK we can do that. I'll let her know.'

I waited in the car for about half an hour, listening to the rhythmic droning of the windscreen wipers. Eventually I saw Myfanwy walking through the parked cars towards me. I flashed the lights. When she got in we were both in near-prefect darkness but even though I couldn't see, I could tell she'd been crying.

'Myfanwy –'

'Don't.'

Silence filled the car and amplified the sounds as we shifted in our seats.

'Can we just drive somewhere?'

'Where?'

'Anywhere, it doesn't matter. Please.'

I turned on the engine.

'Anywhere as long as it's away from Aberystwyth.'

The rain was driving hard, sweeping in from the sea. Outside the hospital car park I turned right, up over Penglais Hill, and on into the darkened landscape beyond. Myfanwy told me about Evans. He'd been found earlier in the day by a man walking his dog. The dog had run off to fetch a stick and returned with a finger. The body had been crudely buried under gorse bushes but little attempt had been made to conceal it. Someone had disfigured it and removed the fingerprints in the time-honoured way of immersion in a mixture of battery acid and local cheese. Police were still hopeful of a positive identification when the pathologists were finished.

We drove to the caravan. I shouldn't have revealed its location to

Myfanwy but I didn't care. The park was quieter than a cemetery when we arrived, the only sound the squeaking of the Fresh Milk sign from the general store and the far-off hum of the ocean beyond the dunes. The rain had stopped. It was cold and damp inside the caravan, but the camping-gas heater soon filled the interior with a cosy yellow warmth. The lamps sighed as they burned. Myfanwy sat at the horse-shoe arrangement of seats at the end, rested her elbows on the Formica table-top and buried her head wearily in her hands. I made two cups of packet soup in the kitchenette, poured a shot of rum into each, and took them over to the table. Myfanwy had found the ludo and was setting out the counters.

'Suppose you tell me about Brainbocs.'

She rolled the dice. Four and a five; you needed a six to start.

'What do you mean?'

I rolled a six and a one, and set off on my journey around the board. How many other people, honeymooners and young families, had made the same journey as the rain swept in from the sea and pounded on the plywood roof of their shoebox on wheels? Families who had driven for two or three hours, stopping occasionally for puking children, to this world of gorse and marram grass, dunes and bingo and fish and chips.

'Your cousin's dead, Myfanwy. Don't you think it's time to stop playing games?'

She picked up the dice and shook. They made a hollow clip-clopping sound inside the cup.

'I'm not playing games.'

'You haven't been straight with me.' Clip-clop, four and three.

'I've told you everything I know.' Double six. 'Oooh!'

I put my hand palm down on the counters before she could move them.

'You didn't tell me you and Brainbocs were lovers.'

It caught her by surprise and she bit her lip. 'We weren't.'

'That's not what I hear.'

'Well whoever told you that was a liar. We weren't lovers. I mean we didn't you know . . . do it.'

'What did you do?'

'Nothing. Honest.'

'Why don't you tell me about it?'

'It's not like you think.'

'You don't know what I think.'

'We weren't lovers, he just had this thing about me. All through school he'd had a thing about me; a lot of boys did. It's not a crime.'

'No,' I said gently, 'but a crime has been committed, and now you have to be straight with me.'

Clip-clop, double five. She paused. 'It started just after I took the job at the Moulin – when he found out about it he was really upset. He came down one night but they wouldn't let him in. So he waited outside. I left that night with a gentleman and I saw Brainbocs just as I got into the car. He was standing in the doorway of Army Surplice and staring like he'd seen a ghost. The next night he was there again. And the next. It came to be a pattern: he'd come down and try to get in, they wouldn't let him, and then he'd spend the rest of the evening standing outside. At first the bouncers tried to frighten him away. But he didn't seem to care. I think he knew there wasn't much they could do to a poor lame boy. When it rained he stood there in the rain, soaked and not even shivering. Eventually the boss asked me to go and speak to him. So I did.'

'When did all this happen?'

The Legendary Welsh Chanteuse stuck her tongue into one cheek like a schoolgirl doing a hard sum.

'It started last autumn. At Christmas he stopped coming. Then at Easter he . . . he died.'

I nodded and wondered at the casual precision with which she recited the dates. Wasn't it all a bit late in the day for a revelation such as this?

'So what happened when they sent you out to speak to him?'

'He said, "Myfanwy, please don't do this." I said, "Do what?" (like I didn't know); and he said, "Work in this establishment." Just like that, "Work in this establishment", like he was straight out of *Oliver Twist*.'

'And then what?'

She sighed and lowered her eyes back to the board. 'So I said, "What do you want?" And he didn't really say anything for a long time. He just kept looking at me like he wanted me to know but didn't want to say it. So I said it again, "What do you want? I've got to go back to work." And then it started to rain and I told him again I really had to go back inside. And then he put his hand on my arm. A hand like a girl's and he said, "Myfanwy, I love you." Just like that, and I laughed. And then when I saw the look on his face, I sort of stopped laughing. He looked like . . .' The words trailed off. Myfanwy's jaw moved silently as she struggled to find an expression appropriate for the abyss of misery to which her careless laugh had condemned the lame, unworldly scholar. But she couldn't. There was no experience in her carefree life to match his despair. How did I know? I, who had never met Brainbocs, and had never observed the scene in the rain outside the Moulin Goch? Oh, I knew. I just knew.

'Anyway,' she said finally, 'he looked really hurt.'

Clip-clop, one and five.

'And he asked me if he could buy me an ice cream the next day after he finished school. At first I said no. And then he pleaded and still I said no. It wasn't that I didn't want to, I just knew that if I said yes, that look in his eyes, I just knew it would come to no good. Then Mr Jenkins appeared in the doorway across the road and tapped his watch. I said again that I had to go. And again he begged me to have an ice cream with him. And then something awful happened.'

She looked up from the board and straight at me.

'Yes?'

'He started unbuckling that metal thing he has on his leg. The what's-it-called?'

'Calliper?'

'And I said, 'Dai what are you doing?' And he said he was going on his knees!'

I shook my head in sympathy at the sad scene.

'So of course I agreed to have an ice cream. But only on condition, I said, that he never came waiting outside the Club like this again and that he didn't go round telling everyone he was my boyfriend, just because I had an ice cream with him.'

'Did he agree?'

'Yes. Next day I met him at Sospan's, but it was a cold day and so we went to the Seaside Rock Café and over a plate of humbug rock he proposed. He asked me to marry him. I told him not to be so stupid. And he said, "It's my leg isn't it?" I said, "No, of course not." And then he said something strange. He said, "Myfanwy, what is the one thing you want more than anything in this world?" And I said "Nothing." But he wouldn't listen. He said there must be something I wanted. He said I must have a dream. I said no. And he said everybody, even a beggar, has a dream. But again I said no. And he went all quiet. Paid for the rock and left. That was in November, and weeks went by and I never saw him. Then as I left the Club on Christmas Eve, there he was again standing in the doorway as the snow fell. And do you know what?'

I raised my eyebrows.

'He had one of my school essays with him. From long ago. I hadn't a clue where he got it. It was about how it had been my dream to sing in the opera in Patagonia, and how I would give my hand in marriage to the man who made my dream come true. I'd forgotten I'd written it. And he held it under my nose and said, "See, you have a dream!" And I laughed sarcastically and said, "No, David, I had a dream. I don't have a dream any more. Now I'm just a Moulin girl with no time for dreams." Then he said, "One day I will make your dream come true, and then you will marry me." I was going to laugh but the look in his eyes . . . well I knew I shouldn't. So I just stared at him. And then he walked away. That was the last I saw of him. Limping off into the snow on Christmas Eve. Then a few weeks later a package arrived for me. There was no letter, just the essay. All about Cantref-y-Gwaelod; I didn't even bother reading it. Then one day I read that he'd been killed.'

'And what did you do with the essay?'

'I gave it to Evans the Boot.'

*

It was sometime between two and three when I pulled up outside the Orthopaedic Boot store on Canticle Street. I was dog-tired and made only the vaguest attempt at parking straight before climbing the sad wooden stairs to my office. It was like climbing Everest. I didn't bother changing, just collapsed on to the bed. As soon as my head hit the pillow I was asleep and as soon as that happened the phone rang.

'Yes?'

'Where on earth have you been?'

'Uh?'

'You've got to come quick.' It was Bianca.

'Bianca? What's up?'

'I'm in trouble. I haven't got much time. Can you come here now?'

'Why what's happened?'

'I've got the essay.'

The hair on my head would have stood on end if it hadn't been too tired.

‘You’ve what?’

‘The essay. I’ve stolen it, when Pickel catches me he’ll –’ There was a scream, and the line went dead.

When I arrived at her flat in Tan-y-Bwlch her front door was ajar. Furniture and fixtures were thrown across the floor, crockery was smashed, papers littered the carpet. There were bloody handprints on the wall and smeared down the gloss white of the door. I looked at the phone and knew I should call Llunos. Things had gone far enough. And for all I knew, the police could be on the way here right now. I looked at the phone. I really should call the police, but I didn’t.

Chapter 14

I FOUND HIM sitting next to the cauldron in a belfry that smelled faintly of gin. Alerted by the sound of stair-climbing he was already looking at the entrance when I walked in.

'What do you want? This is private property.'

There was no wind, no sensation at all except the steady whirr of the clockwork, and the faint smell of gin.

'Where is she? And don't say "who?"'

'Fuck off.'

The floor was a series of boards suspended high up in the tower. In the middle there was a gaping chasm and beneath it the fabulous iron and brass monster of the clockwork mechanism. It was from here that Mr Dombey had fallen or been pushed into the shark's jaw of the cogs. And at the moment it separated me from Pickel. I started to walk round towards the other side.

Pickel picked up a brass rod from the floor. 'You stay where you are.'

'The deal is very simple, Pickel. Tell me where she is, or I throw you into the clock.'

He waved the rod uncertainly and took a step back. 'That's close enough.'

I continued walking and ducked under the horizontal spindle that turned the hands.

'I'm warning you!'

I took another step. 'There was blood on the walls.'

He stepped back again and shook his head. 'Not me.'

'If you've harmed her, I'll kill you.'

'You've got the wrong man.'

'Why don't you tell me who the right man is?'

I looked down at the precipice. Lying on the floor a few feet from the edge was an old blacksmith's anvil. Covered in dust and cobwebs now, but probably used at some point in the past to repair a piece of the machinery. Pickel's gaze landed on it at the same time and the same thought went through both our heads.

'No!' howled Pickel.

I smiled.

'Don't you dare!'

He made a jump towards me but stopped like a fly hitting a window pane the moment I rested my foot on top of the anvil.

'Don't what?'

He was standing on one foot, poised like a relay racer waiting for the baton. Immobilised by the terror that any movement of his might induce me to slide the lump of iron over the edge and into the teeth of his beloved clock.

'Don't do it,' he cried in a softer voice. 'Please!'

'Where is she?'

He held his hands out in supplication. 'I don't know.' It was a simple statement delivered in the beseeching, wheedling tone of a mother begging for her baby back.

I pushed the anvil a bit further until it was lying at the very edge of the precipice. The clock was well built, but still extremely delicate. An anvil crashing through it would do a lot more damage than the emaciated frame of Mr Dombey.

'I don't believe you.'

I could see fear in Pickel's eyes. If I had threatened to throw his mother out of the window, he probably wouldn't have batted an eye, but the prospect of seeing his clock destroyed was too much. I pushed the anvil even further until it was now teetering on the brink, held in place only by the slight extra weight from the sole of my shoe.

'Where is she?'

'Please, they took her.'

I looked at him impatiently.

'Lovespoon and his tough guys. She stole the essay from me, y'see – the stupid bitch. I mean I had to tell them. They'd have killed me if they'd found out; probably will anyway.'

His eyes were riveted on the anvil.

'Where did they take her?'

He shook his head. 'I don't know. Really I don't.'

I let the anvil swing a bit to refresh his memory.

He cried out. 'Why the fuck would they tell me, anyway?'

'Look, you pile of shit, I don't care what they will and won't tell you. I'm trying to find that girl before any of you monkeys harm her. Now either I leave this tower knowing where to find her, or your clock is fucked.'

He sank down on to the floor and supported his head in his hands.

'Lovespoon is up at the school.'

'What's he doing up there?' I asked in surprise.

'He goes there every night . . . to his study . . . to write . . . and –'

He stopped.

'Yes?'

'And to look at his Ark.' He shrugged. 'That's where he goes.'

'Even at four o'clock in the morning?'

'He'll be there. He never sleeps any more.'

I pulled back the anvil and walked to the door. If you're lying, I'll be back with my own anvil.

Nothing had changed: the squeaky floor, the stale smell of feet and disinfectant, and the skeletal coat pegs, empty except for the occasional lonely anorak. But night gave it an alien, ghostly appearance. Breaking in was as easy now as it had been twenty years ago when we used to come and piss in the sports trophies in the assembly hall. I crept down the corridor, my shoes squealing on the tiles like birds in the rainforest. It was difficult to believe Lovespoon would be here at four in the morning, but Pickel was right. At the end of the corridor, across the foyer, I could see a shaft of light coming from the door of his study. The section where the senior masters had their offices was set off from the main foyer and used to be called the Alamo. A powerful Pavlovian reaction, dormant for two decades, was set in motion as I approached. Mouth went dry and ears began to throb in anticipation of being cuffed. I wrestled with the force inside me which was turning me once again into a subservient, defenceless schoolboy. A target for board rubbers, someone to be lifted bodily by the ear and pulled by the hair. To be upbraided with inferior sarcasm and terrorised into not answering back. How would I find the courage to stand up to him? To accuse him of murdering five of his own pupils? What business is it of yours, anyway, little boy? What if he had his cane? I hesitated outside the door and a voice came from inside:

'Come in, boy, don't stand out there dithering!'

He was at his desk, side-on to me, hunched over and marking essays. Without looking round he raised a hand and waved it in my direction, indicating that I should wait. I stood up straight and took my hands out of my pockets and then cursed myself for the cringing subservience. The only light was the lamp on his desk, and from outside the window the reflection from the huge wooden Ark which now filled up most of the scrub grass to the left of the games field. It shone in the intense white glare of the lights, and security patrols could be seen wandering up and down in front of it. Lovespoon finished marking with a dramatic flourish, closed the last exercise book and looked up.

'It's about that girl, isn't it?' And then adding, as he transferred his entire attention from the marking to this new subject, 'Such a silly girl.'

I said nothing and stared.

He scrutinised my face, trying to place me in the endless stream of pustulating, squeaky-voiced adolescent boys that had flowed through his life, boys who perhaps grew to be as indistinguishable as the leaves that littered the drive each autumn.

'Mr Ballantyne the careers master tells me you're a private detective?'

I didn't answer and the old Welsh teacher sucked on his tongue as he considered the merits of my career choice. 'I always had you down for something more clerical. Drink?'

He pulled a bottle of wine out from behind the angle-poise lamp.

'I'm not thirsty.'

'Ffestiniog Chardonnay, the '73. Really quite good.' He poured himself a glass and added, 'I was under the impression that hard-boiled private eyes were constrained by the requirements of stereotype to drink on every possible occasion.'

'Fuck you!'

The teacher flinched slightly and then said, 'Ah!' before drumming his fingers softly on the desk.

'Where is she?'

He smiled weakly and made an almost imperceptible shrug. 'I don't know.'

'Try again.'

'No, really I don't.'

He leaned slightly closer and peered at me. 'I don't remember teaching you actually.'

'You chipped my tooth when you threw the board rubber.'

He reached and picked up a pen, and then put it down again. 'This is all a terrible mess. Apparently she did it for you.'

Even in the dark I couldn't disguise my reaction.

Lovespoon laughed. 'So romantic. Still, you'd make a better match than Pickel, I dare say. So one can hardly blame her.'

'Just tell me where she is, and I won't hurt you.'

'Hurt me?' he said in phoney surprise.

'Not that you don't fucking deserve it, I owe you plenty.'

The Welsh teacher tutted at my language, and ran a hand lovingly along the ornately carved wooden arms of his chair. It was like a throne.

'Do you know what this chair is?'

I knew he was playing for time, trying to think of a way out or hoping someone would come, but it was difficult to resist the drift of his conversation.

'It's the bardic chair from the Eisteddfod. You won it for the poetry.'

'Three times. That's why I got to keep it.'

'Like Brazil in the World Cup.'

He winced. Then stood up wearily and walked through the darkened office to the window.

'That's the trouble with people like you, Knight, you only know how to mock. How to break things. You don't know how to create anything. You never did.'

'Where does killing your pupils fit into the picture?'

'Brainbocs was unfortunate.'

'You'll be telling me you can't make an omelette without breaking eggs, next.'

He shrugged and turned back to face me. 'It's not a bad philosophy.'

'Is that what Bianca is then?'

'Surely you're not going to get all sentimental about a tart?'

I jumped and lunged at him; he stepped back in time and I ended up grabbing his arm. As he struggled to break free we both fell on to the desk, scattering photos, half-marked essays and a pair of scissors.

'She's worth ten of you.'

He laughed wildly. 'She's not worth one of my farts.'

'Tell me where she is!' I shouted. We rolled off the desk on to the floor. Lovespoon struggled to push me off and I fought to get above him, to push him down. He was strong but I had twenty years on him. Soon I was kneeling on his chest. The struggle had knocked the table lamp over and the thin yellow beam pointed at his face.

'Where is she?'

Lovespoon was breathing hard and spoke in gasps. 'I told . . . you . . . I . . . don't know.'

I balled my fingers into a fist and raised it. He looked straight at me with clear, calm grey eyes. There was no fear in them. It was then that I noticed the scissors on the floor. They were those heavy craft scissors with black-painted finger holes. I picked them up and held them hovering above his face.

'Don't make me do it.'

He sneered. 'You haven't got the balls! You never did have, did you? You were too much of a milksop to play rugby – yes I remember you; and now you think you can come here threatening me?'

I brought the scissors down so low that the point was almost touching his eye. The eyelashes brushed against it. I could see him visibly forcing himself to remain composed.

'You can't frighten me, you know. I fought in Patagonia.'

'With Gwenno Guevara.'

He sneered. 'You'll never find her, you know. Brainbocs managed it but he died, and you don't have the brains.'

'What have you done to Bianca?'

'Since when did you care so much about Pickel's tart?'

I tightened my grip on the scissors. 'If you don't tell me where she is I'll put out your eyes so you never see Cantref-y-Gwaelod.'

For a while there was silence except our breathing. Lovespoon stared up at me and I stared down at him and in between were the scissors. Finally he said: 'I'll make a deal.'

'You're not in a position to.'

'Herod has the girl; I don't know where. We'll bring her to you tomorrow.'

'Why should I trust you?'

'Because you haven't got the fucking balls to use those scissors, have you?'

Chapter 15

He was right, of course. Maybe in the heat of a fight I could have used them but not like that in cold blood. Perhaps if I had paid more attention during Herod Jenkins's games lessons I could have done it, but I was, as he said, too much of a milksop.

There was nothing to be done. I left the school and drove aimlessly inland, through Commins Coch and on to Penrhyncogh, and then began a long sweep west towards Borth. As I drove, the words of Lovespoon echoed through my thoughts. Since when did I give a damn about Bianca? I thought of the night I took her home. To perform that act – the one that along with money was responsible for most of the trouble that came in through my door. For years I had sat and watched them all squirming on the client's chair, gored by the suspicion that their partners were cheating on them. Each one thinking that the disaster that befell them was unique, thinking that paying me to confirm it would somehow make them feel better. I had heard it all a thousand times before, like a priest taking confession – me with my phoney absolution. That act that so twisted the heart. Which the newspapers called sexual intercourse, and Lovespoon called sexual congress, and the man in the pub called bonking and Bianca called, paradoxically, making love, and which Mrs Llantrisant didn't even have a name for which she felt comfortable with. That act of cold animal coupling that so often in this town was nothing more than simple rutting. I didn't know why I had done it. Lonely and frightened, and drunk, perhaps. I hadn't given it any thought. Why? Because she was a Moulin girl and we all knew they had no feelings, or the ones they had were invented to suit the occasion. As men we warned each other with smug pride at our worldliness to steer clear of their treacherous hearts. And then this happens. She risked her life to help me; and might now be dead, or worse. A course of action that could only have been prompted by tenderness or love or some feeling she wasn't supposed to be capable of. And I thought of Myfanwy, so much more wise and versed in the ways of the Aberystwyth street, and I tried to imagine her sacrificing herself for me like that. And even as I tried to picture it, I knew with iron certainty that it was out of the question.

The first light was filtering through a veil of grey clouds when I reached Borth. I drove through the golf course and parked at the foot of the dunes and got out. I had intended going for a swim but when I reached the top of the dune, I thought better of it. Instead I sat on the sand and watched the slow, endless advance of the cleansing waves. My eyelids dropped lower and lower, until I slept. It was Cadwaladr who woke me. The war veteran Myfanwy and I had shared our picnic with. He offered me a drink from his can of Special Brew and I took it despite the waves of nausea brought on by the high-alcohol lager hitting an empty stomach. For a while we didn't speak, just stared out at the eternity of the ocean and I asked him the same question that I had asked Lovespoon. Who was Gwenno Guevara? This mysterious soldier Brainbocs had met in the week before he died.

Cadwaladr didn't answer immediately, and when he did he said simply, 'She was a whore.'

'Is that it? Just a whore?'

'Before the war she was a whore. A tea-cosy girl. Then she went to Patagonia and became a fighter. After the war – who knows? She disappeared.'

The old soldier stood up to leave and I called after him.

'You remember what you said about Rio Caeriog?'

He paused.

'You said they didn't teach your version of it in school. Do you remember?'

'Yes.'

'Can you tell me your version? The true story of Rio Caeriog?'

'No.'

'But you were there, weren't you?'

'Oh yes, I was there.'

He shook his head and added before tramping off: 'But I can't tell you that story. It's not mine to tell.'

When I got back to the office, there was a note from Eeyore to call him, and Llunos was once again sitting in my chair. He was picking bits of dirt from underneath his fingernails, and spoke without looking up, 'Have a nice swim?'

'Not bad; you should get out in the sunshine a bit more yourself.'

He continued to talk to his fingernails. 'You're probably right.'

I slumped down into the client's chair across the desk from him and waited for him to say what he had to say. Nothing came. We sat in silence like that for a while. The phone rang.

'Louie Knight Investigations.'

'If you want to see the girl, come to the harbour tonight at midnight. Outside the Chandler's.'

'Who is this please?'

'Come alone or we'll slice her up.' The caller hung up and I put the receiver down while trying to keep the look on my face neutral.

Llunos seemed too bored to even ask about the call. When he finally spoke it was about palaeoanthropology.

'Fascinating discipline,' he said looking up from his fingernails.

'If you've come to borrow a book on it I gave my last one to Mrs Llantrisant.'

'It's quite a hobby of mine, actually.'

I wondered why he was here. Had they found Bianca?

'Chap at the University specialises in it. He's got this wonderful 3D modelling software for his computer. He takes the skulls of stone-age men and scans them in and then slowly builds up the tissue and muscle and things until eventually presto! he gets to find out what Stone Age men looked like.'

'Why bother? We all know they looked like you.'

He flinched, but persevered with the air of studied detachment he'd adopted for the occasion. 'We found some fibres under Evans the Boot's fingernails. Hardly any really, but we gave them to this chap and he put them in his computer and he managed to recreate the knitting pattern. It was a tea cosy. Then we got two speedknitters up from the Bureau in Cardiff and they knocked us out a copy of the original cosy.'

I knew what was coming next.

'I just took it down to Mrs Crickhowell at KnitWits. She said it was the same as that South American cosy that was stolen from the Museum. Funnily enough, she said seen it quite recently – in your hands.'

He stood up and walked over to the toilet. He put his hand on the door handle and added, 'There are police officers posted downstairs in case you don't feel like waiting.' He went in and I dashed across and turned the key.

'I'm sorry about this, Llunos, really I am!' I shouted to the door. Then I walked over to the window and peeked carefully out. He wasn't lying. A police officer looked up and waved. It was time to use the escape route through the attic. It was clear that this time I would be in the cell for a lot longer than overnight, and I was desperate to stay free long enough to see Bianca tonight. Locking Llunos in the bathroom was a high price to pay, though. He wouldn't forgive me for that so easily.

*

Eeyore opened the door, took one look at the man in shaggy blond wig, dark glasses and false moustache and said, 'Oh it's you.' He led me into the kitchen where the smell of recently fried bacon hung heavily in the air.

'I've got someone here who wants to see you,' he said as he filled the old whistle kettle and placed it on the gas oven. 'It's an old friend of mine, from my days in the Force. He knows something about the ESSJAT.' Eeyore pulled up a chair and I sat down.

'He was given the task of breaking the organisation a long time ago; but his cover was blown and they had to give him a completely new identity.' He walked out and a few seconds later came back in with the former agent. A look of surprise consumed my face. It was Papa Bronzini.

'*Buon giorno!*' I gasped.

He smiled sadly and said in a voice filled with pathos, 'It's OK, sir, we can dispense with the *arrivedercis*.'

'So you're not Italian, then?' I said obviously.

He shook his head. 'Alas no.'

An awkward moment followed as I waited for him to explain, but he didn't.

'Well you had me fooled,' I said finally.

'I used to be a bit of an actor in those days – amateur dramatics. I expect you're quite familiar with that sort of thing?'

'I've seen a few plays.'

'Oh really, sir? Which ones?'

'Er . . . *Lady Windermere's Fan*,' I said desperately.

'Tennessee Williams?'

'Er . . . yes!'

He nodded. 'I was into method acting – eat, drink, live and sleep the part – that's the trick.' His eyes misted as he thought back to those days of greasepaint and footlights. 'Ah yes, I used to do a lot of that – *Richard II* . . . "I wasted Time, and now doth Time waste me." Are you familiar with that one, sir?'

'Yes, it's one of my favourites.'

He looked pleased. I smiled politely and stared at the floor of polished red tiles, spotlessly clean although strewn here and there with bits of straw. I'd never known a time when my father didn't have straw somewhere near him. Even in the sitting room it only added to the feeling of cleanliness, this association with the donkeys. What, after all, could be purer than the soul of a donkey? It's probably why my father had taken it as a second career. After years submerged in the moral grime of the Aberystwyth underworld he had turned to the one industry in town which traded innocence. Sospan tried to in a way, of course. He traded in the essence of the nursery, the sugary, vanilla smell of a mother's breast. But there was nothing innocent about the men who stood at his stall and ate, no matter how much they may have yearned inwardly to turn back the clock. Papa Bronzini continued to drone on about the theatre and at one point a donkey, I think it was Mignon, put her head in through the kitchen window and listened for a while before giving me an uncanny look of sympathy and loping off. Gradually the conversation turned to the old days when Bronzini and my father had worked on the Force together, the days when Bronzini had tried to bust the ESSJAT. For me, Bronzini cut a slightly pathetic figure but I saw that Eeyore was in awe of him and watched in uncritical fascination as Bronzini, now Aberystwyth's foremost mobster, described the workings of the ultra-secret elite known as the ESSJAT. He told how Gwenno Guevara had been a streetwalker before the war and had joined up to earn some extra money with the troops. Once overseas she had discovered a taste for fighting and had been good at it.

'That was the thing about Gwenno, you see, sir,' explained the old policeman. 'Whatever she turned her hand to she excelled at. Great hooker, great soldier and great chief of the ESSJAT.'

After the War Lovespoon rewarded her by offering her any job she wanted, not expecting the former hooker to choose a position in the newly formed League against Turpitude. But true to form she not only took the job but excelled at it, rising through the ranks until eventually she sat the top. At which point she simply disappeared. No one outside the organisation knew who she was, or where, although it seemed likely that Brainbocs had found out. But he of course was dead.

It was about ten to midnight when I made my way through the rows of boats, warehouses and lobster pots that made up Harbour Row. In the distance I could hear the whoop of a police siren and the engine howl of a car being driven at high speed. A chase. I took up a position deep in the shadow of a public shelter across the road from the Chandler's and thought about what I had just done. By locking Llunos up like that I had committed myself to a course from which there seemed no way back; it was as if I had been holding on to the precipice of a normal life in Aberystwyth and the last of my fingers had lost its hold.

A cat mewed at my feet and I jumped, my shoes making a harsh scraping sound which my fear convinced me could be heard across the whole neighbourhood. The racing car was nearer, but the police car seemed to have moved off, the klaxon getting fainter and fainter somewhere in the direction of Penparcau. Suddenly a door opened across the way. The hairs on the back of my neck pricked up and I stopped breathing. There was a pause. The beats of my heart louder than kettle-drum notes.

A figure stumbled or was pushed out of the warehouse. A woman's figure. She turned round and looked over to where I was standing. There was no way I could see in the light and with the distance, but I knew it was Bianca. I stepped forward, terrified that a trap was about to be sprung; Lovespoon had given me his word, but what was that worth? Why arrange the meeting at a place and an hour like this? As I walked across Bianca recognised me and opened her mouth to speak, but as she did the car that had been racing through the neighbourhood rounded the corner on two wheels. I darted a glance over – it was a car I'd seen before, very recently. Bianca spun round and a cry erupted in my throat. Confusion and terror swept across Bianca's face, and then there was a bang and Bianca went sailing like a rag doll into the air. Turning, turning, turning, before hitting the ground with a single, sharp crack like an axe hitting a tree. I stood transfixed, unable to move, and watched the car reverse a yard and then slam forwards back into Bianca's broken body. The car door sprang open, a figure leaped out and sprinted round to the other side of the car and down one of the dark alleys between two warehouses. Seconds later I heard from the harbour the sound of an outboard motor being fired up.

I ran over to Bianca's side and knelt down.

She looked up, eyes glazed with pain, and tried to force her mouth to overcome the agony and speak. Far off the banshee wail of the police siren was getting louder. I grasped her shoulders tenderly and ordered her not to speak.

'Louie!'

'It's OK, don't speak.'

She curled the fingers of her hand round my forearm weak as a baby.

'Louie!'

'I'm here, baby.'

And then her index finger detached itself from the rest of her fingers and slowly formed a curl like the finger of the grim reaper; she beckoned slowly towards herself and mouthed a word. I felt myself being pulled down by the finger as if attached by an invisible thread, and when my ear reached so close to her mouth that I could feel the warmth of her breath, she spoke again. Each word making her smashed body quiver like the pangs of childbirth.

'Louie!'

'It's OK, don't speak!'

'I . . . love . . . you!'

'There, there . . .'

'The essay . . .'

'No, no! Don't talk!'

And then as if at the exact moment her spirit left her she gripped me with a terrifying new strength.

'The essay . . .' she gasped desperately, 'it's in the stove!'

The grip broke and her head fell with a thud on to the tarmac glistening with her blood.

The police car skidded into view at the far end of the Prom and I looked at the murderer's car, engine still running, and realised where I'd seen it before. It was mine.

Chapter 16

I SIPPED MY coffee and read Meirion's editorial about Bianca:

> It is almost a week since the tragic death of Sioned Penmaenmawr, better known to the denizens of our notorious entertainment district as 'Bianca'. A girl who cocked her final snook at the society that cast her out by being buried in her night-club costume. By now most people will already have begun to forget about her; and the rest will never have cared in the first place. More fool them. The photo of the miserable funeral at Llanbadarn Cemetery on Tuesday contains a message for us all. There were four mourners at the sad interment. Her close friend Myfanwy Montez; Detective Inspector Llunos; a photographer from this newspaper; and a solitary figure who passing by felt the touch of pity in his heart. Wearing a dirty old coat tied up with packing string, his face dirty and lined with the years of suffering, it was a man only too familiar with the condition of exile from the hearthside of the Aberystwyth good life: a Patagonian War veteran. His lot it was that afternoon to teach us all not only the meaning of the word 'pity', but also alas, the meaning of shame.

The War veteran with the coat tied up with packing string had been me. Had Meirion known? It was hard to see how he could have done. I went to the funeral in the hope of speaking to Myfanwy, but she stayed too close to Llunos the whole time and rushed off in his car immediately afterwards. Llunos said in the newspaper that he was desperate to talk to me in connection with the death, which they were treating as a tragic hit-and-run, but he didn't mention that I locked him in the toilet.

Ever since the night she died I had been hiding in the caravan. I still didn't know how I survived: standing over her dead body, the car that killed her – my car – parked nearby with the engine still running, the police only seconds away. In a situation like that the only thing to do is make a decision. Any one, it hardly matters. The one I made was to jump in the car with Bianca's blood and tissue still smeared across the grille and drive off. She was dead, I could see that. And if by some miracle she wasn't, the police would be better able to help than I was. So I saved myself. As the police car screeched to a halt I did a U-turn, turned right at the Castle and over Trefechan Bridge; then I pulled off on to the track leading to Tan-y-Bwlch beach. From there I abandoned the car and set off on foot across the darkened fields and over the Iron Age hill fort. The plan was to double back, making a wide arc around the town, and head for the caravan in Ynyslas. It took me four hours, but I did it.

Since then, the weather had closed right in with expanses of dove-grey clouds filling the sky; it was cold and windy and moisture hung in the air ready to occasionally spit at the windows of the caravan. I didn't go out much, but when I did, the disguise as a War veteran worked well. Such was the stigma, most folk simply averted their gaze when they saw one.

There was a knock on the caravan door. I opened it and Calamity burst in.

'Take your time, won't you?'

'Sorry, I didn't hear you.'

'It's freezing out there, like the middle of winter.'

'It's all right, I've made coffee, that will warm you up.'

She took off her anorak and walked over to the table. 'I've made some progress.'

'Oh yeah?'

'It could be the breakthrough we've been waiting for.'

She opened her school satchel and pulled out three books. I picked them up and read the titles. '*On Pools of Love* by Joyce Moonweather; *Governing a Sloop* by Captain Marcus Trelawney; *Towards a New Pathology of Slovenliness* by Dr Heinz X. Nuesslin.' I put the books down.

'I got them from the school library. You won't believe who was the last person to borrow them.'

'Brainbocs?'

'No. Guess again.'

'Sorry, chum, that's my best effort.'

'You won't believe it.'

'Amaze me.'

'Evans the Boot!'

I picked up the *New Pathology of Slovenliness* and examined the flyleaf. 'Maybe we misjudged him all along.'

'I don't think so. Look at the title page.'

Obediently I opened the book. Letters were missing from the title page, crudely cut out with scissors leaving jagged edges.

'He got into trouble for it, you see. That's how I knew. I remember hearing this story ages ago about how he turned up at the library one day and borrowed all these weird books. And then when he returned them he'd cut them up. So I checked on his record which ones they were.'

I opened the other two books; each one had been vandalised in the same way.

'OK, clever-clogs, what does it mean?'

As if impatiently waiting for this question she took out a piece of paper and unfolded it.

'These are the letters he cut out: O.V.E.N.L.O.O.P.S.'

'You still got me.'

'Rearrange them.'

I stared at the paper for a second and then it hit me. 'Lovespoon!'

'That's right!'

'So what does it all mean?'

'What do people use cut-out letters for?'

I shrugged.

'Blackmail notes of course. He was blackmailing the Welsh teacher. No wonder they did him in.'

I thought about the significance of it for a few seconds but it did little to lift my depression.

'Don't get carried away with excitement will you?'

'Sorry, Calamity, I'm sitting here wanted for the murder of a prostitute. It's difficult to get excited about things.'

'But this is the way we're going to clear your name.'

'I don't see how.'

'Evans was blackmailing Lovespoon. Why? Because he copied Brainbocs's homework and found out something incriminating about the teacher. What else do we know about Evans? He stole a rare tea cosy from the Museum. Now it's my guess these two facts are related.'

'Sure, but what's the link?'

'I don't know. We haven't got all the pieces of the jigsaw yet.'

'But it doesn't really take us forwards. We already know why Lovespoon killed Evans.'

She looked at me, the frustration bringing tears to her eyes. 'We have to explore every angle, Louie. We have to be thorough, we're building a case, sod it!'

'OK. What else have you got?'

She pushed the books away and placed her palms flat down on the table. 'Operation "stove-search" not so good. Bianca could have hidden the essay in any number of stoves. I tried yours but

Mrs Llantrisant wouldn't let me into the kitchen. She said you wouldn't be needing a stove, clean or otherwise, where you were going. It would be bread and water down at Cwmtydu Prison for you from now on.'

'I'm touched she has so much confidence in me.'

'She said, "You never really know anyone, do you?" Then I went to Bianca's flat and tried there but it was cordoned off and the policeman wouldn't let me in. I said I'd come to clean the stove and he said he'd never heard such a load of codswallop in all his life. I waited till he was replaced by another policeman. Then I tried again and this time I said I wanted to go and see my auntie who lived above Bianca and was ninety years old and very frail and I had to check up on her now and again just to make sure she wasn't dead.'

My eyes widened at that one, but I said nothing.

'So he let me in and I sneaked into Bianca's flat and just as I was checking the stove the first policeman turned up and caught me. He drags me downstairs saying he's going to give me a good hiding and down at the bottom when we got to the gate the other policeman looks up and says, "Sarge, I've heard it all now, there's a woman here who wants to clean the stove!" And do you know who it was? It was Mrs Llantrisant!'

This time we both looked at each other and stared.

'Mrs Llantrisant?'

She nodded

'I don't like the sound of that. Not at all.'

'Not much chance of it being coincidence is there?'

'I'm afraid not. So then what happened?'

'I bit the policeman's hand and ran for it.' She paused and then said, 'Are you angry?'

I blinked in puzzlement. 'Angry? What for?'

'Because I gave the game away.'

'No you didn't!'

'I did. Because of me she found out we were looking in stoves. I screwed up.'

I punched her playfully in the arm. 'Kid you did a brilliant job. I really take my hat off to you and one day – maybe next week – you are going to be a famous private eye.'

Her face brightened. 'Well I'd better get back to them stoves.'

I raised a hand. 'Don't worry about the stoves.'

'No?'

'By my reckoning, counting out my stove and Bianca's which you have checked, there must be about 3,998 left in town. It's hopeless.'

She blew a raspberry. 'What sort of talk is that?'

'Look, the way my luck is going, it will start snowing soon and then every stove in town will be lit up anyway.'

She picked up her coat. 'We don't need to check every stove in town. We just have to work out what her movements were and check the ones she would have had access to. It's simple.'

Later that afternoon I decided to go out. It was not a clever thing to do with half the countryside looking for me, but I decided, what the hell. I might as well be arrested as sit in the caravan doing nothing. I tied the old coat on with the packing string and covered my hands and face with soil. It was bitterly cold out so I stuffed crumpled-up newspaper inside my coat as insulation. Lastly, and this was something I hated most of all, I smeared myself with a liquid I had prepared from rotting fish, boiled cabbage and mouldy cheese. It was the nearest I could get to that sour unwashed cheesy smell that the vagrants seemed to have.

From Ynyslas I walked across the bog to the railway track, climbed on to a goods train, and jumped off a mile before Aberystwyth station. From there I walked through town to the sea front. And then I climbed up to the camera obscura on the top of Constitution

Hill. At the café at the top I bought a tea and a bag of old sixpences for the telescope mounted in the corner overlooking the town. The town astronomy society met here twice a month to use the little sixpenny telescope but there was no one here now. I turned it away from the sky and trained it on Sospan's stall. There was no one there apart from Sospan and so I sat down and drank my tea. After five minutes I looked again and this time found what I was looking for. Llunos enjoying his regular afternoon ice cream. I walked over to the phone.

'Yeah?'

'I didn't do it.'

'Sorry?'

'I said I didn't do it.'

'Who is this?'

'Can't you guess?'

'Louie?'

'I'm just calling to tell you it wasn't me. And you know it.'

'Do I?'

'Run a girl down in cold blood?'

'It was your car.'

'But I wasn't in it.'

'We found your fingerprints on it.'

'Of course you did, it was my bloody car!'

'What do you want?'

'I don't know.'

There was a short silence. Llunos was obviously taken aback by the honesty in the reply.

Then he remembered:

'You locked me in the toilet, you bastard!'

'Look, forget about that now, it's not important –'

'You won't say that when I get hold of you!'

'I mean we can discuss it later; right now I want you to know it wasn't me.'

'All right, Louie, if you're innocent why did you skip town the same night?'

'That doesn't prove anything.'

'It doesn't prove it, but it doesn't look very good, does it?'

'If I hadn't run away I would be locked up by now.'

'You think you won't be when we find you?'

I sighed in exasperation. 'It wasn't me, Llunos.'

'Look, say you weren't involved. Say someone else took your car and ran her over. Just say that for a moment. And you were safely home in bed at the time, why then would you leave town? You wouldn't even know she'd been killed. First thing you would have known was when we came knocking on your door.'

'I didn't do it, Llunos, and you know it.'

'You got an alibi?'

'Not a very good one.'

'Where were you on the night in question?'

'What time?'

'Between eleven and midnight.'

I paused.

'Well?'

'I was at the harbour.'

'That's a great alibi!'

My eyes smarted as I took in the mess I was in. It was hopeless.

'Fuck it all, Llunos, why would I want to kill Bianca?'

'Who did it then?'

'One of Pickel's mob.'

'Why?'

'Ask him.'

'You'll have to do better than that.'

'He was with her that night.'

'He's with her every night.'

'He stole something from Lovespoon and kept it hidden. He shouldn't have had it, but he did. He boasted to Bianca about it, so she stole it. If Lovespoon had found out, he would have killed Pickel so he told him first. The Druids took her and tortured her to find out what she had done with the thing she had stolen. They must have gone too far. Beaten her too much. She was probably going to die. So they arrange a car crash and use my car. Kill two birds with one stone.'

I could tell he was listening hard. It was troubling him, this murder. He probably had enough evidence to send me down. But he knew in his heart I didn't do it.

'What did she steal?'

'Some important papers belonging to Lovespoon.'

'Papers? Why would the girl care about papers? She couldn't hardly read.'

'She did it for me. She thought I wanted them.'

'Did you?'

'Not like that. Not for her to get involved.'

'What was so special about the papers?'

'They could prove that Lovespoon killed those schoolboys.'

There was silence. Had I got him? My heart started to beat a little faster.

'You know where the so-called papers are now?'

'Not really.'

'What do you mean not really? You're hanging by a thread, Louie. You tell me this cock-and-bull story –'

'Look, all I know is she hid them in the stove.'

'Which one?'

'Look, I know it's a big job, but a team of men could probably –'

'Louie!'

'What?'

'Look up at the sky.'

I leaned back and looked out of the café window. It looked like someone had burst a feather pillow in the sky.

'See that white cold stuff?'

I held the phone cradled against my cheek for a few seconds and then hung up.

Snow in June. Five minutes from now, every stove in Aberystwyth would be lit.

Chapter 17

THE SNOW FELL all afternoon but didn't stick, it just turned to a dirty grey slime on the pavement, and soon it was gone. I hung around the deserted town all day, dressed as a veteran and forced to live the life of one, which meant no life at all. There was no bar or café which would allow me in, and eventually I took refuge in Eeyore's stable where I could find warmth among the donkeys. I stayed there until evening and then I wandered over to the south side of Trefechan Bridge and waited in the shadows behind the bus stop. After half an hour I heard Myfanwy clip-clopping down the wet pavement in her high heels. In my veteran's outfit she didn't give me a second glance and came and stood right in front of me.

'Myfanwy,' I whispered.

She ignored me.

'Myfanwy!'

She moved up to the other end of the bus shelter.

'Myfanwy, please!'

She looked round. 'You leave me alone, mister, do you hear?'

'Myfanwy, it's me, Louie.'

She peered at me and then gasped.

'I need to talk to you.'

'Don't come any closer.'

'Do you think I would hurt you?'

'Is that what you said to Bianca?'

I sighed. This was all wrong.

'Myfanwy!' I begged. 'Please. I didn't kill Bianca, it's all wrong what they are printing in the paper. It was the Druids. I can prove –'

She looked back up the street as the green bus trundled up to the lights. They were on red. The yellow electric glow from the interior of the bus looked warm and inviting in the chill evening gloom.

'That's my bus.'

'Get the next one.'

'I can't, I'm already late.'

Without being able to stop myself, I made a move towards her lifting my arm out to touch her shoulder. She started backwards, raising her arms, but then stopped. We both stood frozen in our respective positions. She looked at me and our eyes met.

'I didn't do it,' I said simply.

She nodded. 'Promise?'

'I loved Bianca. You know that.'

She rushed over and I took her in my arms. 'But not as much as me, right?'

I hugged her.

'You smell.'

'I know.'

She breathed deeply and pressed her head into my chest. 'Louie, take me away.'

'Where?'

'Anywhere.'

'OK.'

She pulled away and looked up into my face. 'You mean it?'

'Yes.'

'When can we go? Tonight?'

I shook my head. 'No, not tonight.'

The lights changed and the bus eased forwards.

'Please, Louie, it has to be tonight.'

'A few days won't make any difference.'

'They will, oh they will, Louie, if only you knew.'

The bus approached.

'It has to be now.'

'If I go now, they will track me down. I'll go to prison.'

'We'll go somewhere where they won't find us.'

I shook my head sadly. 'I locked Llunos in a toilet, he'll find me.'

The bus stopped and the doors swished open. Myfanwy broke away and took a step towards the bus, looking back over her shoulder. As she stepped aboard she bit her lip and her face became disfigured with grief.

I walked the seven miles back to the caravan; on the beach between Borth and Ynyslas there was a bonfire surrounded by a group of War veterans. They were cooking rabbits and drinking from cans of strong lager. One of them had a guitar on which he strummed tuneless ditties. I skirted round them, not anxious to come into contact with a group of people who would quickly see through my disguise. But I was too late, they called out to me. I tried to pretend I hadn't heard and carried on walking, but one of the tramps stood up and came towards me.

'Hey, friend, come and share some supper.'

I twisted on the spot, uncertain what to do. Could I convince them I was a real veteran? Almost certainly not. How would they react to an impersonator? Laugh? Or get angry? If they got angry, what would they do? When you're on the lowest rung of society's ladder you don't have a lot to lose. Damn. The soldier walked up to me.

'Come and have some supper. I owe you a dinner, remember?'

'I think you've got the wrong person, my friend.'

He chuckled. 'I don't think so. It's not every day I get to eat strawberries and Black Forest Gateau. Especially in the company of a famous night-club singer.'

He laughed at the expression on my face. 'Do you think you can go round dressed like that and we won't notice?'

* * *

The rabbit was good, and so was the company. There was an easy informality about it and genuine sense of brotherhood. No one asked me the first thing I expected to be asked: what I was doing pretending to be a vet. It seemed to be understood that I must be in dire straits. And these were men with an instinctive understanding for suffering. They could sense my plight and knew better than to make it worse by asking stupid questions. For the first time in weeks I felt good. We sat there until late in the night, sucking the hot juicy goodness out of the roast rabbit and swapping stories; War stories mostly and sometimes stories from that life, impossibly distant to most of these men now, before the War. A life which was distinguished by a boredom and normality for which they could only ache. I'd never understood until now how beautiful a normal life could appear to those who can never possess it. For eight years I had been a private detective in Aberystwyth, never making any money and seldom getting a case that was remotely interesting; certainly never fighting off the hordes of beautiful female clients that Myfanwy was convinced from watching TV were a staple part of my routine. Every day I had bantered with Sospan, wandered up and down the Prom, stroking my father's donkeys and drinking pints in silence with him, a silence which I now recognised could only be enjoyed between two people whose love has gone beyond the artifice of words. And of course I had exchanged the most excruciatingly banal platitudes with Mrs Llantrisant about the weather. And now I was an outcast, wanted for the murder of one of my own friends, and the thought of being able to discuss the weather again with Mrs Llantrisant appeared to me as a distant dream.

I thought about the circumstances which had brought me to this pass, and when finally the conversation died slowly down and the only sound was the crackling of the fire and the distant sighing of the sea I turned to Cadwaladr.

'Remember what you once told me about Rio Caeriog? About the version of events they never tell anyone?'

Cadwaladr threw a bone into the fire, sending bright sparks up into the night sky.

'Yes, I remember.'

'Would you tell me that story now? The true story of Rio Caeriog?'

There was a murmur around the fire. Cadwaladr laughed softly and said, 'By rights there's only one man who should tell that story.' His words hung in the air and were followed by a rustling around the fire as the men shifted their positions and turned their gazes to a man sitting in the shadows next to the guitarist. He eased himself forward into the glow from the fire; an air of expectancy spread round the circle.

'You ask about Rio Caeriog?'

'Yes.'

'Tell me what you know about it.'

'I know what the history books say, that it was a great military victory –'

Scoffing sounds erupted from all sides of the circle.

'Oh yes,' the man laughed bitterly, 'a great military victory. That's why there's no statue of General Prhys outside the museum, and why you never find him mentioned in any of the history books.'

There were more scoffing sounds.

'And what else do you know?'

'I know that they put a radio beacon inside a Rolex watch, that the watch was lost in a rigged card game to one of the bandits who then took it back to the rebel base and then the Legion sent in the Lancaster bomber to home in on the radio beacon.'

The man nodded. 'In these history books you talk of, do they tell you where the card game took place?'

'It was a place called San Isadora, in the foothills of the Sierra Machynlleth mountains.'

'That was a hundred miles behind the lines in hostile territory. Do you know how we got there?'

'Marched, I suppose.'

The man spat. 'Marched.' His voice rose in anger. 'You think you can just walk a hundred miles in hostile territory and no one will notice?'

The guitarist placed a mollifying hand on his shoulder. 'It's OK, Johnny, take it easy. It's not this man's fault.'

Johnny turned sharply towards the man. 'Were you there? Were you there, huh?'

'No, Johnny, I wasn't. I wasn't there.'

'Don't you think I have the right to be angry?'

Cadwaladr answered. 'Yes, Johnny, you have a right to be angry. We all know that. But this man is a guest. He isn't the one responsible for your pain.'

'Tell him the story, Johnny.'

'And us too; tell us about Rio Caeriog.'

'Yes tell it, Johnny!'

Johnny sat back and resumed his story in a calmer voice. 'I'll tell you how we got there; General Prhys made us march those hundred miles disguised as United Nations peace-keepers. He gave us all a tin of blue paint and made us paint our helmets. That's how we did it.'

I whistled, not sure whether I was supposed to be impressed or shocked. Then there was a pause, and as the fire died down to a glow, and with the far-off lights of Aberdovey gleaming behind him, Johnny told the story of Rio Caeriog.

'When we got to San Isadora we billeted and went to the cantina. A young private by the name of Pantycelyn was chosen to play the card game. There was nothing special about him. He was like most of the other kids there. Young and frightened and wishing he could go back to his parents' farm in the shadow of Cader Idris. But he was chosen.' Johhny paused. 'Or maybe he was chosen because he was sober and reliable. The sort of person who could be trusted not to get the watches mixed up. Because everyone had Rolexes in those days, cheap from the PX store.' He stopped again and sighed sadly. 'Yes maybe that was why they chose him.' Johnny stopped and took a sip from his can. 'Do they tell you any of this in your books?'

'Yes, this much I have heard.'

He nodded. 'Everything went well at first. Losing the watch was easy – the only hard part was not making it look too obvious. As soon as they won the Rolex, the bandits rode out of town, shooting their pistols in the air as they went. A Rolex watch was worth ten years' salary in those parts. Then after the game Pantycelyn went to join the rest of the platoon. They were listening to the radio in the front bar. It was the semi-final of the Copa Americana and Brazil were playing Argentina. The entire town was there. When the kid walked in, something funny happened. The radio reception went haywire. The peasants hooted and threw enchiladas at him. And the kid starts to get scared. He realises that he must have got the watches mixed up. The bandits had got the genuine Rolex and he was wearing a radio beacon on his wrist with a Lancaster bomber heading directly for him. So he tries to get the thing off, but he's so clumsy in his terror that he breaks the catch. Well, as you know, a Rolex is made to last: try as he might he can't get the damned watch off. So his mates take him outside to work out what to do. There's about an hour to go and everyone is getting jumpy. Someone suggests to the kid he does the noble thing and get on a mule and ride out of town for five miles. And, of course, he's getting really jittery now and says, "Fuck off, why don't you all ride out of town on a mule?" And they say, "So we can save all these innocent people here," and he says, "Do I give a fuck?

I'm dead anyway." So then the medic pipes up and says, "Why don't we amputate his arm?" This strikes everybody as a good idea, except Pantycelyn who's now only too pleased to ride out of town for five miles, in fact, he's begging to do it. But no one trusts him. So he makes a break for it, and they chase after him. All around the town he runs, with the platoon on his trail. Eventually they catch him. They hold him down, give him a shot of morphine, and amputate the arm – just below the elbow. Then they strap the arm to a mule and fire a gun behind it. Wham! The mule covers the first mile in less than a minute. Leaving Pantycelyn to sleep off his anaesthetic they go back into the cantina. Soon they hear the far-off drone of the bomber approaching above the clouds. By now it's the last five minutes of the game and Argentina are one-nil up. The peasants are on the edge of their seats. They're all betting like crazy on the outcome and the tables are all piled high with money. Well, what do you know! As soon as the soldiers walk in, the radio goes haywire again. Turns out it's just something to do with the radio waves reflecting off the helmets. It means they cut the kid's arm off for nothing. Of course, they're pretty upset, but they agree among themselves not to tell the kid when he wakes up. After all, if there was nothing wrong with the watch on the arm they amputated, then the bandits must have taken the one with the radio transmitter all along. So as the sound of the plane gets louder, everyone goes outside to watch the fireworks. And from the roof of the cantina they watch as the bomber drops 14,000lbs of high explosive and phosphorus on to the orphanage. It seems the bandit had donated the watch to the one of the holy sisters. Twenty-seven children killed. Within hours every hoe, axe, hammer and shovel for two hundred square miles was raised against us. As we started our retreat, the rain came and washed the blue paint off our helmets.'

After he finished, I didn't know what to say. No one did. There was silence for a long while and then one by one people stood up and drifted away. I thanked the veterans for their hospitality and rose to my feet. As I left, Johnny the storyteller gave me a sort of salute of farewell. At the same time, a branch on the fire cracked in the heat sending a flare up that illuminated the whole of one side of his body. And then I knew why of all the assembled people that night, only he could have told me the true story of Rio Caeriog. His left arm was missing below the elbow.

When I got back to the caravan, the one that had been welded together from two crash write-offs and couldn't be traced, the one that couldn't be seen from the road and about which not even the caretaker knew anything, I found a police car parked outside.

Chapter 18

'YOU THINK I didn't know about this crappy caravan? I could have picked you up any time I wanted.'

I put a plastic mug filled with instant soup down in front of Llunos. It seemed like years since I had done the same for Myfanwy. But it was just over a week. The ludo set was still out on the table.

'So why didn't you?'

He ran a pudgy hand through his hair. He looked as if he hadn't slept for a week; and there was something else about him: the air of weary self-assurance was gone. Now he just seemed weary. He looked at me as if appealing for help. 'I don't think I'll have a job by the end of the week.'

I blinked.

'There's a new commissioner of police.'

'Anyone I know?'

'Herod Jenkins.'

'The games teacher?'

'Yes.'

'Fuck.'

'Soon you won't be able to sneeze in this town without a note from your Mam.'

I topped up the mugs of soup with rum.

'The man's a nutcase.'

Llunos gave me a 'tell me about it' look. He pulled out a bag from under his chair and slid it across the table to me. It was a child's school satchel.

'We took this from Brainbocs's house just after he disappeared.'

I looked at the policeman and he shifted uncomfortably in his seat as if he couldn't believe what he was doing. He was helping me.

'It's no fucking use so don't get all excited.'

I undid the buckles and opened the satchel. There were four objects inside and I laid them side by side next to the ludo set: a field guide to edible mushrooms; Job Gorseinon's *Roses of Charon*; an invoice from Dai the Custard Pie's fancy-dress basement; and, perhaps most curiously of all, a nineteenth-century nautical primer: *Corruption of the Deep: The Captain's Guide to Last Rites and Burials at Sea.*

I picked each one up in turn, examined it briefly and then put it down in its original place.

No one spoke.

Llunos stood up to leave. 'I told you it wouldn't help.'

I followed him to the door and for a while we stood there facing each other awkwardly on the step. It was as if the components of our universe had shifted like fragments in a kaleidoscope and we now found ourselves fighting on the same side. He stuck out his hand and we shook.

'If I was you,' he said, 'I'd leave town.' And then, through the wound-down window of his car, 'Did you hear about Ma Brainbocs?'

'No, what?'

'She was spotted at Cardiff airport yesterday boarding an Aerolineas Argentina flight.'

When I awoke late next morning, one thing was clear to me: it was time to get out of town. If Llunos had known all about my hiding hole plenty of other people probably did as well. And I'd had enough of skulking around disguised as a War veteran. With the games teacher running the police force we were all in the shit. I threw a few things into a zip-up hold-all and put the veteran's disguise on for what I hoped was the last time. Maybe Myfanwy and I could get the train to Shrewsbury.

At Myfanwy's flat the door was ajar and the place deserted. Not empty with the atmosphere of a room from which the tenant has nipped out to buy milk, but with air of a nest in which the eggs are cold and the parent birds have been frightened away. There was nothing concrete to suggest it, but sometimes you know these things without needing evidence. Bras and panties were left drying on cold radiators. T-shirts and inside-out jeans were strewn across the floor. Mugs of instant coffee covered in green fur cluttered every surface next to wine bottles and beer cans filled with cigarette ends all glued down with sticky rings of stale beer. There were half-eaten take-away meals and tins of tuna stuck to the carpet, with forks sticking out of the jaggedly opened tops. Clothes draped on hangers hooked over door handles, Schwarzenegger and Stallone videos, Lady Di souvenirs, posters of Bon Jovi, shiny vinyl cases from which make-up bottles spilled out on to the floor. Birth-control pills and tampons. And everywhere the air was rank with the smell of old beer, candles and stale farts. It was as if a butterfly had emerged from a chrysalis on a dung heap. But the butterfly had flown.

I almost didn't care. Like a regularly beaten dog I was too tired to yelp. The fall of the stick had become routine. Myfanwy had pleaded with me to take her away and I had been too stubborn and now it was too late. What did I expect? Everyone knew you don't get two bites at a cherry like that. With her gone I no longer had any desire to leave, or to stay, or in fact to do anything. Maybe, I thought, I should just go back to my old flat and wait for Herod's men to arrive. I wandered down to the harbour and then on down past the castle and stood for an hour on the Prom leaning on the sugar-white railings and staring emptily out to sea. The waters were a chill unwelcoming gunmetal colour and the breeze stiff and salty. Above my head the Noddy illumination swayed and creaked eerily and I thought grimly of the likely consequences if a man turned up in this town wearing a red hat with bells. Eventually I headed for the only suitable place for a man whose world has collapsed: the Whelk Stall.

The boy was reading the newspaper on the counter when I arrived and gave no sign of stopping. I stood pointedly in front of him for a while but still he ignored me. This was not a wise policy. I slammed my hand down on the page he was reading.

He looked up with hatred in his eyes. 'Sorry, Smelly, we don't serve tramps.'

I gasped in disbelief. Didn't he know what I had been through recently? Didn't he know that I was an outcast, wanted for murder? That this filthy coat was just a disguise? Didn't he know I had lost Myfanwy? Didn't he know how dangerous that made me? Didn't he know any of this? Of course he didn't but that was just tough. There comes a time when someone has to pay and it doesn't matter whether it's the wrong bill or not. Someone has to pay.

'What did you say, Sonny Jim?'

'I said, fuck off, granddad, and stop stinking up my stall.'

I nodded slowly and thoughtfully. And then I hit him. He flew backwards more from surprise than from the force of the punch and fell heavily into a pile of saucepans. Before he could recover, I jumped over the counter, paused for a second while I recovered my balance, took aim, and kicked him in the stomach. He grunted and struggled desperately to escape on all fours, unable to get to his feet. I picked up a frying pan and swung it against the side of his head. I could feel the cartilage in his ear cracking and vibrating through the handle of the pan. 'No, please, no mister, please,' he cried. But it was too late. Two weeks too late; the invoice was in his in-tray and he was going to pay it. He scuttled away still on all fours and the sight of his desperation served only to increase my fury. I ran forwards and grabbed the scruff of his neck, pulled him backwards and slammed the frying pan full into his face. Blood from his nose spattered on his dirty white chef's tunic. 'Please, mister!' he cried, and I pushed him into a pile of cardboard boxes and waste bins. Trapped, with nowhere left to go, he turned to face me, cowering and pulling back at the same time. I picked up a knife with a long blade from the counter and advanced another step. This time he was too frightened even to speak. I could smell urine as his hands clutched at his groin.

'Right then,' I hissed. 'Are you going to serve me some fucking whelks or not?' The knife pointed at the end of his nose and he stared at it in cross-eyed fascination. He nodded.

'Yes sir,' he whispered. 'It'll be a pleasure.'

While he prepared the evening special which we had agreed would be on the house I read the newspaper. Back page first. Then I turned to the front; the main story was Herod's appointment, complete with a photo of the games teacher smiling through that familiar horizontal crease in his face. The same teacher who had sent a consumptive schoolboy out on a run in the worst blizzard to hit Cardiganshire in more than seventy years. The only other story was a small one-column piece on the right under the headline VICE GIRL GRAVE DESECRATED. I turned the page angrily. Then stopped like a cartoon animal that has just run over the edge of a cliff. I turned the page back and re-read the headline, my eyes wide open with shock. It was about Bianca's grave. Feverishly I skimmed the article. Two nights ago someone had dug the coffin up at Llanbadarn Cemetery and broken open the lid in what the paper described as a sick and motiveless crime. The attackers had used a power saw to open up a rectangle eighteen inches long and ten wide in the lid covering Bianca's face. Nothing had been taken, and the corpse hadn't, as they put it, been interfered with.

I pushed the paper away and sat there stunned. Aberystwyth was shocked and baffled by the crime. No one could imagine who could do such a thing. But I could. It was the same person that killed the Punch and Judy man.

Chapter 19

TO THINK OF all the millions of useless, pointless, empty, cruel, vain, proud, mean, obscene and utterly valueless words we spit out during our lives; to think of all those words and all those syllables, more syllables than grains of sand on Borth Beach. Oh Bianca, all you needed was just one more. What evil jinni stood on your shoulder and robbed you of that last, crucial puff of air? To think of all the nonsense you talked. All the lies and flatteries you spent your nights pouring into the ears of pink-faced Druids! All those empty, wasted words. If only you could have bitten your tongue just once: withheld a word and kept it on credit for that rainy day when an extra syllable could have changed the world. One syllable, perhaps the only one in your whole life, that could have made anything better. The essay is in the stove, you gasped. Oh no! You didn't put it in the stove. You who cocked a final snook at society by wearing your night-club costume in the coffin. You put it in your stovepipe hat!

Chapter 20

THE DOORSTEP WAS smeared with dust, cats' piss and muddy boot prints. And someone had daubed 'murderer' on the wall. I climbed the stairs. The door to my office was ajar and I could see Mrs Llantrisant sitting with her feet on the desk eating peanuts. So lost in her own world, she didn't notice me. Mechanically she reached into the brown paper bag, withdrew a handful of nuts, cracked them between her fingers and threw the shells willy-nilly across the floor, cackling to herself as they spattered against the portrait of Noel Bartholomew. The smell of peanutty breath was overpowering even out in the stairwell. I pushed the door open and she let out a gasp.

'You!'

I stared at her through narrowing eyes.

She cast a furtive glance across the desk to the phone, silently judging the distance and deciding against it. She recomposed her features and forced them into a beam of joy.

'You're back!'

'Got tired of swabbing, did you?' I said in a cold monotone.

The beam of joy became a pantomime of anxious concern.

'Oh, Mr Knight, it breaks my heart it does to see the step like that, it really does. It was the police, you see, told me not to touch anything – not that I think for one moment that you . . . I mean, all those things they're saying . . . never heard such . . .' The words trailed gently off into the ether. She cast another look at the phone and smiled at me with less conviction this time.

'Still, it's nice to see you back. Will you be staying long?'

I walked across to the desk. She moved back unconsciously pressing herself against the back of the chair.

'I don't know. How long does it take to beat the crap out of an old lady?'

I yanked out the phone cable. Her pupils flashed open.

I sat on the edge of the desk and leaned across. 'Where is it?'

'Where is –'

The words stopped as I raised my index finger.

'Please don't say "where is what".'

She looked at me without saying a word.

'I have to hand it to you,' I said, 'you're a real dark horse.' I started flicking the broken telephone cable against the desk. 'I mean, you give the impression that you haven't got two brain cells to rub together, but you certainly worked the stovepipe hat out a lot quicker than me.'

She said nothing, just continued staring at me wondering how much I knew and what I was going to do.

'But then you don't get into the upper echelons of the Sweet Jesus League without being smart, do you? Not into the ESSJAT you don't.'

'I'm not in it, Mr Knight.'

'Not in what?'

'In . . . in what you said.'

'What did I say?'

She looked at me uncertainly. 'That organisation you mentioned; I'm not in it.'

'What's it called?'

'Er . . . I don't know.'

'Then how do you know you're not in it?'

'I . . . I . . .'

'You're a lieutenant in the ESSJAT, Mrs Llantrisant.'

She shook her head in desperation. 'No . . . no . . . no I'm not, I'm not!'

'All these years you've been swabbing my step and all the time you've been listening at the keyhole.'

'No, Mr Knight, no!'

'That's how you found out about the Punch and Judy man.'

She shook her head and put her hands to her ears. 'No!'

I leaned closer until my face was only inches away from hers. I could smell the musty reek of Eau de Maesteg.

'You killed him, didn't you?'

'Who?' she whined. 'I haven't killed anybody, Mr Knight. Honest I haven't. I'm just a step-swabber. I'm sorry about the peanuts –'

I whipped the end of the phone cord across her face and the words stopped in mid-sentence. A fine pink groove appeared in the thickly plastered foundation cream.

'It wasn't enough for you to destroy his life: knock him off the pedestal he stood on for thirty years and force him to scratch a living in the Punch and Judy tents of Aberaeron. You had to throw the poor man off a cliff.'

'No, Mr Knight, not me, not me!'

'It was you I fought with that night down at the harbour, wasn't it?'

'No, please, Mr Knight. You've got it all wrong.'

'Have I? Have I?' I shouted. 'I don't think so.' I paused, breathing heavily, and waited for myself to become calm again. I needed to stay in control.

'Tell me, Mrs Llantrisant. Are you familiar with the works of Job Gorseinon?'

She looked at me blankly.

'Brainbocs was. They found a copy of Gorseinon's *Roses of Charon* in his satchel. It's an enquiry into the darker side of Greco-Roman horticulture. Have you ever read it?'

She watched me, confused and suspicious. 'I don't think I have. Good book is it?'

'Ooh, curate's egg really. But there's one nice bit where Gorseinon describes how Livia is alleged to have murdered

Augustus. He was a wily old bird, you see, Augustus. A bit like you if you don't mind me saying so. And he was paranoid about being poisoned. With good reason as it turned out. It got to the point where he wouldn't eat anything except fruit he had picked from his own orchard. So Livia smeared the figs on the tree with deadly nightshade. Ring any bells does it?'

She looked at me with an empty face like a poker player.

'The story reminded me of that occasion just before Easter when you were taken ill all of a sudden from eating that apple pie. Remember how you called the priest? How he took your deathbed confession? It's funny because we also found in Brainbocs's satchel a book on how to perform the last rites and a fancy-dress hire ticket from Dai the Custard Pie's. It doesn't say what costume he borrowed but I bet if I went down and looked at Custard Pie's ledger I'd find it was a Catholic priest's outfit. What do you say?'

Slowly a change came over Mrs Llantrisant. As if she had decided that the time had come to drop the mask. She brought her hands down from her ears and looked me in the eye. The silly, frivolous old gossip faded away and in its place there sat a different woman. Self-possessed and steely with an expression of stone. Suddenly she darted sideways out of the chair. I leaped after her grabbing at the tails of her housecoat but she moved like a cat and was almost at the door when I managed to grab her ankle. She was strong and fast and would have got away, but my nails caught on her old varicose vein scars. The sharp pain pulled her up for a split-second and made her gasp. It was all I needed. I reached higher and took a firmer grip on her coat. Then her training took over, banishing pain, and focusing every sinew on the task in hand, she turned and sized me up in one cold, robotic look. She lowered one knee, transferred her weight and then spun round driving a backhand smash into my face. I reeled and fell backwards and she moved in with cold precision.

In came the elbow, ramming into my head above the ear and I started to go down. The room swirled and birds sang inside my head. I could see the knee moving up now, the confusion in my brain slowing its hideous progress down to a crawl. A crawl that I felt powerless to avoid. I remember seeing insignificant details with a strange detachment: how the housecoat parted and revealed the elasticised bottom of the bloomer, slightly above the knee. The knee, fish-white and blue-veined like Gorgonzola cheese, slamming upwards like a ramrod. At the last second I jerked to the side and the knee crashed into the filing cabinet. I could see, almost feel myself, the fireworks of pain that shot through her. A deep gash appeared, blood splattered, and she fell to the floor.

I bent over her and suddenly jumped backwards as she jabbed at me with a hatpin which she had pulled from her boot; the hypo-allergenic calfskin boot made in Milan. I dodged the pin and she tried again, but crippled by the wound to her knee she could only lunge and crawl dementedly. I stepped clear of her range of action. Took a careful look round the room and spotted what I wanted. Among the fire irons in the grate was a big cast-iron poker. I picked it up and walked over to where Mrs Llantrisant lay. She looked up at me too convulsed with hate to display any fear. With bitter deliberation I smashed the iron down on her knee. She screamed like a wolf, her spit-covered dentures jettisoning out on to the carpet. Then she blacked out.

When she came round she was sitting in the client's chair, bound at the ankles and wrists with the flex from the TV. I threw a washing-up bowl of cold water with ice cubes into her face. She lifted her head and looked at me, her face still twisted and contorted with misery. I smiled. Then kicked her in the knee; she jerked and writhed, straining at the flex with a power that looked as if it might break the back of the wooden chair.

'That was for killing the Punch and Judy man.'

She spat blood on to the carpet but said nothing.

'Now when you're ready I have some questions I'd like to ask you.'

'Bugumph a dwonba frum ga fum paschtad!'

I screwed up my face 'What!?'

'Ga fhaard bu mon get aggyfun oumpa me ga frunbin pash schtern!'

I picked up the dentures and shoved them back into her mouth.

She started manipulating them furiously with her tongue, making obscene gob-stopper mounds in alternate cheeks. When they were in place she shrieked at me, 'I said you won't get a fucking word out of me, you bastard!'

I kicked her in the knee and she squealed in agony. I spoke to her in a soft bedside manner.

'You know, something puzzles me.' She looked up, interested despite her attempts not to be. 'You're always whingeing to me about the amount of time your friends have to wait at the hospital to get their hips done, and here I am fucking up your knee and you don't seem bothered. Why is that?'

She looked at me coldly and said, 'Your threats are useless. I spit on them.'

'Why did you kill him?'

'Who?'

'Iolo Davies – the Museum curator.'

'My orders were to remove him and so I removed him. He meant nothing to me. It was just a job.'

'Like swabbing the step?'

'He was just a filthy semen-squirting little toad.'

'So where's the essay?'

'Fuck off!'

'OK,' I smiled.

I walked to the kitchen and filled the kettle. I was troubled. What if she had been trained to withstand pain? You heard of such things. My resolve would soon give way. I had already shown that with Lovespoon. My gaze wandered round the kitchen and I was struck at how totally she had made the place her own. Four new housecoats hung up, doubtless paid for out of my petty-cash tin. Groceries from Safeway littered the side. There was even a trunk containing her orthopaedic-boot collection. And then it struck me: even Mrs Llantrisant had an Achilles heel.

I picked up the industrial-size meat mincer which had lain in the corner gathering dust since the time when Mrs Llantrisant and Mrs Abergynolwen had made the sausage rolls for the Eisteddfod. I dragged it into the office and placed it down a few feet in front of Mrs Llantrisant. She looked at me with a look of withering contempt.

'Gonna mince me leg off, are you now, Mr Knight? Or is it me arm? Mince away for all I care, I shall just laugh at you.'

'It's not your leg you should be worried about, Mrs Llantrisant.' I bent down and started unlacing her orthopaedic boot. The brash confidence disappeared and a look of naked terror swept into her cold, pitiless eyes. She struggled like a fish on a hook but the TV flex held her firmly bound to the chair. I took off the boot and stuffed it into the top of the mincer where the chopped meat usually goes and grabbed the handle.

'Better start singing, Mrs Llantrisant, or your boot will be mincemeat.'

'You wouldn't dare! They cost eighty quid they did!'

'You're Gwenno Guevara, aren't you?'

'Fuck off!'

I gave the handle a slight turn. The teeth of the mincing mechanism made contact with the leather. Mrs Llantrisant gasped. I stopped turning the handle and peered to look at the damage to the boot.

'They're just a bit scuffed at the moment; bit of shoe polish would get that off. It's your last chance.'

She started struggling to break free of the flex which bound her to the chair and I gave the handle a full heave. There was a sickening crunching, gristly sort of noise as the spiral teeth cut into the solid wall of the boot. Mrs Llantrisant let out a long, blood-curdling howl, like a tortured wolf.

'You're Gwenno Guevara, aren't you?!' I shouted.

'Yes! Yes! Yes!' she screamed.

'The supreme commander of the ESSJAT?'

'Yes!'

'Is that why Brainbocs came to see you? Why he took your deathbed confession?'

'Yes!'

'Why was he so interested in you?'

She just shook her head sadly and gasped for breath. 'I don't know. I really don't know. All I know is the boy was trying to reunite Lovespoon's bomber crew. Lovespoon, Herod, Dai the Custard Pie . . .'

'And Frobisher?'

'He was dead. He didn't matter. But Brainbocs was trying to track down the remaining survivors from the Rio Caeriog mission. I was the only one he couldn't find.'

'So where's the essay?'

'It's in my handbag on the chair in the kitchen.'

I looked over to the kitchen and then back at her. This was all a bit too easy.

'If you're lying, your boot's fucked.'

She shook her head.

'I mean it! I'll do every single fucking one of them!'

'In my bag, go and see.'

I went to the kitchen and opened her handbag. Inside was a manila envelope. I pulled it out. It was marked on the front in ball-point pen: 'David Brainbocs, spring term assignment, Cantref-y-Gwaelod'. Next to that was a date and the St Luddite's school stamp, initialled by Lovespoon. I tore it open and pulled out the essay. There were about thirty pages of A4 filled with a closely packed schoolboy hand, interspersed here and there with technical-looking diagrams. It was perfect. The essay that half of Aberystwyth had been looking for. There was just one thing wrong. As I leafed through the pages I could hear from the other room a horrible raucous cackling that went straight through me like a graveyard wind. Mrs Llantrisant was laughing. I could mince up every orthopaedic boot in Aberystwyth and it wouldn't make a hap'orth of difference this time. The essay was written in runes.

Chapter 21

WEARILY, I SET off on the half-hour walk across town to the light industrial estate on the site of the old engine sheds. That was where the new Witches' Co-op could be found next to the DIY emporium, the computer superstore and the frozen-food wholesalers. It was a far cry from the cubby hole the shop had formerly occupied in the side of the castle ramparts next to the Coronation Muggery. The shop itself was an uneasy mix of traditional and modern. In front of the warehouse-like building of corrugated iron and sand-coloured brick was a car park in which the parking bays were marked out in whorls and vortices corresponding to the lines of power beneath the tarmac. The staff wore bright cotton overalls covered in half moons and stars like Hallowe'en costumes, but the security guard had a wolf on a leash. The lighting was mainly fluorescent, except for torches burning at the ends of the aisles.

At my approach, the glass double doors opened as if by magic and one of the assistants pointed me in the direction of the R&D facility at the back. The door was marked 'authorised personnel only' but I walked through regardless and found myself in a laboratory. It was empty except for Julian, the cat, who was peering into the eyepiece of a microscope, his paws balancing on the knurled focusing wheel. He looked up and gave me the usual look of disdain and then, intimidated perhaps by the expression of determination on my face, flicked an ear back towards the far side of the room. My gaze followed the direction of his ear to a large glass window set in the wall and through the glass I could see Evans the Boot's Mam sitting on a broomstick in what appeared to be a wind tunnel. Julian returned his gaze to the eyepiece of the microscope. The door to the wind tunnel had a red light above it and, not wishing to compromise the research, I went up to the window and waved. Mrs Evans saw me, signalled to one of the white-coated technicians in the room, and dismounted. She came out carrying the broomstick and took off the helmet which looked like one of those worn by Olympic racing cyclists. Then, struggling to get her breath back, she tossed me the broomstick; it was lighter than a feather.

'Not bad eh?' she panted. 'Carbon fibre frame, hollow inside and polypropylene bristles – drag coefficient about the same as a seagull.'

'I'm impressed.'

'I hear Myfanwy left town. I thought you two were an item.'

'So did I but you just never know, do you?'

I took the essay out of my pocket and handed it to her. She held the papers up to her nose, and slowly leafed through them, making soft grunting sounds as she went. Unfortunately, she didn't have her runing glasses with her but agreed that she would start transcribing tonight and send Julian over every half hour with the pages as she finished them. At the mention of his name, the cat looked up again from the microscope, stared long and hard at us, and then reapplied his eye to the eyepiece.

'You're staying in that old caravan aren't you?' Mrs Evans added as I left. 'The one no one knows about?' As I retraced my steps through the whorls and vortices of the car park I thought sourly of Eeyore and his so-called untraceable caravan. I was tempted to curse him, but if you did that in this shop it set off an alarm.

The sun was setting when I got back and the caravans were bathed in golden fire, like an Inca city. I wasn't expecting to see Julian with the translated pages until later in the night and so I slept for a while. When I awoke, the caravan was in darkness. I got up and took down a tin of pilchards from the cupboard as a reward for Julian and went out for a walk. A breathless hush had fallen, the sort sometimes found in the hour or two between the end of a perfect summer's day and the onset of evening. Under a sky darkening to indigo I walked through the caravan park, aware with a tinge of envy that the rest of the inhabitants would be sitting down inside their two-wheeled homes to their homely meals: dinners scooped out of tins, heated over camping-gas burners and served on picnic crockery. Children tingling with the raw memory of swimming in the sea and burning on the hot sands. A nameless sense of foreboding had found its way into my heart. I headed for the dunes that edged the park; there was something eternally beautiful and reassuring about them, the sharp spiky marram grass that stung our knees as children looked soft now, like fur ruffled by the fondling breeze. I climbed and sat down facing the ocean looking out to a world which ten thousand years ago had still been land, and which Dai Brainbocs had persuaded his Welsh teacher to try and reclaim. The scheme seemed no madder than some of the other things that had been happening and I could no longer find the strength to be convinced that it wouldn't work. It was the normal world that was difficult to believe in now. The first stars flickered faintly and from far away the voices of playing children came, weak as ghosts. It was going to be a long night. I took out the hip flask and had a drink of rum, then reached into my pocket for a notepad and pencil. I thought for a few seconds and wrote on the pad: What are the lessons of Noel Bartholomew? I took another drink and savoured the fiery liquor as I contemplated the answer to my question. Never try and save a woman who can't be saved? I stuck the pencil in my mouth and looked at the new sentence. No. I crossed it out. Always try and save a woman who can't be saved? I scratched that one out too. Don't try and save a woman if it's you who needs saving? I put the notepad down and took another drink. Calamity, who thought all private detectives should drink whisky, once asked me what was the difference between the two drinks. I thought at the time it had to do with the taste, but I was wrong. People are wrong about everything. What is the difference? They both taste fiery and get you drunk, they both look the same and cost the same. But one is the distilled essence of cold, wet, miserable Scottish highlands. And one is the succulent ichor made from sugar and the distilled sunshine of far-off places. I knew which one Bartholomew would have chosen. Bartholomew the dreamer, the romantic, travelling upriver against all advice, lured ever further inland by tantalising rumours and contradictory stories . . . All this time I had been telling Calamity to ask the right question and had been asking the wrong one myself. I knew now that he never found Hermione, and it wasn't the Chinese shopkeeper who faked the pictures but he himself before he left Aberystwyth. A few sprigs of foliage from Danycoed Wood, a girl from a harbourside tea-cosy shop paid a farthing to dress up, and a studio in Terrace Road.

And the question was not whether he found her or not but why he went all that way just to die? I looked out over the quiet grey landscape, the colour slowly leeching out. The answer is etched in all the faces you meet in Aberystwyth. No one has the courage to be saved. Not the Moulin girls seeking escape in the one place they'll never find it. Nor Sospan grinning sadly behind the invisible bars of his vanilla prison.

A lone figure came running along the beach from the direction of Borth. One tiny figure running with the arrow-straight desperation of one whose errand might still save the world. I watched her approach, a school satchel swinging at her side, as she ran up the beach over the stones and into the foothills of the dunes. Her pace suddenly halved on the soft sand as her footholds gave way and the air around her turned to treacle. But she just redoubled her efforts, racing against the tumbling mounds of sand and contemptuous of their attempts to thwart her. It was Calamity and the fire of belief within her still burned strong. At the top she ran up to me and threw herself into my arms, she was sobbing uncontrollably.

'He . . . he . . .'

'It's OK.'

Her face was washed over with a silver film of tears and her efforts to speak juddered into nothing as each time a fresh bout of sobbing took her.

'He . . . he . . .'

'What is it?'

'He's going to destroy Aberystwyth!' and at the thought of it she squealed and burst into another fit of weeping.

I reached into my pocket and found a pack of tissues to hand to her. Staring out over Ynyslas sands in the deep calm of this night, I was able to receive the news that someone was going to destroy Aberystwyth with strange detachment. I waited patiently as the sobs slowly subsided. Calamity took out a tissue and blew her nose. She looked up at me, her face wet and glistening.

'He'll destroy everything!'

'Who will?'

'Lovespoon.'

Another sob interrupted but through the tears she said:

'You said you didn't know how he was going to get the Ark to the sea?'

I nodded.

'It was the wrong question. He's going to take the sea to the Ark!'

As we retraced our steps, carefully now as all the light from the world had gone and the paths through the dunes had disappeared, we saw a bonfire burning on the horizon, somewhere in the direction of Tre'ddol. In the dark midsummer night there was something unnervingly ancient and pagan about the sight. We watched for a long time until our reverie was startled by the mewing of a cat at our feet, the sharp scent of burned fur pricking our nostrils. It was Julian, with a badly singed ear. An entire story was contained in that sharp burned cat smell and we apprehended it in an instant. We set off at a run across the hills in the direction of Ma Evans's house, through the caravan park, across the road and out along the bog towards the railway line. I knew what to expect before I got there. Mrs Llantrisant had outwitted me yet again. When we arrived the area was bathed in the familiar flashing blue light. A team of firemen was hosing down the house and some ladies from the St John's Ambulance Brigade were reassuring Ma Evans who sat huddled under a blanket drinking tea. Some yards away stood the makings of an ugly pyre. And beyond that, held back by the police and making angry grumblings, was the mob of disgruntled villagers who had no doubt set the pyre. I didn't know what Mrs Llantrisant had said to them – such a task would have been child's play for an agent of her experience. Sheep not lambing, or cows not calving, or milk going inexplicably sour; any of the myriad natural mishaps of everyday life could have been ascribed to witchery and used against Ma Evans. The pyre had been extinguished but the house, set on fire deliberately but made to look like the work of an accidental spark, was beyond saving. As I surveyed the scene, Ma Evans looked over to me, the tears still glistening on her cheeks, and tried to somehow explain things to me with her expression. I waved it aside; it was me who should be doing the explaining; I had brought all this upon her. A group of men walked over and pointed shotguns at me and I slowly raised my hands. From behind the house came a figure, an old lady who used to be a hunched and bent old spinster but now walked with a back ramrod straight and an authoritative purposeful air. It was Mrs Llantrisant, her sense of having achieved her destiny compromised only by the big black gap in her front dental plate which made her look like a cartoon pirate. Julian the cat ran up to her. A wave of despair and fury hit me as she took a large kipper out of her shopping bag and handed it to the cat. 'You fucking Judas!' I screamed, and ran forwards, lashing out viciously with my foot at the ring of Julian's arse. The cat yelped and jumped out of the way just as the stock of a shotgun smashed into the side of my head. I twisted slightly as I fell and the last thing I saw before losing consciousness, as I looked up, was Herod Jenkins and that horizontal crease in his face they called a smile.

Chapter 22

I OPENED MY eyes in a dark room, my cheek pressed against a cold, gritty concrete floor. Three stripes of light ran down the wall from a barred window and my head and ribs throbbed. I drifted back into unconsciousness. When I woke again the shadow of the bars was fainter as the first pale glimmer of dawn filled the room. I dragged myself to my feet, wincing at the shooting pains from my ribs and shuffled to the window. The view was from the side of Pen Dinas overlooking the harbour towards the station. It was Blaenplwyf prison. I felt the ribs with my fingers – they didn't appear to be broken, but someone had given me a good kicking. From my vantage point I could see Victory Square between the station and the museum and I could see what it was that had so upset Calamity. The Lancaster bomber was gone. Finally, when it was too late to do anything about it, I understood. That dramatic change of course in Brainbocs's research that started all the trouble. It could mean only one thing. All along we had been puzzled how they were going to get the Ark to the sea. And Calamity had worked it out. They were going to take the sea to the Ark. After all, everyone knows you need a deluge to launch an Ark. And Brainbocs's Promethean ego was going to supply one. Brainbocs was going to reunite Lovespoon's old bomber crew, the one that flew the mission over Rio Caeriog, and blow up the dam at Nant-y-moch.

The sounds of a prison slowly coming to life filled the air. Iron doors clanged open and shut, and harsh voices echoed down the hard corridors; keys jangled; men moaned. Calamity had worked it out as well. And it had been too much for her. She didn't need to be a Dai Brainbocs to know what the mountain of water released with the destruction of the dam would do to the town. I had sent her off in search of Llunos in the faint hope that he might have some officers still loyal to him. Maybe they could do something. Stop the plane or devise a plan to get the townspeople to higher ground. If they commandeered the Cliff Railway, it might be possible. But it was all beyond my control now. Shortly before 8am the door opened and a tray with bread and a brown drink in a plastic beaker was placed inside. The drink was sweet and warm but I couldn't tell whether it was coffee or hot chocolate. Maybe it was neither. The beaker had chew marks all along the rim. Some time after that the door opened again and the guard told me my lawyer was here to see me.

I followed the guard down a long corridor through a series of barred doors, until eventually I was shown into another cell at the end, smaller than mine and with a simple wooden desk in the middle. A little man with a boyish face sat at the table. He was smartly dressed in a well-cut three-piece suit and was resting his two small hands, both gloved, on top of a malacca cane. A mauve handkerchief billowed out of his top pocket. He stood up as I entered and pointed to the chair.

'Please, sit down.' His voice was thin and weaselly. 'Smoke?' He took out a packet of cigarettes and held them aloft. I shook my head and he threw the pack down on the table. 'Neither do I; beastly habit. Still didn't quite know what else to take a man in prison. Not much practice at this sort of thing.'

I said nothing, just stared at him. There was something unpleasant, almost otherworldly about him, like those pictures of aliens said to be living in Area 51.

He looked at me and smiled weakly. 'Do you know who I am?'

'I know you're no lawyer.'

He chuckled. 'We've never been introduced, of course.'

The side of my head where I was hit with the shotgun was sore and pounding, but my mind was becoming clear. A suspicion slowly took concrete shape in my mind, a suspicion that had been floating there like fog for some time now. I had no reason to know he was, but I did. It was simple really.

'You're Dai Brainbocs.'

He giggled.

'I suppose it was a spare calliper you threw in the vat at the cheese factory?'

'No. I just made a replacement – out of Meccano – quite an improvement on the original design actually; much better articulation. I might apply for a patent.'

'And the teeth?'

'They were real too; milk teeth. Shows you what a wanker that police pathologist was.'

I nodded as I slowly took it in.

'Why go to all that bother of pretending to be dead?'

'Because Lovespoon was going to kill me.'

He walked over to the window and looked out. 'You should get a good view of his Ark from here, that's one of the reasons I chose this place.'

There was something in his tone that made my skin crawl. A sort of wheedling, taunting, smugness that suggested he had planned everything right down to what shirt I wore this morning.

'Eight cubic kilometres of water. I calculate it will take about twenty minutes to reach Aberystwyth. A very respectable effort for one's first deluge, don't you think?'

'It'll destroy everything.'

'No great loss to architecture.'

'Why are you here?' I said bluntly.

He paused. I knew the answer already: he was here to boast.

He looked at me and tapped the top of his cane.

'I wanted to thank you.'

'What for?'

'For saving my life.'

'I thought you were already dead.'

'Ah! But for how much longer would I have been allowed to rest in peace?'

I shook my head. 'I thought Lovespoon adored you.'

He began talking to the air, as if rehearsing his defence in case St Peter ever asked.

'Herod Jenkins, Custard Pie, Zachariah Lovespoon and Arthur Frobisher. One dead; the other three respectable members of Aberystwyth society. Each one well known. Each one in the phone book. But where was the fifth member of the crew, where was Gwenno?' He turned to face me and wagged his finger. 'If only I hadn't asked that question. If only.'

I said nothing but watched him intently. Impressed despite my disgust that this tiny fragment of humanity, a boy with the physical presence of a grasshopper, could have created such a whirlwind in the affairs of men through brain power alone. I was conscious of despising him, not for the evil that he wrought, but for his pale, sickly decrepitude. I who had automatically taken the side of such people against the steamroller insensitivity of Herod. Was this how Herod felt about me?

Brainbocs continued. The wistful tone in his voice suggesting that he was already addressing posterity rather than me.

'When I found out it was Mrs Llantrisant, I couldn't believe it. It was impossible. That daft, weather-obsessed, step-swabbing moron? The leader of the ESSJAT? How could it be? That's why I devised the poisoned apples and the deathbed confession: I needed to be certain. All I wanted was her to say yes or no. But the silly old bag had other ideas. She was convinced she was going to die and said she had this terrible secret on her conscience which she didn't want to take to the grave. I tried to shut her up but she wouldn't listen. I suppose she saw it as her big moment and wasn't going to be cheated of it.'

'And you found out that Rio Caeriog wasn't a military triumph after all?'

Brainbocs shook his head sadly. 'Oh no, far worse than that. I already knew it was a military disaster. That much I could have come to terms with. No, I found out something far worse. Something that spelled death for the whole project. The land reclamation, the beautiful boat, the whole Exodus – kaput!'

It was as if the air was slowly drained out of him. He leaned forward, put an elbow on the table and placed his chin softly into his cupped hand. The messianic fervour was gone and he looked at me; almost as if he was appealing for help.

'Lovespoon is English.'

I gasped. Brainbocs nodded his head slowly and closed his eyes.

'Imagine how I felt? The man to whom I had devoted my life, for whose glory I had created my masterpiece, the Cantref-y-Gwaelod reclamation scheme, was an impostor. From Slough.'

For a while neither of us spoke. A quiet so absolute filled the room that I could hear the sound of each of us breathing. Gradually Brainbocs gathered himself together again.

'There were five of them in the bomber. Mrs Llantrisant, Dai the Custard Pie, Herod Jenkins, Lovespoon and Frobisher. Lovespoon is actually Frobisher.'

'The English volunteer?'

'Yes. The real Lovespoon died when the Lancaster ditched in the Rio Caeriog after the mission. Or rather, he died soon after it. Apparently he wasn't going to make it anyway, so they all helped him along a bit. They were all in it. They hit on the plan to finish him off and Frobisher would take his identity. Then after the war they would share the money. The real Lovespoon was rich, you see. As the icing on the cake, they cut off his John Thomas and stuffed it in his mouth to make it look like the work of Indians.'

'Don't tell me, it was Herod who did that.'

'Gwenno . . . er . . . Mrs Llantrisant actually.'

I nodded gently as I slowly absorbed the enormity of what he was telling me.

'This is what Mrs Llantrisant told me during her deathbed confession. It might still have been OK. But I was so staggered by what I heard that right in the middle of the confession I cried out "fucking hell!"' He smiled sadly. 'I'll say one thing for Mrs Llantrisant: she's a smart woman. She knew instantly what was up. That was when I made my first mistake: my only one, in fact. I should have killed her right there in the bedroom.' He looked at me. 'I could, you know. I know how.'

I nodded and Brainbocs continued.

'But instead I ran away. From that moment on it was only a matter of time before Lovespoon came to hear about it.'

'So what was all this stuff about the tea cosy?'

Despite his gloom, Brainbocs chuckled. 'The tea cosy depicted *Mhexuataacahuatcxl*, the Mayan shape-shifter. He was supposed to represent Frobisher because he had taken the form of a man who had had his John Thomas cut off. It wasn't a serious blackmail attempt. But you get the idea. I needed to find out how Lovespoon would react to his secret being out. So I led him to think Evans and his cronies had copied my essay and were trying to blackmail him – test the waters sort of thing. When he killed all four of them I knew the water was pretty hot. So what was I supposed to do? You can imagine my problem. The police couldn't be trusted – I was sure they would hand me straight over to the Druids. That's why I thought of you. And now I just wanted to thank you.'

'But I haven't done anything – I failed. Didn't I?'

He smiled, stood up and walked over to the door. 'Actually,

you're playing your part very well. Even if you don't know what it is.'

As the guard let him out, I called out:

'So when does the plane take off?'

'Tonight.'

'And Aberystwyth gets destroyed?'

'They'll build another one. Don't worry.'

Chapter 23

GETTING A MESSAGE to Llunos proved to be easier than I expected. He was lying on the floor of my cell when I got back, his face bruised and swollen. It looked like he'd finally fallen down his own police station stairs. I bathed his cuts and waited while he gradually recovered consciousness. When he did I explained the situation to him and he went to the door and banged on it to bring a guard. After ten minutes he gave up. No one came for the rest of the day. And so the hours passed. Every half hour or so, Llunos would look over and ask the time. I would tell him and he would bang his fist into his palm and say, 'There must be some way.' But neither of us could think of one. At the end of the day we went to the window to watch the sunset. And as the sky turned pink we heard the clatter of propeller engines starting up from the fields of the Ystwyth flood plain.

Llunos looked at me. 'That will be the Lancaster then?'

'Yes.'

'Do you think it will work?'

'What?'

'Their plan.'

'Which part of it?

The old policeman considered. 'The bit about blowing up the dam.'

'I don't know. If they get the plane to take off, then they can probably do it. I mean with things like that Brainbocs is pretty good. Making the bombs would be a piece of cake for him and the rest, getting the right flight approach and trajectory and all that, is just mathematics.'

'Do you think the water will come this way?'

'Where else can it go?'

He thought about that one and didn't say anything more for a while.

'I suppose there's a lot of water behind that dam.'

'Eight cubic kilometres.'

'How much is that?'

'It's about the size of a small mountain.'

He nodded as if I was confirming his own calculations. 'That's a lot of water to be released all at once isn't it?'

'Yes, a lot.'

'A fuck of a lot actually.'

'Yes.'

'A hell of a fuck of a lot.'

'Yes.'

'What do you think it will do to Aberystwyth?'

It wasn't an easy question to answer. How do you describe something no one has ever seen before? Even Brainbocs would have struggled. I looked at Llunos. He was never a particularly jovial man but tonight he looked especially dejected. Maybe he was taking the whole thing as a personal failure. I struggled to find an analogy that he would understand.

'Well?'

Suddenly an image popped into my head.

'Imagine Aberystwyth is your testicles and the water is a rugby boot.'

The first street lights in town were starting to flicker into life when we heard a key in the lock. We both spun round, cursing ourselves that we hadn't made a contingency plan to overpower the guards or something. Anything no matter how foolhardy would have been better than standing looking out of the window admiring the view. The keys jangled harshly in the lock and the door opened emitting a faint, familiar whiff of gin. It was Pickel and Calamity. Pickel was holding an elaborately bent coat hanger he'd used to pick the lock; he looked from me to Llunos and then back at me.

''Ere! This girl says Lovespoon is going to knock me fucking clock down with a tidal wave!'

We drove to Plascrug recreation field on the back of Pickel's pick-up truck, arriving just as the plane began to taxi. Calamity and Pickel sat in the cab. The runway had been marked out with oil drums and flashing amber lights stolen from council road works. Pickel drove at full speed into the car park and then straight over the kerb on to the grass. We could see the plane at the opposite end of the field lumbering towards us, and Pickel drove straight at it. Half a minute later and we would have been too late; the Lancaster bomber would have picked up enough speed to take off before we reached it. Instead we hurtled towards each other in a head-on face-off. The giant bomber lurched and bumped across the turf, gradually gaining speed, torn between two conflicting forces: the drag of gravity on its lumbering frame and an invisible force sucking it up into the night sky. The gap between us rapidly shrank until it was only a matter of yards, the plane jumped violently and the wheels left the ground for seconds at a time before crunching back on to the turf. There were three possibilities: the plane would leave the turf at the last moment, there would be a head-on collision, or one side would veer off at the last minute. It turned out that both sides veered off at the last minute.

The manoeuvre worked in our favour. After the plane and truck had performed two unwieldy circles on the field Pickel managed to bring us alongside the fuselage and match the speed of the plane. We stood in the back of the pick-up opposite the entrance in the fuselage beneath the dorsal turret used by the Museum visitors. We could have clambered aboard but Hades had lent the aviators one of its gatekeepers. Herod Jenkins, dressed in his track suit and holding a cricket bat, stood in the entrance and grimaced with hate as he recognised us. A shudder ran through my loins; even after twenty years I was still scared of him. Slowly, as he realised the predicament we were in, that familiar horizontal crease spread across his face. Herod was smiling, just like he did the day Marty died; but this time, for once, he had miscalculated. The wheels hit a lump in the turf and the plane bounced violently. Herod flew backwards into the plane and didn't reappear. Llunos and I jumped in just as the wheels left the turf and this time there was no bump back down to earth. We found ourselves rapidly rising; the pick-up truck getting smaller and smaller. The last I saw of it was Calamity Jane leaning out of the window waving.

We stood up in the cramped tunnel of metal beams and girders and stumbled to get our balance like drunkards. Herod Jenkins lay slouched against the side of the plane, unconscious, a red smear on the fuselage wall indicating where he had hit the back of his head. The policeman gave me a brief glance, I nodded. He picked up the cricket bat and smashed the games teacher on the head. Then we turned our attention to the front of the plane. Through the hatch at the front we could see the shoulders of the crew, their two faces peering at us through the doorway. The pilot was Dai the Custard Pie and the bombardier, Mrs Llantrisant. There was a split-second of mutual recognition and then the thunder roared and we were hurled against the cold hard metal as the plane crashed into turbulence.

It was the fairground ride to end them all. The plane leaped and jumped and plummeted as the ferocious summer storm pounded upon the aluminium skin with giant anvil bows of thunder. Forks of lightning danced on the wings and we were hurled from side to side inside our tin box. We hit our heads, our knees and our elbows on the sharp metal innards of the plane, but we didn't stop. We had come too far and suffered too much. This was our moment. I stood up and moved forwards. Suddenly a huge hand grabbed me by the collar and pulled me backwards. It was Herod again. I wriggled free just as the plane hit another bank of turbulence and we all lost our footing and were rocketed into the ceiling. When I clambered to my feet, Llunos was behind me and Herod stood between us and the cockpit. The lightning flashed, filling the inside of the cabin with a ghostly incandescence. Herod, maddened by the blows to his head and looking for someone to blame, roared above the din like a space monster in a B-grade movie. He took a step towards me.

There are many defining moments in a life. In all our lives. Like rivers and mountain ranges they stretch across the topography of growing up. There is the day we discover that our parents – those twin repositories of all our trust – lied about Father Christmas. Or the moment we realise our father didn't really drive a tank in the war. Nor play for Manchester United. And later there is the time when a process that has been gathering force for many years quietly slips into focus like the image in a telescope and we realise that we have eclipsed our father. That stern, towering embodiment of manhood and authority, the unassailable protector, who always knew everything there was to know, and whose inner resources were a match for any of the contingencies that life could throw, has fallen. Has become a frail and flawed old man.

And then there is that other final oedipal Rubicon beyond which lies the territory of manhood: the day a boy faces down his games teacher. As the thunder roared and blinding blue-white flashes filled the sky, I squared my shoulders and looked into his eyes, that track-suited Minotaur who dwelled in the labyrinth of my heart.

'Come on then, son, do you want some?'

The plane disappeared. In its place was the swirling, murky vision of the games field from long ago: that patch of turf where all the rules we learned in school were overturned, where might was right and intellect a curse. A field where it was death to be clever and where the only cleverness lay in being invisible. The field where Marty fell on his sword for us, and then ran off into the clouds and never came back.

'Come on then, son, want to rumble, do you?'

I looked and sized him up. He was older, of course, but not frail. Not by a long chalk. He was maybe more squat, and fatter, and greyer, but he was still a formidable opponent and he knew it. And he still thought I was a poofter. Like the commando officer who makes it a point of principle to be harder than any of the younger men in his outfit, so the games teacher never relinquishes the belief that he can beat up any of his former pupils.

'Come on then, darling, show us what you're made of.' He grinned through that sour crease in the face.

I looked over my shoulder to Llunos who watched transfixed. He could have intervened, could have rushed forward to take my place. But some primordial instinct held him back. Some knowledge that this was my battle, felt rather than understood, which perhaps men have possessed throughout history, from the streets of Troy to the streets of Dodge City and Aberystwyth. Even though he was only a few yards away, the core truth of the scene excluded Llunos. Wordlessly, he handed me the bat. I took it with one hand and Herod laughed. He took a step towards me, still grinning. Lightning flashed again.

'Move out of the way, Mr Jenkins.'

'Why don't you make me?'

'If I have to, I will.'

He took another, careful step forward.

I cried, 'Out of the way now!'

'You won't do it.'

'By God I will.'

Herod paused, just outside the range of the bat and the universe held its breath. He looked at me, and I at him, and we stared into each other's eyes. Probably the only time he had looked at a pupil that way. Unfamiliar emotions skimmed across the waters of his eyes and when he spoke it was in a soft, hoarse tone that I had never heard him use before. 'You never forgave me, did you? All these years, you and the rest of them.'

I tightened my grip and Herod reached out a hand towards me.

'How do you think I felt? Did you ever stop to consider that?'

'It was your fault.'

'The Inquiry didn't think so – that note from his Ma was a fake. He forged it. He always did. You know that.'

'What does that prove?'

'He was fit to run.'

'Because of a piece of crappy paper? Is that it? Is that what you think?'

'There have to be rules, boy!'

'Fuck you, Herod!' I cried and lifted the bat. Herod dropped the placatory pose and darted forwards and as he did another scene from long ago swam into my mind. A vision of a small frightened boy in cricket pads being harangued by a man ten times his size. 'Not like that, like this, you stupid little boy! Hold it like this. No! Higher up! Now swing! Not like that, like this!' The words like the lyrics of a hymn sung every morning in assembly came to me across the years. And I thought of Marty and Bianca, and also of Noel Bartholomew, the man who took a picture of a tuppenny whore all the way to Borneo in the back of his camera. Suddenly, I knew he must have died laughing and the rogue gene he had passed on to me wasn't for madness or failure but balls. Herod took a final irrevocable step towards me and, using his own medicine against him, I did as he had commanded all those years ago. I strengthened my grip, spread out my feet and swung. Swung, swung with all the synchronised and focused strength in my body. And the slab of willow, anointed with linseed oil, slammed into the side of the games teacher's head. Astonishment flashed across his face as he found himself knocked for six. I watched in shock and with a creeping sense of pride at my late-developed athletic prowess as he cartwheeled sideways out of the door and the last words I heard him say before he disappeared into the void were: 'Good shot, boy!' I ran to the door and looked out as, still smiling, he spiralled down through the misty shreds of cloud, getting fainter and fainter, wispier and wispier until the tendrils of steam like the waters of the ocean covered that horizontal crease in his face they once called a smile.

For an instant I stood transfixed by the enormity of what I had done, then Llunos gave me a thumbs-up sign and the spell broke; we rushed forward. A sheet of lightning lit up the valley and for a second the vast, metallic sheen of Nant-y-moch reservoir lay illuminated below us in such awesome majesty that we were all struck dumb. Then the flickering electric discharge from the clouds went out and darkness consumed the vista again. A darkness broken only by two spotlights slung beneath the Plexiglas nose of the plane which were trained on the surface of the water. I knew without needing to ask that Brainbocs had rigged them up after watching *The Dambusters*. They were to indicate the correct altitude for dropping the bomb. When the two lights merged on the surface of the water, the plane would be at the correct height and they could release the payload. They were now only yards apart, skimming across the surface of the reservoir, getting closer and closer, as Custard Pie levelled the plane for the final approach. The vast concrete wall of the dam loomed up ahead and Bombardier Llantrisant – her eyes buried in the bombsight – screamed out above the din.

'Six seconds! Five seconds! Four seconds!'

And Llunos and I stood in the entrance to the cockpit and exchanged glances of disbelief.

'Three seconds!'

Mrs Llantrisant's hand, oblivious to us and everything else except those twin pools of light on the surface of the lake which were now less than a second or two apart, moved forward to the lever which would release the bomb. The hour had come. We only needed to retard the moment of release by a second or so and the angle would be wrong, the bomb would drop harmlessly and sink.

'Two seconds!' Ma Llantrisant screeched. Custard Pie held the joystick steady in a grip of iron, just as he must have done so many times all those years ago in Patagonia; just as he must have done, in fact, on that infamous approach over the clouds above San Isadora when they dropped the bombs on to the orphanage. The twin pools of light converged and became one, the hand hovered over the lever, waiting to deal the final blow to Aberystwyth, that once-lovely town by the sea.

'One second' shouted Mrs Llantrisant and then in an orgasm of triumph, 'Go! Go! Go!' as Llunos and I shot our hands forward to hold the release lever and stop the bomb.

Chapter 24

THE POLICE HORSE stamps and whinnies as the wind driving in from the sea makes the windcheaters crackle like fireworks. Dogs howl and babies cry as the townspeople mill around the Cliff Railway base station, pushing in confusion and shoving to board the trains. 'Keep back, at the barrier!' the policeman shouts. 'Women and children first! Able-bodied men take the footpath! No season tickets!' Then a mighty lamentation goes up as the outriders rushing in from the outskirts bring their tales of the advancing wall of water. Tales of tree trunks being tossed about on the surface of the raging foam like matchsticks; of caravans shaken along like dice in a ludo cup; of trains being catapulted down the main street of Borth; of the apocalypse at Talybont, where the waters hit the mill wheel with such fury that the mill building itself had started to spin. Panic spreads and the police horses rear up, neighing in terror and foaming at the bridle as the funicular trains creak and groan under the strain. Each carriage is weighed down with a cargo that spills out of the windows like bunches of human grapes. Never in the entire history of funicular railways has there been such an imbalance between the up and down cars. The hawser joining the two counterbalancing carriages stretches thinner than piano wire and the rails glow so hot in the night that the people down the coast in Aberaeron think Jacob's Ladder has returned to Earth above Aberystwyth.

As the credits began to roll I followed Calamity out of the cinema, blinking into the bright afternoon sunshine.

'I don't know why we keep going to see it,' I laughed.

'It's rubbish!' Calamity agreed. We exchanged guilty glances –

we both knew why we went: we loved it. The warm July wind blew a curtain of blonde hair across her face. The spiky hair was gone now, and the tomboy had given way to a burgeoning air of sophistication and self-possession. She punched me on the arm.

'I'd better get moving, don't want to keep him waiting.'

I nodded and she strode off, adding, 'See you at the harbour!'

I looked at my watch; there was still just enough time for a coffee at Sospan's before the meeting at the harbour with the Vatican envoy. I ordered a cappuccino and carried it over to one of the new tables set before the kiosk. Above my head a seagull wheeled in a lazy arc before floating down to land on the railings. He was a big bird, old and fat, almost as big as a cat, and probably remembered the days when Sospan's was a little wooden booth that sold ice cream. I proffered a piece of almond biscotti but he seemed unimpressed. 'Yes, old bird,' I said, 'we all remember those days. But these plastic tables with the central parasols are an improvement, aren't they? Progress isn't always a bad thing.' In the old days, of course, there was no room for such frippery; there was just the ice-cream booth, a few yards of pavement and then the railings. But that was the old days. I wasn't sure whether they had moved the road back or extended the sea wall but the new Prom – or 'Esplanade', as we would have to learn to call it, was much wider and airier. Noddy had gone, too, but he wouldn't be missed. Cartoon characters had no place illuminating the espressos and ristrettos of Sospan's terrace café. Nor indeed at the 24-hour Moules Marinière booth which had replaced the Whelk Stall at the foot of Constitution Hill.

A voice intruded on my thoughts and I looked up to see Llunos, now Commissioner, walk up to my table. He took a seat and gave his order to the waitress.

'Skinny double decaf' latte please.' He looked at me. 'Afternoon!'

I nodded. 'How's the new police station coming along?'

'Almost finished. Still a few teething problems with the central locking for the cells; and the mural, what a pain that is!' He rolled his eyes. 'Should have been finished by now. But he's flattened the perspective too much for my liking; the bit where the ocean divides.'

'You wouldn't want it too photographic, though.'

'That's what he says. He says he's done it deliberately to compress the narrative focus. I mean, that's all very well, but to Joe Bloggs it just looks like a mistake. We'll get there eventually.'

The waitress brought the coffee and Llunos took a thirsty gulp that left his mouth edged with foam.

We sat in silence for a while like a couple of Darby and Joans and enjoyed the shimmering tranquillity of the afternoon. Llunos was in no hurry to return to work, and I could afford to relax. Calamity took care of the day-to-day stuff and she was a lot better at it than I had been. It was only a matter of time before she took over entirely. I watched Llunos from the corner of my eye and felt an upsurge of warmth towards him. It had been a long journey that we had undertaken together but we had emerged as firm friends. Sospan, moving among the tables near the café, raised a hand in greeting and I smiled. He was a busy man these days, checking on his chain of bistros, or meeting with EU officials to discuss grants. We seldom saw much of him. There was still so much to do.

From where I was sitting I could see a tattered poster of Myfanwy Montez, the Legendary Welsh Chanteuse, still pasted to the wall of the old Bandstand. It made me think of that peculiar blemish in the new tarmac down at the harbour and Father Renaldo who had come to see it.

* * *

Llunos interrupted my reverie again. 'It's been a rum two years hasn't it?'

I grinned. 'You can say that again.'

'Do you think Brainbocs intended to sell the movie rights like that?'

I shook my head. 'I think he was just lucky. The newspaper serialisation rights were always part of the plan. But not Hollywood.'

Llunos wiped away the beard of milk with the back of his hand. 'I hear one of the dealers in Cardiff has bought the original essay. Half a million pound.'

'Lot of money for a schoolboy's homework.'

'Bloody madness. I mean, how do you know it's real?'

I allowed myself a secretive smile. Llunos wasn't wrong, but strangely this time, after all the red herrings and false trails, I suspected that the real essay had surfaced. In fact, I was willing to bet on it. 'I think this time it could be for real.'

He looked at me sceptically. 'You think so?'

'I've got this funny feeling.'

He snorted. 'Fake Brainbocs essays coming out of the woodwork for months. What's different about this one?'

I reached into my trouser pocket and handed him the letter that had arrived for me last month from Argentina. It was from Myfanwy and inside there was a photograph of her taken after one of the concerts at the Estada della Caeriog.

The policeman examined it. 'Brainbocs looks well.'

'Yes. That's what the Florida sunshine does for you. He went there to get his leg straightened by one of those fancy Miami surgeons.'

'And who's this in the big hat?'

'Ma Brainbocs. Looks quite the part doesn't she?'

He let the photo fall to his lap and looked at me. 'I don't see that this proves anything.'

'Look at Myfanwy.'

He peered once more at the picture and then looked up. 'What about her?'

'Notice anything different?'

'Seems the same as ever.'

I chuckled and Llunos started to get irritated. 'What are you driving at?'

I pointed at the picture of Myfanwy pasted to the Bandstand wall. Though old and faded, it was still recognisable. It contained a detail that was missing from the photo in the letter. But you needed sharp eyes to see it.

'Do you remember where Brainbocs said he'd hidden the essay?' I prompted.

'A well-known beauty spot,' he said, snorting at the stupidity of such a hiding place and looking at me for support; all he saw was a big wide grin. His brow screwed up and I grinned wider and wider as he looked at the picture in his hand and at the picture on the Bandstand and then finally, the penny dropping so loudly it almost frightened away the seagull, he cried out: 'My God!' And then, running his hand through his hair in disbelief, 'My God!'

He looked up, eyes shining and I nodded encouragement at him. 'The mole!' he cried. 'It's gone! Myfanwy's mole has gone!'

He stared at me open-mouthed as saliva dribbled down his chin, and I held my breath watching the cogs whirr and the truth slowly come to light.

'Well bugger me!' His face was one of pure astonishment. 'He hid the fucking essay in a micro-dot!'

I laughed. 'The cheeky bastard!'

'All that time we were checking out the picnic spots and lovers' leaps and things!'

'I must have walked past that fucking micro-dot photo booth at the museum a hundred times. And never even considered it.'

'And all the time,' said Llunos, 'the answer was staring us in the face.'

And so we both laughed. What else was there to do? Brainbocs hadn't just outwitted us, he had waltzed around us and danced the Charleston on our heads. The essay had been in front of us all along – right under Myfanwy's nose. And we sat in the Moulin every night staring at it, and never knew. Llunos looked at me and I returned the gaze and we both burst out laughing again.

I left him still laughing into his latte and made a leisurely stroll along the Esplanade to my appointment. Father Renaldo had flown all the way from Rome and I didn't want to keep him waiting. It was a beautiful day and as I passed the audacious architectural hybrid of Edwardian ironwork and swooping Perspex that was the new Pier I struggled with the tumult of emotion in my breast. It was at moments like this that I continually returned to the same question: did it really happen the way I think it did? That night two years ago aboard a plane where a terrible secret was born? The secret that joins with unbreakable glue Llunos and me in friendship but about which, paradoxically, neither of us dare speak? Did it really happen the way I think it did? 'Five seconds! Four seconds! Three seconds!' the bombardier had shouted as lightning forked off the wing and the shining waters of Nant-y-moch loomed up before us in the Plexiglas nose. 'Two seconds, one second! Go! Go! Go!' And in that second our hands shot forward to stop the release of the bomb and save the Town. Yet as they did, they came together with a touch as soft as the beating of butterfly wings and there was that hesitancy – I'm sure it was there and that we both felt it – that strange feeling almost of telepathy between us as we became aware of the god-like power that had been given to us in that twinkling of an eye. We looked at each other and saw in a moment of shared vision the unleashed fury of the waters racing down Great Darkgate Street; saw the proud white horses of the waves crashing their hooves down on to the fudge shops and the slate paperweight shops; saw the windows of the Moulin explode and the tea-cosy shops on Harbour Row washed into the sea; we saw the end of the amusement arcades and toffee-apple dens. And in that scintilla of time we thought of everything that had been, and of all the things that might be, or might not be, and that look passed between us, and we sort of said 'fuck it' and withdrew our hands. And the bomb fell. It's a scene you won't find in the movie.

I'll never be certain. The world is full of mysteries. No trace of the Ark has been found, for example, if you discount the odd bits of gopher wood that wash up now and again. And then there is this other matter. The blemish that keeps appearing in the tarmac down at the harbour and which Meirion has called municipal stigmata. This is the fourth time they've laid down a new surface – those pragmatic bare-torsoed men from the Council with their cauldron of bubbling tar and stripy canvas hut. And once again it has appeared; as if the blood that was spilled that night had contained photographic fixative. Normally I would have no trouble dismissing the whole affair as the prattle of superstitious fools. And I certainly don't believe in ghosts; I even told her that, damn it! But as I push my way impatiently past the pilgrims and stalls selling relics, as I take my place among the ranks of the credulous and stare down at the stain in the tarmac, I have to wonder. Because no matter how hard I try, there are two things I find impossible to deny: the mark really is on the exact spot where Bianca died. And if you screw your eyes up tight you really can make out the outline of a girl in a basque wearing a stovepipe hat.

A NOTE ON THE AUTHOR

After a brief career as the world's worst aluminium salesman, Malcolm Pryce worked as an advertising copywriter, in London and later in Singapore. During this time he created campaigns for the famous Singapore Girl, and also wrote tourist promotional advertising for the former headhunting tribes of Borneo – a group of people he describes as the most civilised clients he ever dealt with. In August 1998 he quit his job, booked a passage on a cargo ship bound for South America, and set to work writing *Aberystwyth Mon Amour*. The first draft was completed somewhere off the coast of Guyana. He now lives in Bangkok.

A NOTE ON THE TYPE

The text of this book is set in Fournier. Fournier is derived from the *romain du roi*, which was created towards the end of the seventeenth century for the exclusive use of the Imprimerie Royale from designs made by a committee of the Académie of Sciences. The original Fournier types were cut by the famous Paris founder Pierre Simon Fournier in about 1742. These types were some of the most influential designs of the eighteenth century, and are counted among the earliest examples of the 'transitional' style of typeface. This Monotype version dates from 1924. Fournier is a light, clear face whose distinctive features are capital letters that are quite tall and bold in relation to the lower-case letters, and *decorative italics, which show the influence of the calligraphy of Fournier's time.*